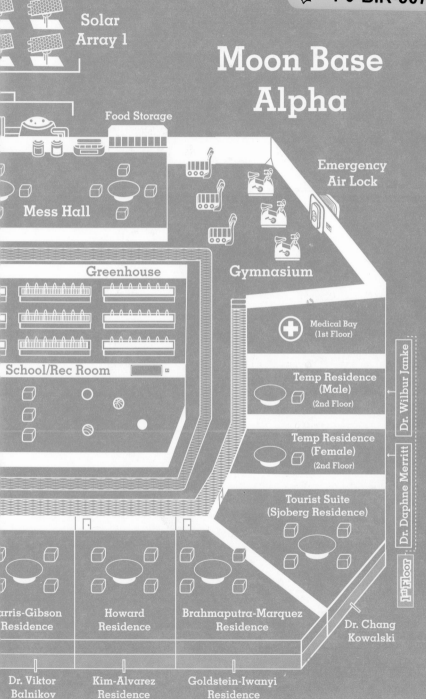

Solar
Array 1

Moon Base
Alpha

Food Storage

Mess Hall

Emergency
Air Lock

Greenhouse

Gymnasium

Medical Bay
(1st Floor)

School/Rec Room

Temp Residence
(Male)
(2nd Floor)

Temp Residence
(Female)
(2nd Floor)

Tourist Suite
(Sjoberg Residence)

Dr. Wilbur Janke

Dr. Daphne Merritt

1st Floor

rris-Gibson
Residence

Howard
Residence

Brahmaputra-Marquez
Residence

Dr. Chang
Kowalski

Dr. Viktor
Balnikov

Kim-Alvarez
Residence

Goldstein-Iwanyi
Residence

P9-BIK-507

waste of space

STUART GIBBS

waste of space

A **moon base alpha** NOVEL

Simon & Schuster Books for Young Readers

New York   London   Toronto   Sydney   New Delhi

SIMON & SCHUSTER BOOKS FOR YOUNG READERS
An imprint of Simon & Schuster Children's Publishing Division
1230 Avenue of the Americas, New York, New York 10020

SIMON & SCHUSTER BOOKS FOR YOUNG READERS
is a trademark of Simon & Schuster, Inc.
For information about special discounts for bulk purchases, please contact
Simon & Schuster Special Sales at 1-866-506-1949 or business@simonandschuster.com.
The Simon & Schuster Speakers Bureau can bring authors to your live event.
For more information or to book an event, contact the Simon & Schuster Speakers Bureau at 1-866-248-3049 or visit our website at www.simonspeakers.com.
Book design by Lucy Ruth Cummins
Endpaper art by Ryan Thompson
The text for this book was set in Adobe Garamond.
Manufactured in the United States of America
0318 FFG
First Edition
10 9 8 7 6 5 4 3 2 1
Library of Congress Cataloging-in-Publication Data
Names: Gibbs, Stuart, 1969– author.
Title: Waste of space : a Moon Base Alpha novel / Stuart Gibbs.
Description: First edition. | New York : Simon & Schuster Books for Young Readers, [2018] | Summary: In 2041 on Moon Base Alpha, thirteen-year-old Dash must solve the mystery of how Lars was poisoned before the base loses oxygen, forcing the colonists to return to Earth.
Identifiers: LCCN 2017007147| ISBN 9781481477796 (hardcover : alk. paper) | ISBN 9781481477819 (eBook)
Subjects: | CYAC: Mystery and detective stories. | Poisons—Fiction. | Interpersonal relations—Fiction. | Space colonies—Fiction. | Moon—Fiction. | Extraterrestrial beings—Fiction. | Science fiction.
Classification: LCC PZ7.G339236 Was 2018 | DDC [Fic]—dc23
LC record available at https://lccn.loc.gov/2017007147
ISBN 9781534431669 (B&N proprietary hardcover)

For the *real* Violet,

the best daughter in the universe

acknowledgments

I know that I have already thanked Garrett Reis-man on this page in the previous two Moon Base Alpha books, but I'm doing it again. An ex-astronaut and the current director of human space flight operations at SpaceX, Garrett has always given me a great window into what space travel is actually like—and he's incredibly funny as well. Without Garrett there would never have been an MBA. I would also like to thank Matthew Golombek for his exceptional tour of the Jet Propulsion Laboratory and his insights into the future of space exploration.

Additional thanks to Simone Francis, Garrett's better half; my amazing editors, Kristin Ostby, who got this whole MBA ball rolling, and Liz Kossnar, who has taken up the helm; my publisher, Justin Chanda, who has always been amazingly supportive; my incredible cover designer, Lucy Ruth Cummins; my exceptional agent, Jennifer Joel, to whom I owe my entire career as a middle-grade writer; my brilliant researchers, Emma Soren and Nate McLeod; and, of course, my family.

My parents, Ronald and Jane Gibbs, fostered a love of science and writing in me. My father was always happy to bring me to the hospital where he did research and taught the doctors of tomorrow, while my mother was willing to do things like drive me all the way across the city at night when I was a young boy so we could see Halley's Comet. And huge thanks to my wife, Suzanne, and my children, Dashiell and Violet. Though we say it every night, it seems appropriate to do it here as well: I love you to the moon and back, infinity and beyond.

contents

Moon Base Alpha Resident Directory

Upper floor:

Residence 1 *(base commander's quarters and office)*
Nina Stack, moon-base commander

Residence 2
Harris-Gibson residence
Dr. Rose Harris, lunar geologist
Dr. Stephen Gibson, mining specialist
Dashiell Gibson (13)
Violet Gibson (6)

Residence 3
Howard residence
Dr. Maxwell Howard, lunar engineering specialist for
Moon Base Beta
Kira Howard (12)

Residence 4
Brahmaputra-Marquez residence
Dr. Ilina Brahmaputra-Marquez, astrophysicist
Dr. Timothy Marquez, psychiatrist
Cesar Marquez (16)

Residence 4 *(continued)*

Rodrigo Marquez (13)

Inez Marquez (7)

Tourist Suite

currently occupied by the Sjoberg family:

Lars Sjoberg, industrialist

Sonja Sjoberg, his wife

Patton Sjoberg (16)

Lily Sjoberg (16)

Residence 5 *reserved for temporary base residents (female)*

Residence 6 *reserved for temporary base residents (male)*

Residence 7

Former residence of Dr. Ronald Holtz. Currently
reserved for new moon-base physician. *(Note: selection
still in process. Not due to arrive until Mission 8.)*

Lower floor:

Residence 8
Former residence of Garth Grisan. Reserved for new moon-base maintenance specialist. *(Note: selection still in process. Not due to arrive until Mission 8.)*

Residence 9
Dr. Wilbur Janke, astrobiologist

Residence 10
Dr. Daphne Merritt, base roboticist

Residence 11
Dr. Chang Kowalski, geochemist

Residence 12
Goldstein-Iwanyi residence
Dr. Shari Goldstein, lunar agriculture specialist
Dr. Mfuzi Iwanyi, astronomer
Kamoze Iwanyi (7)

Residence 13
Kim-Alvarez residence
Dr. Jennifer Kim, seismic geologist
Dr. Shenzu Alvarez, water-extraction specialist

Residence 14

Dr. Viktor Balnikov, astrophysicist

Residence 15

Chen-Patucket residence

Dr. Jasmine Chen, senior engineering coordinator for
Moon Base Beta

Dr. Seth Patucket, astrobiologist

Holly Patucket (13)

*(Note: Arrival has been pushed back until Mission 9. This
residence will be used as housing for temporary base workers
until then.)*

THE OFFICIAL NASA PROCEDURES FOR CONTACT WITH INTELLIGENT EXTRATERRESTRIAL LIFE

WARNING:

The documents contained within this dossier are highly classified. Only government employees with level AAA security clearance are allowed to read them. If you do not have level AAA security clearance, it is a felony to read, scan, or even peruse the following pages, punishable by a minimum of five years in a federal penitentiary. If you have the appropriate clearance *and* believe that contact with intelligent extraterrestrial life has taken place—or is imminent—then break the seal and continue reading.

ILLEGAL BASEBALL

Earth year 2041

Lunar day 252

Really freaking early in the morning

For my thirteenth birthday, my father gave me the greatest present I could have ever hoped for: He took me outside to play catch.

Now, before you start thinking that my father was the biggest cheapskate on earth, there are a few things you need to know:

For starters, my father couldn't have been the biggest cheapskate on earth, because we didn't live on earth. We lived on the moon.

We were some of the first lunar colonists. Along with

a handful of other scientists and their children, we lived at Moon Base Alpha, the first human settlement in outer space. When NASA had recruited us, they had made it sound like MBA would be the most exciting, amazing, incredible place in the universe.

It wasn't.

It turned out, living on the moon was far more difficult than anyone had predicted. But as hard as it was for the adults, it was even worse being a kid there. Not only did we have to deal with the same lousy dehydrated food and cramped sleeping spaces and sadistic toilets as the adults, but there were a host of other problems for kids.

Like making friends. There were other kids at MBA, but I hadn't been given any choice in selecting them. I was just stuck with them, and the only other boy my age, Roddy Marquez, wasn't much fun to hang out with. You know how, on earth, parents will sometimes drag you to their friends' house for the night and ask you to hang with their friends' kid, even though they know the two of you don't really get along? Well, imagine that, instead of going over to their friends' house for one night, you've gone over for three years. And you can't leave.

That was another problem with being a kid on the moon: You couldn't go outside and play. Ever. Leaving Moon Base Alpha was extremely dangerous. There were a hundred ways you could die on the lunar surface; we had already lost one person out there and nearly lost another. For this reason, NASA forbade children from ever going outdoors, meaning that we were supposed to spend our whole time on the moon inside a building smaller than your standard Motel 6.

Despite it being against the rules, I had experienced the dangers of the surface myself. I had been outside on the moon four times: once while walking to MBA from the rocket that had brought me there and three times due to emergencies. I had nearly died on two of those excursions, which was a 50 percent near-death-experience rate. The same as flipping a coin. Not great odds.

And yet I still desperately wanted to go back outside again.

I was going nuts cooped up inside Moon Base Alpha. So were all the other kids. Even my six-year-old sister, Violet, who was normally as cheerful as an animated cartoon chipmunk, was starting to go stir-crazy. After eight months on the moon, she had watched every episode of her favorite TV show a thousand times and was constantly hounding Mom and Dad to let her go outside and play.

To which they'd inevitably have to reply, "You can't."

"Whyyyyyy nooooooooot?" Violet would whine. "I'm bored inside. There's nothing to do on the moon."

"That's not true," my parents would tell her. "You could play a game. Or read a book. There are thousands of books we could upload."

"I want to ride my bike," Violet would say.

"Your bicycle is back on earth."

"Then I want to go out in a lunar rover. Dash got to go out in a lunar rover."

"That was an emergency. And Dash was almost killed by a meteorite shower."

"At least he got to have some excitement. I never get to almost die. I never get to do *anything*. I hate this stupid base!"

At this point my parents would get a little flummoxed. Ideally, they should have argued that "hate" was a strong word and that the base wasn't stupid, but the fact was, neither of them was a big fan of MBA. I think both of them were feeling really guilty about having volunteered our family for service on the moon. Which would also explain why Dad ended up waking me at two a.m. on my birthday to play catch.

"Dash," he whispered, shaking me lightly. "I have a surprise for you."

I sat up groggily on my inflatable mattress and promptly bonked my head on the low ceiling of my sleep pod. Even after eight months at MBA, I still hadn't gotten used to the fact that our sleeping areas were as tiny as coffins. I glanced at my watch and groaned. "Dad, it's the middle of the night . . ."

"I know."

". . . on my *birthday*."

"Sorry. It's just that this is the only time I can take you outside without Nina noticing us."

"Outside?!" I exclaimed. "What for?"

"Shh!" he warned. "I thought you'd like to try out some extreme low-gravity sports."

I blinked at my father in the darkness, trying to figure out if this was a bad joke or a good dream. "It's illegal for me to go outside."

"I figured we could make an exception for your birthday. What do you say?"

I was out of my sleep pod before he could even finish the sentence, yanking on a T-shirt and shorts over the boxers I'd slept in. "What about meteors?"

"They shouldn't be an issue. I've run a dozen atmospheric scans. No known clouds of potential meteors or space debris are anywhere within two hundred thousand miles. But we'll stay close to base anyhow, just in case."

"Okay." I knew that, should a meteorite hit me directly, it wouldn't matter how close to base I was; I'd be dead. But the risk of that was nonexistent if the skies were clear. Dad wouldn't have taken the chance if he didn't think it was safe. "And Nina . . . ?"

"Asleep. She was on the ComLink with earth until two hours ago, but I haven't heard a peep out of her since then."

Nina Stack was the moon-base commander. She was

tough as nails and had the emotional range of a blender. (For this reason, all the kids called her Nina the Machina.) Her quarters were right next to ours, and the walls were thin; if you pressed your ear against one, you could hear *everything* in the next room. So if Dad said Nina was asleep, she was probably asleep.

"Won't opening the air lock trigger some sort of alert?" I asked.

"Normally, yes. But Chang showed me how to hack the system." Chang Kowalski was my father's closest friend at MBA and the smartest person I had ever met; if anyone knew how to hack the system, it was him.

"C'mon," Dad urged. "Before we wake your sister."

Since he hadn't mentioned Mom, I glanced toward her sleep pod. She was awake, peering out of it, looking a little jealous that Dad was getting to go with me, rather than her. "Happy birthday," she whispered. "Have fun out there."

"Thanks, Mom."

She gave me a bittersweet smile. "I can't believe I have a teenager. I'm old."

"You don't *look* old," Dad told her. "You look the same as the day I met you."

"That's just the low gravity. Wait until you see me back on earth."

"You'll look even better there, I promise." Dad gave

Mom a kiss (which I averted my eyes from), then grabbed our baseball and led me out the door.

It took another fifteen minutes for us to get outside. Space suits are difficult to put on, and you don't want to make a mistake. Otherwise you could freeze to death. Or suffocate as your oxygen leaks out. Or both. All of which were things we obviously wanted to avoid. So Dad and I took great care suiting up, then double-, triple-, and quadruple-checked each other.

"How's the suit feel?" Dad asked me. With our helmets on, we were now using radios to communicate, even though we were standing right next to each other.

"All right, I guess," I reported. "Seems a little tighter in the shoulders than it was last time I went out."

"Really?" Dad asked, surprised. And then understanding flooded his face. "Oh my gosh," he sighed. "Of course."

"What is it?"

"You've grown."

I would have smacked my forehead if I hadn't been wearing a space helmet. Over the past few weeks, I'd begun a growth spurt. It was only an inch so far, but still, that had very different repercussions on the moon than on earth. The few T-shirts I had brought were getting tighter and shorter on me, so we'd had to ask NASA to send new ones on the next supply rocket. The same applied to the single pair of sneakers I had brought; in the meantime, I'd had to slit the tips off with a paring knife to make room for my toes. And as for my space suit . . .

Everyone on the moon had a suit specifically designed for them and no one else. Many parts of mine, like my helmet, had been sculpted specifically to my own personal measurements, meaning that someone significantly bigger or smaller than me wouldn't be able to use it. However, it appeared that NASA—which had only made space suits for adults until recently—had forgotten something very important about kids: We grew. And in the significantly lower gravity of the moon, there was a chance we might grow even faster than we did on earth. Meaning that, after being on the moon for three years, our suits might not fit us anymore.

Of course, I hadn't thought about this myself, and apparently no one else had either until that moment.

"Do you think it's still safe for me to wear it?" I asked.

"Yes," Dad said reassuringly. "You haven't grown *that* much. But I wonder if your sister's still fits *her*. She's sprouted a bit since we got here, and she hasn't tried her suit on in eight months. She ought to, though. And all the other kids should too."

"Especially Roddy," I said, meaning Rodrigo Marquez, the only other boy on base my age. The one I was stuck on the moon with. "I don't think he's any taller, but he's definitely rounder than when we got here."

Roddy was the only person who had actually gained weight at MBA. He was one of the few Moonies who actually found space food appetizing and he had staunchly avoided the two hours of exercise a day we were required to do to combat low-gravity bone and muscle loss. There was a decent chance that, once we got back to earth and its stronger gravity, Roddy wouldn't have the strength to stand up.

Dad didn't say anything in response, though. A cloud of worry had formed over his face.

"Dad?" I asked. "Is something wrong?"

"Hmm?" He turned back to me, then seemed to snap back to the present. He gave me a smile, but I could tell it was forced. "No, I was just thinking about the suits. Remind me to make sure we test your sister's on her, first thing tomorrow."

"First thing?" I asked. "We're not leaving here for another two and a half years. If we're lucky."

"Still, there could always been an emergency and we might have to evacuate." While that was true, I got the sense something else was on my father's mind. Before I could press the issue, though, he said, "Looks like we're good to go. Let's get out there before someone comes along and sees us."

With that, he picked up the baseball, opened the interior

door of the air lock and stepped inside. I followed him.

I was quivering with excitement.

I had expected to be more nervous after my previous life-threatening trips onto the surface, but those had been very different. Each of those times, I had been in a rush, and lives had been on the line. This time I was going outside simply to have fun. And my father was with me, which made a big difference.

Honestly, the whole point of going to the moon is to walk around on the surface. For as long as people have dreamed of going there, the dreams have never been about being cooped up in a moon base. The dreams have been about being making boot prints in moon dust that will last forever, climbing mountains that no human has ever climbed, and staring up into the sky and seeing our home planet in the distance. All anyone remembers about humanity's first visit to the moon is the two and a half hours Neil Armstrong and Buzz Aldrin spent on the surface, not the additional nineteen hours they spent in the lunar module.

The air-lock chamber depressurized, and then a green light lit up by the outer door, indicating that it was okay to head outside.

"Sun's out," Dad said. "Lower your visor."

I was already doing it. The moon doesn't have an atmosphere, so in the direct sunlight it's more than four hundred degrees. Without the protective mirrored visors in our helmets, our heads would have cooked like microwave popcorn.

Dad lowered his visor too. His face disappeared and was replaced with a warped mirror that reflected me back at myself.

Then Dad opened the exterior air-lock door and we bounded out onto the moon.

Since the sun was out, the entire plain of moon dust before us was lit up. Above us, the sky was pitch black, save for earth, hanging in the air by the horizon. I stopped and stared at it for a few seconds, thinking how beautiful it was—and wishing I was back there.

Dad seemed to sense this—he was probably thinking the same thing—and so he made a blatant attempt to distract me. He bonked me on my helmet.

"Hey!" I said, wheeling around toward him.

He held up the baseball and said, "Go long."

So I did. I bounded across the lunar surface. It wasn't easy, as the moon dust was thick and slightly adhesive, and the weight of my space suit counteracted the low lunar gravity. But it was still a joy to be playing outside at all.

The last time I had played catch with my father had been more than eight months before. It had been our last trip back home to Hawaii before setting off for the moon. We had returned from training at the Johnson Space Center in

Houston to say good-bye to family and friends, to take a few last hikes in the mountains, to surf a few last waves. It had been a bittersweet visit, knowing that we wouldn't get to do anything like that again for three years, but at the time we'd all been very excited about heading to the moon. We were blissfully unaware of how much worse life would be at MBA than NASA had prepared us for.

In the last eight months, I *had* been able to play ball inside MBA, but it wasn't the same as doing it outdoors. And every time I did it, Nina inevitably showed up and ordered me to stop it before I hurt someone or broke something. This also happened whenever I and the other kids tried to do anything physical, like tag or hide-and-seek or blindman's bluff. Officially, the only place approved for strenuous activity at MBA was the gymnasium, but the gym was too small to play in. Yet another reason why being a kid on the moon was lame.

Technically, we weren't even supposed to bring balls to the moon because of the potential for injury, but Dad had found a loophole. We were all allowed to bring a few special "personal effects" to remind us of home, so Dad had faked the signature of Sandy Koufax on the ball and claimed it was a family heirloom.

I got forty yards across the moon and spun back to face my father.

He tossed the ball my way. Only in the low gravity, he

didn't know his own strength. It rocketed out of his hand and sailed several stories over my head. "Oh, crap!" he exclaimed.

I spun around and ran for the ball again. Thankfully, it wasn't hard to track. Against the pitch-black sky, it glowed like an oncoming headlight. I charged through a small impact crater, tracking the ball as it fell, then dove for it. I snagged it out of the air and landed on my belly, carving a long furrow in the moon dust. But the ball stayed in my gloved hands. I got back to my feet and realized I was now nearly a football field away from my father. I raised the ball triumphantly for him to see.

He gave a whoop of joy. "Way to go, Dashiell! That has to be the greatest catch in human history! It puts Willie Mays at the Polo Grounds to shame!"

I whooped as well. Diving for the ball had been reckless and childish. I could have smashed into a moon rock and damaged my suit—and it was now so covered with moon dust, it would probably take an hour to clean. But I still felt exhilarated. "Let's see if I can get it back to you!" I said.

"Be careful," Dad warned. "I didn't even throw it that hard. If you use all your strength, you'll send it into orbit."

"All right." I gave the ball a light flick, the same way I might have chucked it across our yard back in Hawaii. Sure enough, it flew all the way back to Dad—and then some.

It shot over his head, ricocheted off the air-lock door, and plopped into the moon dust at his feet.

"Okay," Dad said. "I think we've got the hang of this. Let's see how far we can go. I'll bet we can easily set the record for the farthest game of catch of all time."

I took a few steps backward and Dad tossed the ball to me. Now that he had a better idea of how to throw in the low gravity, he was much more on target. I caught the ball, took a few more steps backward, and winged it back to him. We kept on like that for a few more minutes, until the distance between us was nearly two football fields. Definitely a record. And yet we still weren't even throwing that hard.

The only thing that kept us from going any farther was that it was now getting hard to see each other. My father was only a little dot on the horizon. He had to alert me as to when he was throwing the ball so I would know it was coming. If I lost it in the field of moon dust around me, we'd never find it again—and the closest sporting goods store was 250,000 miles away.

And yet I kept finding my attention drawn to the earth hanging in the sky above me.

I desperately wanted to go home.

I hadn't taken a breath of fresh air in eight months. I hadn't gone on a hike, or ridden a bike, or seen an animal that wasn't part of a lab experiment. Almost every bit of food

I'd eaten had been dehydrated, irradiated, thermostabilized, and reduced to little cubes of gunk; I was dying for a taste of ice cream, or fresh salmon, or a salad.

I missed water most of all.

I hadn't expected that, but it was true. I had never realized how much I took water for granted until I barely had any. I missed standing under a warm shower. (On the moon, we had to clean ourselves with a cold, measly trickle of water—and we only got to do that once every few weeks.) I missed swimming in the ocean. I missed being able to open the tap and drink water that had recently fallen from the sky, instead of water that had been consumed, urinated out, and recycled two thousand times already. I missed every single thing about rainstorms: the feel of the drops on my body, the rumble of thunder, the shimmer of a rainbow, the smell after the rains had passed. That had all been missing from my life for the past eight months.

Except for one, all-too-brief moment.

A month before, with the help of an alien named Zan Perfonic, I had mentally traveled to earth to see my best friend, Riley Bock. For approximately two seconds, I had the experience of standing on Hapuna Beach in Hawaii. It wasn't like I was merely watching it on a screen; it was as though I was actually there. I could feel the ocean breeze on my skin and the cool wet sand beneath my feet; I could smell the salt in the air; I could sense the warmth of the setting sun and the earth all around me.

And then I lost contact.

I know, I sound like a lunatic. Like all the time cooped up on the moon drove me insane and made me start hallucinating.

But I wasn't crazy. Zan was real. She had first approached me two months earlier. Originally, she had been in contact with Dr. Holtz, but after he was murdered, she reached out to me, hoping to continue her contact with the human race. I was the only person she spoke to, and she did it through thought alone. She could project herself into my mind and communicate with me through some sort of highly advanced intergalactic ESP. (This cut down on the need to spend several hundred millennia flying between planets to talk face-to-face. It also allowed me to speak to her in private, which was good, because she wanted to keep our contact a secret.) I had no idea how she did it. In fact, I had no idea how I'd done it myself. I had been desperately trying to replicate the experience ever since, but without any luck. Zan tried to explain the process to me many times, but I couldn't even begin to understand what she was talking about.

In a way, being back on earth for two seconds was even worse than having been removed from it altogether. My moments there reminded me of what I was missing and left me desperate for more. It was like tasting the tiniest morsel of chocolate and then being told I couldn't have any more for the next two and a half years. And my inability to get back again—or even grasp how it had happened at all—was insanely frustrating.

Staring up at the blue planet now, all I could think was how wonderful it would be to be submerged in all that water.

"Dash! Heads up!"

Startled by my father's cry, I snapped back to attention to find the baseball hurtling right at me. While I'd been distracted, Dad had launched a pinpoint throw to me. I didn't even have enough time to react. The ball clonked me right in the face shield. I staggered backward, stumbled over a moon rock, and fell on my butt.

Dad burst into laughter. "What happened?" he asked. "Did you just zone out for a bit?"

"I guess." I staggered back to my feet and found the ball in a pile of moon dust a few feet away.

"Were you looking at the earth?" Dad asked, sounding a lot more serious all of a sudden.

"Yeah," I admitted. "I can't believe it'll be another twenty-eight months until we can go home. Eight hundred and sixty-eight days. Not that I'm counting."

Dad didn't say anything right away. I wasn't sure if he was feeling guilty for bringing me to the moon, or mulling over what to say next—or maybe our radio connection had simply dropped. Finally, he spoke. "About that. There's something we need to discuss."

There was a sadness in his tone that unsettled me. Like he had very bad news to deliver. "What is it?" I asked.

Before Dad could answer me, though, another voice interrupted our conversation. It was Nina Stack, and she was angry. "Stephen and Dashiell! What are you doing out there?"

Rather than be cowed by her, Dad answered cheerfully, knowing it would annoy her. "Good morning, Nina! Dash and I were just conducting some scientific research on the physics of spherical projectiles launched on the lunar surface."

Nina didn't think this was funny. But then again, Nina didn't think *anything* was funny. "Do you have any idea how many safety protocols you are violating by being out there?" she asked.

"Seventeen?" Dad ventured.

"Seventy-six," Nina corrected. "I want you back in here ASAP."

"C'mon, Nina, be a sport," Dad pleaded. "It's Dashiell's birthday. And we're not doing anything dangerous. . . ."

"*Any* foray onto the lunar surface is dangerous," Nina told us. "You two should know that better than anyone.

With everything else that's going on here right now, the last thing I need is for another disaster to crop up."

I wondered what Nina meant by "everything else that's going on here right now." But I didn't have a chance to ask.

"Can you give us another ten minutes?" Dad asked.

"No! I'm watching you right now. If I don't see you head back here this very moment, I will cite you for insubordination." Nina spoke like she was scolding a kindergartner, rather than talking to one of the world's foremost geologic scientists.

"You'd do that?" Dad asked. "After everything I've done for you?" Even though it sounded like Dad was teasing, I knew there was more to it than that. Nina had broken some rules herself at MBA recently—far more serious than the ones we were breaking—and she could have been relieved of her duty for it. Although Nina had reported her actions to NASA, Dad, Mom, and the other Moonies had issued statements in support of her, claiming there had been extenuating circumstances, and Nina had been allowed to keep her position as commander.

"What's your point?" Nina asked coldly.

"I would like to let my son spend another ten minutes on the surface of the moon for his birthday," Dad replied.

"It's okay, Dad," I said, not wanting my father to get in trouble. "We can go back—"

"No," Dad said firmly. "You have been a model citizen at

our base for the last eight months—even when other people haven't." This last part was obviously directed at Nina. "You deserve this. In fact, you deserve a hell of a lot more than this. So I think the least Nina can do is—"

He didn't get to finish the sentence. From the other end of the radio came a shrill, terrified scream.

Even though it was diluted over the radio, it still made me jump.

The scream wasn't from Nina. It was too distant, like it had come from someone else far away inside MBA. I couldn't tell who had screamed—or even whether they were male or female—but one thing was clear:

Someone back at Moon Base Alpha was in serious trouble.

Excerpt from *The Official NASA Procedures for Contact with Intelligent Extraterrestrial Life* © National Aeronautics and Space Administration, Department of Extraterrestrial Affairs, 2029 (Classification Level AAA)

PROBABILITY OF CONTACT

Over the last few decades, it has become evident that there are a vast number of planets in our galaxy. Virtually every other star we have aimed a telescope at has a planet that orbits it, if not multiple planets. Granted the majority of these are not conducive to life, but since there are more than 100 billion stars in our galaxy alone,[*] if even only a fraction of a percent have a habitable planet around them, then there would still be hundreds of millions of planets capable of supporting life. It stands to reason, then, that there could be millions of planets out there where intelligent life has evolved, and certainly some of them may be far ahead of us technologically, possessing the ability and desire to travel to planets such as ours. Therefore, it is not so much a question of *if* we will ever have contact with intelligent life from another planet—but *when*.

This manual has been designed to facilitate such a landmark event. NASA's Department of Extraterrestrial Affairs (DEXA) has been planning for this eventuality for decades, assembling an incredible staff of astronomers, astrobiologists, linguists, doctors, engineers, and military specialists who are all working together to ensure that when the date of alien contact arrives, everything will proceed without a hitch.

---

[*] And 100 billion galaxies in the universe

SPACE MADNESS

Lunar day 252

Still awfully freaking early in the morning

"Who was that?" Dad asked over the radio, sounding worried.

Instead of answering, Nina told us, "Come back right now. That's an order." Then she was gone.

Obviously, we were no longer her number one priority.

"Dash . . . ," Dad began. I could hear the sadness in his voice. He obviously felt bad about cutting off our catch.

"I'm on my way back," I told him. Goofing around on the lunar surface didn't seem right if someone was in trouble.

I bounded back toward MBA as quickly as I could, concerned about what might be happening. NASA had assured us that life on the moon would be as safe as life on earth, but like so many other promises the agency had made, that hadn't turned out to be true. Dr. Holtz had been murdered, Nina had almost died when her space helmet broke, and Kira and I had nearly been killed by a meteorite shower— and that didn't include the dangers of rocket explosions, malfunctions in the base's life-support systems, or dozens of other potentially deadly issues. Life on the moon was basically long stretches of boredom punctuated by quick bursts of terror.

Dad and I entered the air lock, shut the outer door, depressurized the inner chamber, and clambered out of our suits. Normally, we would have cleaned the moon dust off them right away, but since this was a potential emergency, we left them piled on the air-lock floor and slipped back into the base.

Even though it was extremely early in the morning, MBA was now buzzing with activity like a stirred-up anthill. Our fellow Moonies, wakened by the scream, were drowsily staggering out of their residences, rubbing sleep from their eyes and trying to figure out what was going on.

There were two levels of residences at MBA. The upper one exited onto a catwalk that overlooked the air-lock staging area, so we could see everyone on both levels as they emerged. Upstairs, Dr. Ilina Brahmaputra-Marquez, our astrophysicist, was advising her children, Cesar, Roddy, and Inez, to stay in their room while she investigated the situation—although her husband, Dr. Timothy Marquez, our base psychiatrist, looked more nervous than any of his children. (Back on earth, Dr. Marquez had written a best-selling book on psychiatry, but as my parents often pointed out, that didn't actually mean he was a *good* psychiatrist.) Next door to them, Kira Howard, the only girl my age at MBA, wasn't getting any instruction at all from her father. As usual, Dr. Howard's mind seemed to be somewhere else. He was constantly thinking of new ways to improve life at MBA—and since so many aspects of our lives needed improving, he was always getting distracted, even in the midst of a possible crisis.

Downstairs, Dr. Iwanyi, one of our astronomers, had emerged from his room without his family, which proba-bly meant his wife, Dr. Goldstein, our botanist, and their seven-year-old son Kamoze, were still asleep or had opted to stay in the room. Meanwhile, Dr. Daphne Merritt, our roboticist, looked like she *wished* she were still in bed. Nor-mally, Daphne was joyful and chipper, but now she seemed groggy and grumpy. Drs. Kim and Alvarez, our geologist and water-extraction specialist respectively, were struggling to put on their robes and slippers, while Dr. Janke, the Peruvian astrobiologist, was engaged in urgent conversation with Dr. Balnikov, the hulking Russian astrophysicist.

Meanwhile, Chang Kowalski had already leaped into action. In addition to being our geochemist and resident genius, Chang was also in far better shape than anyone else at MBA. On earth he'd been an extreme athlete; now he still worked out in the gym up to four hours a day. Although Chang lived on the first floor, he had already scaled the steps to the second-floor catwalk.

He was racing toward the Sjobergs' tourist suite—which led me to believe that the terrified scream had come from there.

I suddenly didn't feel quite so concerned anymore.

Up to that moment, I had been worried that something bad had happened to someone I *liked*. However, I hated the Sjobergs. I hated them even more than I hated using the space toilet, which was really saying something. They were a family of trillionaires who'd coughed up a ton of money to be the first space tourists, and they were the worst people I'd ever met in my life. I wasn't the only one at MBA who felt that way; everyone else despised them too. Lars and Sonja, the parents, were amoral, abusive, and downright nasty. Patton and Lily, their sixteen-year-old twins, were brutal and mean. In addition to their general awfulness, the Sjobergs had recently sabotaged the base's robotics system to bolster their own investment in a rival lunar-tourism business. As punishment, Nina had taken away all their ComLink privileges, so they could no longer communicate with earth. Since this removed the few things that had given them pleasure—contact with friends, movie and book downloads, access to virtual-reality games—the Sjobergs were miserable. But rather than apologize and make amends, they had responded by becoming even more obnoxious than before.

Even so, it wasn't like I was *happy* that something bad might have happened to one of them. But I would much rather have had something bad happen to a Sjoberg than anyone else at MBA.

All the other Moonies were so focused on the Sjoberg residence that no one noticed Dad and me returning to base through the air lock.

Then Mom emerged onto the catwalk. Violet trailed behind her in purple *Squirrel Force* pajamas, still half asleep. Except for Nina's residence, ours was the closest to the air lock, almost directly above it. Mom glanced toward the staging area, probably wondering if Dad and I had made it back from outside. So Violet looked our way as well and caught Dad in the act of closing the inner air-lock door. She was suddenly wide awake. "Were you just outside?" she exclaimed.

Even though Violet was quite loud, there was enough going on that no one else heard her. Except Chang Kowalski. He spotted us, but instead of saying anything, he simply gave Dad a conspiratorial wink and continued on toward the Sjobergs'.

Dad decided to deal with Violet's question by ignoring it. He quickly sealed the inner air-lock door, then called up to Mom. "What's going on?"

Before Mom could answer, Violet demanded, "Why did Dash get to go outside again and not me?"

Mom shushed her and said, "I'll explain later."

Violet put her hands on her hips and gave the biggest pout she could. "It's not fair!"

She was making a big enough scene now that other Moonies paused to look at us, but by this point, there was no way to tell that Dad and I had just come through the air lock. Now that we'd shrugged off our space suits, we were in our usual, everyday clothes. As far as anyone else knew, we might have been coming from the communal bathroom, which was on the opposite side of MBA from our residences.

"Violet, please . . . ," Mom began.

"I never get to do anything fun!" Violet argued.

In exasperation, Mom simply clamped her hand over Violet's mouth and told Dad, "I don't know what's happening. I only heard Sonja scream."

Violet continued trying to argue, even though Mom's hand was over her mouth and we couldn't possibly understand her.

By now the rest of the Moonies had gathered around the door to the Sjobergs' suite. There was a sudden commotion as Nina and Lars emerged into the crowd.

I figured Nina must have run right there after cutting off radio communication with us.

Even though it was the middle of the night, Nina was in her official moon-base commander jumpsuit. I would have assumed she had slept in it, except that it didn't have a single wrinkle. Everything else about Nina was perfectly shipshape as well, from her polished shoes to her tightly shellacked hair.

Next to her, Lars Sjoberg was completely the opposite. The man was normally slovenly, but now he was disturbingly disheveled. His eyes were glassy, what little hair he had was standing on end, and he was even paler than usual, which was hard to believe. When Lars had arrived at MBA, he had already been the palest person I had ever met; an additional five months on the moon without any sunlight had rendered him as white as a block of tofu. But tonight there was something unsettling and ghostly about his pallor. He leaned on Nina for support, as though his legs weren't working properly, and he seemed very confused. He was still being a total jerk, though. As usual. "Where are you taking me?" he asked Nina angrily. "I demand to know!"

"I've already told you three times," Nina said calmly.

"We're going to the medical bay. We need to find out what's wrong with you."

"Nothing is wrong with me!" Lars snapped, pulling away from her. "I'm perfectly fine!"

"Darling, you're not," Sonja Sjoberg said, following her husband out onto the catwalk. She looked worse than usual as well, only in her case this was because she wasn't wearing any makeup. Sonja had undergone dozens of plastic-surgery operations, vainly reconstructing every bit of her face. Unfortunately, all the adjustments had been designed for earth's gravity, and on the moon things had gone horribly wrong. Her lips, which had been delicately inflated on earth, had ballooned to three times their normal size, while the helium micropockets injected into her face to keep her skin from sagging now rose too high. Normally, Sonja could conceal some of this with makeup, but without it she looked awfully scary. Several of the Moonies gathered around the door recoiled in fright.

Lars responded to her in something that might have been their native Swedish, or possibly delirious gobbledygook. I wouldn't have known the difference.

Patton and Lily Sjoberg lurked in the doorway to their tourist suite. Lily looked concerned about her father, although not nearly as hysterical as her mother. Patton looked like he was annoyed at his father for waking him in the middle of the night.

"Let's go," Nina said, tugging on Lars's arm.

"For the last time, I don't need your help!" Lars snapped. "I'm healthy as can be!" He yanked his arm away from Nina with such force that he stumbled backward, slammed into the catwalk railing, flipped over it, and tumbled to the floor below.

"Lars!" Sonja screamed.

On earth, such a fall might have badly injured Lars. But in the moon's low gravity, he didn't land heavily enough to break anything—although he *did* bonk his head pretty hard. It sounded like a baseball getting thwacked for a home run. Sonja shrieked in horror: the same ear-piercing wail I'd heard over the radio. But now, inside at close range, it was shrill enough to set my teeth on edge.

Dad instinctively hurried to Lars's side to see if he was all right, and I followed. Since everyone else was up on the catwalk, we got to Lars first. He was lying on the floor, spread-eagled, looking even more dazed than before. "How do you feel now?" Dad asked.

"I want a panda," Lars said dreamily.

Rather than circle all the way back to the stairs, Nina and Chang both leaped over the catwalk railing and landed next to us—even though Nina would have chewed me out if she'd ever caught me doing that.

Dr. Marquez stayed on the catwalk and peered over the

railing. "He's obviously suffering some sort of delirium," he announced.

"You think?" Chang asked sarcastically. He had a very low opinion of Dr. Marquez's medical skills. Given that Chang was a genius on the level of Einstein, I would have bet he was right.

Unfortunately, we didn't have another doctor at MBA. Our previous one had been murdered, and his replacement wasn't due to arrive for another week. For the time being, we were making due with Chang's general knowledge of medicine and Dr. Marquez's questionable knowledge of it.

Sonja was now crying hysterically and babbling in Swedish. Mom and Dr. Brahmaputra-Marquez did their best to comfort her, leading her back into her suite to sit her down.

"There's no need to panic," Mom said reassuringly. "Lars is in good hands."

Sonja gave another teeth-rattling wail in response.

Lars was still lying on the floor, smiling vacantly at us, apparently unaware of his wife's concern. "Would any of you like a panda?" he asked us. "I'm buying them for everyone."

"Me!" Violet exclaimed, raising her hand excitedly. "I want *two* pandas!"

"Lars is a lot nicer when he's delirious," Dad observed.

"By a factor of a thousand," Chang agreed. "We should have whacked him on the head five months ago."

Nina frowned, once again failing to find the humor in anything. "Do you think it's hypoxia?" she asked Chang.

Hypoxia is oxygen deficiency. Since there is no oxygen on the moon, we had to generate and recycle it. And since humans can only survive without oxygen for about three minutes, oxygen levels were among the most carefully monitored data at MBA. Everyone, even the little kids, had been instructed in how to recognize the signs of hypoxia, so I knew them well: shortness of breath, elevated heart rate, sweating, wheezing, confusion, and dramatic change of skin color. Although most people associate blue skin with oxygen deprivation, the skin of a hypoxic person can turn other colors, like cherry red.

Now that I thought about it, Lars's breathing sounded a bit labored—although his skin certainly hadn't changed color. It remained as pale and colorless as skin could be.

To my surprise, Chang gave me an uneasy glance before answering Nina, as though concerned that she had mentioned this in front of me. Then he said, "I don't think this is hypoxia."

"Then what is it?" Nina asked.

"I don't know," Chang admitted.

Nina scowled, disappointed. "You don't have any ideas at all?"

"I have plenty of ideas," Chang said. "But I don't know if

any of them are right. We need to call Mission Control and talk to a doctor."

"I'm on it," Nina said, then hustled into the medical bay.

"Why don't you let me look at him?" Dr. Marquez said, even though he had made no effort to check on Lars so far. "*I'm* a doctor."

"I meant a *real* doctor," Chang corrected. "One who actually knows what he's doing."

Dr. Marquez grew offended. "I *am* a real doctor! And I wrote a best-selling book about medicine!"

"About pop psychology," Chang reminded him. "If Lars has trouble finding his happy place, we'll call you. But for now we need to get him to the medical bay." He looked to Lars. "Can you stand up?"

"I can do lots of things," Lars replied cheerfully. "I can even sing 'I'm a Little Teapot' in Dutch. Would you like to hear that?"

"No," Chang said quickly. "I would like you to stand up and walk to the medical bay with me."

Lars tried to get to his feet. He also decided to show us that he could sing in Dutch anyhow. *"Ik ben een beetje waterkoker . . . ,"* he began.

Lars still looked unsteady, so Dad and Chang grabbed his arms and helped him stand. The medical bay was only a few feet from where Lars had fallen, so it didn't take long to walk him there. Lars kept singing the whole way. He had a terrible singing voice. It sounded like someone was strangling a cat. I was relieved once they got inside the clinic and shut the door, muting the sound.

By now, many of the Moonies had made it downstairs. Violet, Kira Howard, and Roddy Marquez joined me.

"What do you think is wrong with him?" Kira asked. Although she had only been at MBA two months, she was my best friend there. (Not that she had much competition for this.) Kira was scary smart, although she tended to think that rules were for other people.

"Yeah," Violet said, mimicking Kira's posture. "What do you think is wrong with him?" Violet had really taken to Kira, and often modeled her behavior reverently.

"Looks to me like he has space madness," Roddy said, which was his go-to explanation for any inexplicable behavior at MBA. Roddy was always quick to offer up his opinion on things, whether you wanted it or not. He generally had a 50 percent chance of being right. He knew a lot about science, but he also got too wrapped up in sci-fi conspiracy theories.

"There's no such thing as space madness," Kira said disdainfully.

"Yeah," Violet seconded. "There's no such thing."

"Yes, there is," Roddy insisted. "But NASA has covered it up. Half the people who came up here to build this base went crazy. Spending long periods of time away from earth and in cramped spaces can seriously damage your brain."

"Well, it's certainly damaged *yours*," Kira said. "Or were you already a psycho when you got here?"

"Boom!" Violet crowed. "She got you good!"

"Ha-ha," Roddy sneered. "If space madness doesn't exist, then what's going on with Lars right now? He looks pretty insane to me."

"I'd guess ergot contamination," Kira said.

"Yeah," Violet agreed. "It's probably blursnot conflammination."

"Ergot contamination," I corrected. "Ergot is a fungus that grows on cereals. If you eat it, it can cause hallucinations and things."

"What kinds of cereals?" Violet asked, worried. "Like Frooty Puffs?"

"Not cereals like that," I said. "Stuff like rye and wheat."

Violet heaved a sigh of relief. "Whew. Because I love Frooty Puffs. I don't want my head getting conflamminated."

"Frooty Puffs are made from wheat, dummy," Roddy said. "And besides, NASA irradiates all our food and then hermetically seals it before it comes up here, so it couldn't possibly get contaminated." He gave Kira a superior smirk.

"So," Kira said, "you think NASA has this huge conspiracy to keep us from learning about space madness—and yet you completely trust them with the safety of our food?"

Roddy's smirk faded. "Well . . . I . . . uh . . ."

"Who's the dummy now?" Violet asked him. "Here's a hint: It's you!" She raised her hand for a high five and Kira slapped it.

Around us, the other Moonies were also discussing what could possibly be wrong with Lars. Most of them seemed to think either some form of food contamination or stress was behind it. Although Cesar Marquez, Roddy's dim older brother, was suggesting that it might have been "some kind of Swedish brain disease." I overheard Dr. Merritt tell Dr. Iwanyi, "I don't know what it could be, but if it keeps Lars from being a jerk, we shouldn't cure it."

Mom emerged from the Sjobergs' suite on the catwalk, looking frazzled after dealing with Sonja. Everyone looked up to her expectantly. I noticed that Sonja's wailing had stopped.

"She's calm now," Mom reported. "Ilina gave her a sedative."

Dr. Janke asked, "Did Sonja give any indication what happened with Lars?"

"Only that it came out of nowhere," Mom replied. "She said she woke up and found him pacing around their suite, babbling deliriously."

"Space madness!" Roddy exclaimed triumphantly. "Just as I thought!"

"Give it a rest, loser," Cesar chided.

Violet giggled at this.

Roddy turned the color red we were supposed to associate with hypoxia. Most likely, he was upset because Cesar had insulted him in front of Kira, who he had a crush on. "You want proof I'm right?" he challenged. "Let's get proof. Nina's probably on the ComLink with a doctor right now. Let's see what she says." He stormed toward the door of the medical bay.

"Roddy!" Mom yelled. "Do not disturb them! This is an emergency!"

Roddy didn't listen. He was too determined to prove he was right.

Mom looked to me for help, as I was a lot closer to Roddy than she was. "Roddy, wait," I said, and started after him.

Before I could stop him, though, Roddy sprang the last few steps to the medical-bay door and threw it open. So I ended up with a very good view of what was happening inside.

Lars was laid out on the examination table. Dad and Chang were pinning him down while Nina held a syringe. A small yellow case marked with a skull and crossbones sat on the table.

A doctor was talking them through the procedure on the ComLink, her face taking up the entire SlimScreen. "Once he has inhaled the amyl nitrate," she was saying, "then give him the shot."

The adults all wheeled on Roddy as he entered. "Roddy!" Nina barked. "Get out of here!"

She was so angry, even Roddy understood not to push his luck. He quickly backed up and closed the door.

But I had seen and heard enough. I had paid plenty of attention to our medical briefings, and I had dutifully read all the sections about emergencies in *The Official Residents' Guide to Moon Base Alpha* as well. So I knew exactly what the yellow case with the skull and crossbones was for.

Lars Sjoberg didn't have space madness.

He'd been poisoned.

Excerpt from *The Official NASA Procedures for Contact with Intelligent Extraterrestrial Life* © National Aeronautics and Space Administration, Department of Extraterrestrial Affairs, 2029 (Classification Level AAA)

HISTORICAL IMPACT

Before reading on, it is important to take a moment to consider the impact of contact with intelligent extraterrestrial life. This event will be, without question, one of the most significant events in all of human history—if not *the* most significant. How it is handled will have incredible repercussions for the future of humanity. Therefore, while initial contact cannot necessarily be controlled,* it is imperative that secondary contact and communication be handled by trained professionals who will be appropriate representatives of Planet Earth. If this is not done, the ramifications for the survival of life on earth could be disastrous.

---

* It is likely that alien civilizations will come to earth with little understanding of our own civilization, and thus it is impossible to predict whom they might initiate primary contact with. They might not approach the proper government officials at first, and might instead attempt to initiate primary contact with laypeople, children, or even animals.

RIDICULOUSLY INTELLIGENT LIFE

Lunar day 252

Still very early in the morning

It was cyanide poisoning, to be precise.

Nina had hoped to keep that a secret, because she didn't want to start a panic. However, Roddy also knew exactly what the yellow box with the skull and crossbones meant. Before I could stop him, he announced to the entire moon base, "Someone poisoned Lars Sjoberg!"

The base immediately erupted into chaos. Everyone spoke at once, insisting that they couldn't believe anyone would have done such a thing—and then quickly professing their innocence.

I understood exactly why they felt the need to do this.

Every single one of them had probably wished Lars Sjoberg dead at some point. Lots of them had even said it out loud in public. (I know that *I* had. Plenty of times.) The man had been absolutely horrible to every one of us. He had insulted, berated, tormented, and threatened us. In the most loathsome and vile family I had ever encountered, he was the most loathsome and vile by far.

So it wasn't *too* hard to imagine that, faced with the prospect of being cooped up with the king of all jerkwads for another few months, someone had decided to simply bump him off instead.

And everyone else seemed to be thinking the exact same thing.

So Nina moved quickly to restore order. Once the cyanide in Lars's system was counteracted, she left Dad and Chang to keep an eye on him and exited the medical bay to speak to all of us.

"Although Lars has been poisoned by cyanide," she announced, "that does not mean someone actively poisoned him."

"Yeah, right," Roddy muttered beside me.

"There are many ways in which Lars might have been exposed to cyanide other than a murder attempt," Nina continued.

"Like what?" Dr. Balnikov asked suspiciously.

"Yes," Dr. Brahmaputra-Marquez agreed. "Are there any environmental hazards that we need to be aware of at the base?"

A murmur of concern rippled through the crowd.

"There is no cause for alarm," Nina insisted. "As you know, NASA is constantly monitoring our habitat, and they haven't seen anything to be concerned about."

"Today, at least," grumbled Dr. Alvarez.

His wife, Dr. Kim, gave him an angry elbow in the ribs. "Shenzu!" she hissed, then glanced toward Roddy, Kira, and me, as though worried we'd overheard him.

It occurred to me that I had gotten a lot of worried glances that morning.

"We all have a very busy day tomorrow," Nina informed us. "Your residences are safe to return to, so please go home and try to get some sleep. Perpetuating rumors like this is childish and counterproductive." Then she spun around and returned to the medical bay, confident that we would all dutifully obey her after she had just insulted our behavior.

Of course, no one obeyed her. Everyone *acted* as if they were obeying her, making a show of heading back to their residences, but instead of going inside and returning to bed, they all simply lowered their voices so Nina couldn't hear them from the medical bay. It was kind of like being at camp, after the counselors inform a cabin full of amped kids that it's bedtime, but no one wants to sleep.

Even Violet was wide awake, given the early hour. "Why would someone poison Lars Sjoberg?" she asked Mom.

"No one poisoned Lars," Mom told her. "Didn't you hear Nina?"

"Yes, but why *would* someone do it? To kill him?"

"It's very late," Mom said, looking uncomfortable. "You ought to get back to bed."

"Would *you* be happy if Lars died?" Violet asked. "I know Dad would."

"Violet!" Mom gasped, glancing around to see if anyone had overheard. Of course, plenty of people had. "Why would you say something like that?"

"Because Dad said he wanted to kill Lars the other day. After Lars threatened Dash."

"Let's go," Mom said, taking Violet by the hand. "Back to bed right now."

"But I'm not sleepy!" Violet protested. "No one else is going to bed! I still don't even know what cyanide is!"

Mom started to rush Violet up the stairs, then paused as she passed me. A look of regret washed over her face as something occurred to her. "Dash, I know this isn't what we'd hoped for on your birthday. . . ."

"It's okay," I assured her. In truth, with all the commotion,

I'd briefly forgotten about my birthday. Then I lowered my voice so no one else would hear. "Thanks for letting me go outside. It was amazing."

"I'm sorry it got interrupted like this."

"I think Chang wanted to kill Lars too," Violet said. "I heard him say it a bunch of times."

Mom sighed, exasperated, then dragged Violet toward our room. In her haste—or maybe because she felt bad for me—she didn't insist that I return to bed myself.

Not that I would have anyhow. Because Zan Perfonic had just appeared to me.

Even though Zan communicated with me via thought, she still projected an image of herself into my mind to make our communication seem more like a normal conversation. Furthermore, she projected herself as a human being, rather than what she actually looked like. The human form she had chosen was that of an extremely beautiful woman, with olive skin and blazing blue eyes.

I had no idea what Zan really looked like. She hadn't shared that with me yet, despite my begging her to. But I was quite certain that she didn't look anything like a human being.

Zan tried to make her arrivals seem as normal as possible to me. She wouldn't simply pop into existence all of a sudden, as that tended to startle me. (We had learned this through experience. The last time Zan had appeared too quickly, I had yelped in surprise in front of the entire mess hall, and then I'd had to blame my strange behavior on accidentally biting my tongue.) Now she made it seem as though she had walked around the corner from the gym and waved at me through the crowd.

"Hey," Kira said to me, unaware that Zan was there. "I almost forgot: Happy birthday."

"Thanks," I said.

"That was almost a heck of a present someone got you: Lars Sjoberg dead."

Across the room, Zan frowned at this. Even though she was projecting herself as being several yards away, she was aware of everything I was thinking, so now she had just learned about Lars.

"I didn't want Lars dead," I said quickly.

"Well, everyone else sure did." Kira lowered her voice. "Who do you think did it? It could've been almost anyone."

"I don't know," I said. "Can you excuse me? I need to go to the bathroom."

"Sure. Have a nice birthday poop. I'll catch you after."

I quickly slipped through the crowd, trying to avoid a conversation with anyone else. I actually headed for the bathroom, not because I really had to go—or wanted to spend any more time there than I had to—but because there weren't many options for privacy at MBA. The base wasn't big to begin with, and now my fellow Moonies were all milling about in most of the public areas, discussing Lars's potential murder. Dr. Balnikov and Dr. Janke were in the rec room. Dr. Marquez and Dr. Iwanyi had wandered into the mess hall to get coffee. Kira's father, Dr. Howard, was standing by himself next to the greenhouse, staring at the plants. He might have been thinking about Lars Sjoberg, but it was equally possible that he'd forgotten all about Lars and was now thinking of some new way to produce more tomatoes in low gravity.

So I went to the bathroom, and then I entered one of the three stalls, locked the door, and sat on the space toilet. I kept my pants up, though. I didn't need to have a conversation with a higher life form while my pants were around my ankles.

Zan appeared in the stall a second later, simply materializing out of thin air this time. There was no point in her making a show of clambering under the locked stall door. "It's your birthday today," she said. "The end of your thirteenth earth orbit around the sun?"

"Yes." Even though there was no one else in the bathroom, I didn't say this out loud. I only thought the words, wanting to keep the conversation silent. It wasn't easy—speaking out loud was a tough habit to break—but I'd been getting much better at it over the past few weeks.

"I wasn't planning on appearing to you this early today," Zan told me. "But then I sensed you were already awake, and

I wanted to wish you a happy anniversary of your emergence from your mother's uterus."

"Um," I said. "We usually just say 'happy birthday.' I don't suppose you had anything exciting planned for me? Like maybe showing me what you really look like?"

"Actually, I *had* wanted to do something like that."

"Really?" I was so excited, I almost said the word out loud. I had been dying to learn more about Zan for months, but she had been very tight-lipped with information, preferring to grill me about humanity instead.

"Yes. I thought you deserved to know some more things about my species." Zan sighed. "But now I'm afraid I have to ask what happened with Lars. Did someone really try to kill him?"

I frowned, upset for two reasons:

First, learning some things about Zan's world really would have been a great present, but now Lars's poisoning had put that on hold.

More importantly, another potential murder at MBA made humans look pretty bad.

There was a great deal at stake in my contact with Zan. Quite likely, the fate of earth hung in the balance.

A few weeks before, Zan had told me that humanity was in grave danger of destroying itself. In a sense this wasn't a massive surprise, because anyone paying attention could see that we were destroying pretty much every life form on earth: hunting rhinos, elephants, and gorillas to extinction; burning down forests; cranking up the heat on the planet by several degrees; and killing one another by the millions in dozens of wars, genocides, and other conflicts over the last decade. But still, it was unsettling to hear that the end could come *soon*, rather than at some vague point in the future. Zan had likened humans to an asteroid bearing down on our own planet, capable of wiping out all forms of life.

But there was hope. Zan's species—and several others in the galaxy—knew of a way to solve many of our problems.

Unfortunately, most of them didn't want to share it with us.

Their solution had the potential to be dangerous if misused, and they had perceived (correctly, I had to admit) that humans had a disturbing track record of taking new technology and trying to kill people with it: gunpowder, planes, nuclear bombs, and so on. If we tried to weaponize their technology, it could have far-reaching effects across the galaxy that would doom those other civilizations as well. So they had written us off as a lost cause.

Only Zan hadn't. She saw potential in us that most others didn't. While our tendency to kill one another was certainly a bad thing, there was good in us as well. We had invented things no other civilization had: Music. Art. Poetry. Love. Some other members of her species were in agreement, but not many. Zan wasn't supposed to be in contact with me at all—and she was taking a great risk by doing it.

Passing on the technology would be a much greater risk, though. Zan didn't even have the authority to do it; she'd be breaking the law, which would put her in danger. So she was still trying to figure out what to do.

Which was where I came in.

Essentially, humanity was on trial, and I was the defense lawyer in an uphill battle. In the two months that I had known Zan, there had already been one murder at MBA, as well as many other acts of greed and duplicity. To make matters worse, this was all happening in a group of only twenty-five people, some of whom were among the smartest humans alive.

We also had the Sjobergs, prime examples of the worst that humans could be.

So I already had my work cut out for me. And now I had another potential murder—or attempted murder—to explain.

"I don't know if someone tried to kill Lars or not," I told Zan. "Nina says it was probably an accident of some sort."

"But you don't believe Nina." It was a statement, not a question. Zan could read my thoughts and feelings well enough to know the truth.

"I'm not sure what to believe. I don't really know much about this. It all only happened just now."

"Nina has lied to you before. Plenty of times."

"You've lied to me too," I pointed out.

"I was trying to protect you."

"So is Nina, I think. She's trying to protect all of us."

"How?"

"By keeping us from getting worried."

"But there could be a killer among you again. Don't you think all of you *should* be worried about that?"

"If there *is* a killer, yes. But we don't know that for sure yet. This might just have been an accident. Maybe Lars got poisoning from the food."

"If your food is poisoned, that sounds like something you should be worried about too."

"Um . . . yes," I admitted. "The thing is, Nina's trying to do the right thing. We all are—"

"Except for whoever tried to kill Lars."

"If someone actually tried to kill him at all. Which there's no proof of. While plenty of us have been doing very nice things for the Sjobergs. I mean, my Dad and Chang just helped save Lars's life, and he's always been awful to them. And Mom and Dr. Brahmaputra-Marquez were taking care of Sonja, too."

"They are," Zan agreed, then considered this for a while. Eventually, she asked, "Do humans *like* killing each other?"

"What?" I asked, aghast. "Why would you even think that?"

"You seem to do it so often."

"Not really," I said, defensively.

"There are only twenty-five people at this base—and there has already been one murder and one poisoning here. That's quite a lot, isn't it?"

"Well, like I said, that poisoning might have just been an accident."

"And I understand that on earth there are thousands of murders every day."

"That sounds a bit high. . . ."

"Well, you have people dying in wars. There are many of those taking place on earth right now, yes?"

I frowned. Somehow the conversation had grown even worse. "Yes."

"And there have been hundreds of wars throughout your history. Thousands, maybe. Why would you do this so often if it wasn't enjoyable?"

"It's . . . um . . . well, it's complicated. But no one *likes* killing people. I swear."

"A great many of your movies feature people killing one another. And those are made for your enjoyment, yes?"

My frown grew larger. The only way Zan even knew about those movies was because I had shown them to her. "Yes."

"Millions of people die in *Star Wars* alone. Garth Schmader blows up an entire planet."

"Darth Vader," I corrected. "And he's the bad guy."

"But the good people kill too. And they're supposed to be heroes."

"I thought you liked *Star Wars*," I said, trying to change the subject again. "And all the other movies I showed you too. I thought you said they were one of the great things about humanity. Along with all our other forms of entertainment."

"The innovation that you employ to amuse one another is certainly unusual. I find it all very fascinating. It's amazing that you can create such wonderful stories and yet still enjoy killing each other."

"We *don't* enjoy killing each other!"

"Then why do you do it so often? Why do you spend so many billions of dollars on weapons? Why are your armies so big?"

"Now hold on," I said. "Are you telling me that, on your entire planet, members of your species *never* kill each other?"

"Yes."

"Really? You settle all conflicts without wars?"

"Of course."

I did my best to hide my surprise. Perhaps it was a bad reflection on me as a human, but I had a hard time imagining how that was even possible. "And this applies to all species that you know of across the galaxy?"

"The intelligent ones."

"So . . . there are some others who kill?"

"Oh yes. But we do our best to avoid them."

"Look," I said. "I can't really explain why people kill each other. I don't get it myself. But I know we don't enjoy it. No one *wants* to do it."

"Then why do so many of your video games involve the simulation of it? Your friend Roddy spends several hours a day playing those."

"Roddy isn't my friend. He's just someone I'm stuck here with."

"But he's not an anomaly, is he? You have said yourself that those games are extremely popular."

I sighed, exasperated. "Zan, it's my birthday. And I can think of a million ways I'd rather spend it besides having this conversation while seated on the space toilet."

Zan blinked, startled. "I'm sorry. I'm simply trying to understand your species. . . ."

"Well, there are things about us I just can't explain. I'm only a kid. I don't know the reason humans do half the things we do. I don't have any idea why we kill each other. Or pick our noses. Or say 'cheese' when someone takes a picture of us—"

"You name a dairy product during the act of photographic recording?"

"Yes! And I don't know why! It makes no sense. But we do it anyhow. That's just the way things are sometimes."

Zan nodded, then lowered her eyes, looking a bit ashamed. "You have made a good point, Dashiell. There are things about my species that I couldn't explain either. Sometimes I ask too much of you. I forget how young you are, how quick your revolutions are around your sun."

"What do you mean by that?" I asked.

Zan returned her attention to me. "Surely you must realize that the time it takes a planet to orbit its star varies greatly throughout the galaxy? In your own solar system, it can take as little as eighty-eight days for the planet you call Mercury, or one hundred sixty-five years for Neptune."

"Sure, I knew that," I said, then admitted, "But it never occurred to me that that would make time different for aliens on other planets."

"Very different." Zan smiled. "My intention in coming here today wasn't to interrogate you. It was to share things about myself with you. So perhaps this is a very good place to start. The way you view time, from seconds all the way up to millennia, is very different from the way we view it."

I smiled as well, pleased to be off the topic of humanity's bloodlust and onto something I was excited to learn. The mere idea that there might be some other way to think of time was fascinating to me. "So how do you view it?"

"I'm afraid it might be too complicated for you to understand, but to begin to put it in your terms, our planet is a bit farther from our sun than you are from yours. So what you would think of as our years are a bit longer."

"How much?"

"Approximately twice as long as yours."

"So if I lived on your planet, I wouldn't even be seven yet?"

"Again, that's not exactly how we see it, but as far as the basics are concerned, you're correct."

"If your planet is so much farther from your sun, isn't it cold?"

"No. Our sun is larger than yours, and it burns a bit hotter. So my planet is quite . . . I think the word you would use is 'pleasant.' Or 'balmy,' maybe?"

A question occurred to me, and it startled me that, in all the time I'd known Zan, I'd never thought to ask it. I had always assumed that she was around the same age as the version of herself she projected to me, but I now realized that might not be true. "Zan, how many times have you gone around your sun?"

She smiled coyly. "I thought that, on your planet, it was regarded as bad manners to ask a woman her age."

"This is for science. And, to be honest, you're not a woman. The same rules don't apply."

"I have orbited around my sun one hundred eighty-six times.

I gaped at her, my mind blown. I had expected Zan to be older than me, but nowhere near anything like this. "What? That's like . . ." I tried to calculate quickly in my head. "Over three hundred fifty years old!"

"Three hundred seventy-two of your earth years. More or less."

I sat back, stunned, unsure what to say. All I could come up with was, "Wow. You look great."

Zan smiled again. "You tease. My real form is nothing like this."

"About that," I said. "You know what would be an incredible birthday present? Showing me what you *really* look like."

Zan considered that for a while. Eventually she said, "I suppose it would."

Before I could ask her to do it, though, the bathroom door banged open and Roddy stormed in.

"Dash!" he yelled. "Are you still in here?" I heard him drop to the floor to peer under the wall of the toilet stall. I tried to yank my feet up before he could see them, but I didn't move fast enough.

"Aha!" he cried. "There you are! Wrap it up. Nina wants to see you."

"Now?" I asked, incredulous. Although, after speaking to Zan in my head for so long, I actually forgot to say it out loud.

Roddy banged on the stall door, rattling it wildly. "No use giving me the silent treatment. I know you're in there."

"Tell her I'm going to be a while," I said, out loud this time.

"Really?" Roddy asked. "'Cause you've been in there for like half an hour as it is. What's taking so long? You didn't bust the evaporator again, did you?"

"No. I just need a little privacy is all."

"Sorry, pal. No can do. Nina gave me express orders to bring you to her right away. So finish up fast."

Zan looked to me sadly. "This sounds important. I'll let you go."

"No!" I said, so upset that this time, I actually said it out loud.

"No?" Roddy asked, thinking I was talking to him. "I'm not going to sit around here waiting all day for you. I've got better things to do." This from the guy who routinely took up one of our three toilets for hours at a time because he got engrossed playing video games on the stall SlimScreen.

I looked to Zan desperately and spoke inside my head. "Please. You can't leave now."

"I'll come back soon," she told me. "Once things have calmed down. I promise."

And just like that, she was gone.

Excerpt from *The Official NASA Procedures for Contact with Intelligent Extraterrestrial Life* © National Aeronautics and Space Administration, Department of Extraterrestrial Affairs, 2029 (Classification Level AAA)

RADIO CONTACT

While we do not want to rule out the possibility of direct encounters with intelligent extraterrestrial life (from here on referred to as IEL), due to the great distances between planets in our galaxy (and thus potential civilizations) it is far more likely that initial contact with IEL will be via long-distance transmissions, most likely radio waves, which will be picked up by large satellite facilities such as the Very Large Array. For this reason, radio transmissions to and from these facilities are closely and carefully monitored at all times. Should anyone who works at one of these facilities believe they have detected an actual transmission, then they are duty-bound to report the detection to the appropriate office at once.

BAD LUTEFISK

Lunar day 252

Still way too early in the morning

"Lars wasn't poisoned by accident," Nina said.
"Someone tried to kill him."

We were in her residence, which also served as her office,
facing each other across her desk. Both of us were seated on
the InflatiCubes we had to use at MBA instead of chairs.
Given the early hour and my exhaustion, I was struggling to
sit upright on mine. Meanwhile, Nina sat ramrod straight,
everything about her compulsively neat and tidy as usual.
All Moonies had been allowed to bring a few personal items
from earth; it spoke volumes about Nina that she had chosen
to bring an iron.

I stared at her, stunned. Even though I had suspected someone had been trying to murder Lars, I had been really hoping I was wrong. The confirmation that we had a second murderer loose at MBA was extremely unnerving.

I was equally surprised that Nina was sharing this information with me. I had been half expecting her to punish me for sneaking out onto the lunar surface, so this caught me completely off guard. I couldn't fathom why she was doing it, but I had other questions to ask first.

"How do you know?" I asked.

"Your father and Chang pumped Lars's stomach. They found cyanide among the contents of his last meal. Someone poisoned his food."

"The cyanide couldn't have gotten in there by accident? Like through some kind of contamination?"

Nina shook her head. "The safety of our food at this base is one of NASA's highest priorities. Given that we have no natural source of food on the moon, contamination of our food supply would obviously be a disaster. So the agency takes extreme steps to make sure that doesn't happen. There is no way that any poison could end up in our food. Not by accident, anyway. And certainly not at the levels that your father and Chang found in Lars's stomach."

"Do we have any idea if any of the rest of our food has been poisoned?" I asked, worried.

"No," Nina admitted. "However, we have reason to believe that this wasn't a random act. The killer appears to have been targeting Lars specifically."

"How?"

"The food that was poisoned was lutefisk."

"Ah," I said, understanding completely.

Lars Sjoberg was the only person at MBA who ate lutefisk. The entire supply of it had been packed for him personally.

Lutefisk is a traditional Scandinavian food of dried cod treated with lye for several days until it turns gelatinous. It was one of the most disgusting things I had ever tasted in my life.

In the defense of the Scandinavians, let me say that I had never tasted lutefisk back on earth. Although the mere idea of jellied fish made my skin crawl, there was a chance that some people could actually make a tasty version of it. However, I had only experienced the NASA version. I had accidentally tasted a bit from a package of space food that had been mis-labeled. I had expected scrambled eggs and ended up with a mouthful of lutefisk instead. It was so vile, I nearly had to get up close and personal with the space toilet afterward.

As Nina said, NASA had to go through a lot of trouble to make sure our space food would last for a long time without going bad. It was dehydrated, irradiated, thermostabilized, and ultimately reduced to cubes and pastes that bore little resemblance to actual food anymore. Even things as delicious as pizza, hamburgers, and cupcakes often wound up tasting like cardboard by the time the food engineers got through with them. Thus, lutefisk—which was probably an acquired taste on earth to begin with—ended up as a horrifying rancid sludge. It was disgusting on every level. It looked like pus, smelled like sewage, felt like a live snail on your tongue, and tasted even worse.

I wasn't the only one who had a problem with it. Everyone else at MBA did as well. Even the other Sjobergs, who willingly consumed lutefisk back on earth, found the NASA version nauseating. Chang Kowalski said it tasted like "punishment for everything you've ever done wrong in your entire life."

Lars Sjoberg actually liked it.

Since Lars had paid nearly a billion dollars to come to MBA as a tourist, he was allowed a few perks. One of them was that NASA would stock a few of his favorite foods. Lars loved lutefisk, so the food engineers took a crack at it—and failed miserably. Even they admitted it was disgusting, and these were the people who actually considered the chicken liver pâté they'd created to be "suitable for human consumption." (We Moonies didn't eat the pâté, although we had been using it as caulk.) The engineers had planned to incinerate the entire batch of lutefisk, but somehow Lars got ahold of it, tried some, and declared it the best thing that NASA had produced so far. NASA was shocked, but agreed to ship the vile substance up to the moon for Lars's enjoyment.

Throughout the Sjobergs' time at MBA, we had all been waiting for Lars to come to his senses and realize that the space lutefisk was vomitous, but if anything, his fondness for it grew. He claimed it reminded him of his childhood. (To which my father responded that Lars must have had the worst childhood imaginable.)

Therefore, if someone wanted to poison Lars, the lutefisk was a good way to do it. Since no one else ate it, there was little chance of poisoning the wrong person by mistake.

"Do you know how the killer got the poison into the food?" I asked.

"Not exactly," Nina replied, "But it wouldn't have been difficult. They could have simply injected some into the package with a syringe. A hole that small would have been easy to seal up. Sticking the descriptive label over it would have done the job."

That made perfect sense. All our food was sealed in metallic foil packets, and thus it all looked exactly the same. So each packet had an adhesive label to describe what was inside.

"Why do we even have cyanide on the base?" I asked.

"We *don't*," Nina stressed. "At least, we're not supposed to. Cyanide has certain industrial uses, but NASA was concerned enough about its lethality that they made sure no products at MBA contain it—or any other toxins."

"You mean, they were worried that someone might try to kill someone else with it?"

"No, they were concerned about accidents. Leaks, accidental ingestion, that sort of thing."

"So we don't know where the poison came from?"

"No."

I considered that, then had an idea. "Aren't there security cameras around the food-storage area?"

"Of course."

"So can't you just review the footage and look for whoever tampered with the lutefisk?"

"Unfortunately, the nature of this crime makes that pointless. We have no idea when the killer actually poisoned the lutefisk. They could have done it anytime within the last few months. Every single person here has access to the food storage—and there's no guarantee that they injected the poison there. They could have easily swiped a package of lutefisk, taken it someplace without cameras, such as their room, injected it, and then covertly returned it. It would take thousands of hours to comb through the past few months of security footage, while the chances of finding any evidence are infinitesimal."

"I see." I shifted uncomfortably. It seemed the time had come to ask my burning question. "Nina, why are you telling me this?"

Nina paused before answering, as though she didn't like what she had to say. "Because I need you to help me find out who poisoned Lars."

"Really?" I asked, surprised.

"Two months ago, you helped solve a murder case here."

"A case you didn't want me to investigate," I reminded her.

"You also helped figure out what had happened to me last month," Nina went on, ignoring my comment. "Therefore, it is evident that you have some talent at solving mysteries, and right now I need this mystery solved as quickly as possible. We can't have another killer on the loose here."

I was at once flattered by Nina's faith in me and worried about having to track down a killer for the second time. In truth, I was worried about there being another killer, *period*. The last time I'd faced off against a murderer, I had almost ended up dead, squashed like a fly by the base's robotic arm. "Nina, I'm just a kid . . ."

"I'm well aware that you are only twelve, Dashiell."

"Actually, I'm thirteen. It's my birthday today."

"Oh." Any other human being would have wished me a happy birthday, but it didn't even occur to Nina to do that. Sometimes she could be even more alien than Zan was.

Instead she said, "That doesn't change my opinion that you can contribute to this endeavor."

"But there are a lot of people on this base who are way

smarter than I am," I said. "Almost everyone here is a genius. Why aren't you asking *them* to help?"

"For starters, I want to keep the fact that Lars was poisoned a secret. There are two reasons for this. First, I don't want to start a panic. Especially among the younger children. Second, I want whoever poisoned Lars to think they got away with it. If they don't know we are onto them, they might let their guard down. . . ."

"And try again?" I asked.

"Perhaps," Nina replied. "If they do, then we'll catch them."

Although she didn't mention it, I could think of a third reason she would want to keep the murder attempt quiet: bad publicity. If the Moonies all knew Lars had been poisoned on purpose, sooner or later somebody would share that information with someone back on earth. NASA monitored and censored all our communication, so they could theoretically keep the public from finding out—but it was possible that Nina didn't even want NASA to know what was going on. Under her command there had already been one murder, and she herself had gone missing after violating several protocols. This might be another big strike against her.

I didn't bring that up, though. It would only annoy Nina.

"Other than you and me, only your father and Chang know the truth about the poisoning," Nina went on. "And I have asked them to keep this to themselves. We are going to tell everyone else that the poisoning was accidental. That Lars ate some contaminated lutefisk. I expect you to stick to that story as well."

"Sure," I said, then asked, "Are you at least going to have Dad and Chang help investigate too?"

"Of course. However . . ." Nina paused before continuing, as though she was choosing her words very carefully. "The reason I have come to you is that I have suspicions about Chang myself."

"Oh." Even though Chang was an adult, I considered him a friend. He was one of the only adults at MBA who talked to me like I was an equal, rather than just a kid. However, I understood exactly why Nina suspected him. Chang was usually easygoing, but when crossed he could be scary—and he was easily the smartest and strongest person on the base. He could outsmart you or beat you to a pulp. Or maybe both. And he had locked horns with Lars Sjoberg many times.

"As you know, Chang and Lars don't get along very well," Nina said, which was a massive understatement. The men loathed each other. "I consider it possible that Chang might have been behind this attempt. If so, he might try to cover his tracks and destroy any evidence that leads to him. Therefore, I would like another person on this case."

"So you want me to keep an eye on Chang?"

"Yes. But also I want you keeping an eye on everyone else."

"Everyone?"

"Sadly, given the victim of this crime, I can't rule out anyone on this base. There is no other person at MBA as disliked as Lars Sjoberg. He has made life miserable for everyone here. It is possible that anyone might have finally had enough."

"Well, not the kids," I said.

To my surprise, Nina didn't agree with this right away. She took her time, then finally said, "I suppose it's unlikely that Violet, Kamoze, or Inez would have the wherewithal to figure out how to poison Lars this way. But even Kira or Roddy could have done it."

Which made me wonder if Nina suspected me as well. It was completely possible that she did, and that she had asked Chang to keep an eye on *me*. After all, I'd had my share of run-ins with Lars Sjoberg.

"In fact," Nina went on, "I'd like you to pay particular attention to the children at this base. Being a child yourself, you can probably question them without raising much suspicion, while Chang, your father, and I don't have that luxury."

"Okay," I agreed. I didn't believe Kira would have done anything so horrible, but truthfully, I wasn't sure about Roddy. And Cesar was a possibility as well. Maybe they had even done it together.

"Very well, then," Nina said, as though we had been discussing something far less disturbing than a potential murderer. "I need you to get started on this right away."

"It's four thirty in the morning," I pointed out.

"It's a known fact that with every hour that elapses after a crime is committed, the killer has an exponentially better chance of getting away with it."

"But like you said, the killer might have committed this crime months ago. All they had to do was poison the lutefisk, then sit back and wait."

"I'm well aware of the difficulties this case presents," Nina said, sounding annoyed at me. "If it was easy to solve, do you think I'd be asking a twelve-year-old for help?"

"I'm thirteen," I reminded her.

"Congratulations," Nina said coldly. "If you learn anything important, I want you to tell me about it immediately. Do you understand?"

"Yes."

"Good. Now could you please get to work before I have another dead body to deal with?"

With that, she turned her attention to the computer on her desk, signaling that our conversation was finished.

I got up off the InflatiCube, walked out the door, and went to hunt for the murderer.

SIGNAL ASSESSMENT

The primary directive for any radio transmission detected from IEL is to determine what is trying to be communicated. It is presumed that such signals will fall into one of two categories:

1) Communication not intended for humanity, which we have intercepted.

2) Communication that is intended for humanity. This can further be broken down into two categories:

a) Friendly communication

b) Threats

It is imperative to determine which of these forms of communication we are dealing with as quickly as possible. Type 1 communication might be exceptionally hard to translate, as it is not intended for us, whereas type 2 communication will theoretically be constructed in some manner that we can interpret, most likely via mathematics, as mathematics are universal.

ANGRY SWEDE

Lunar day 252

A slightly more reasonable hour of the morning

Instead of beginning the investigation immedi-ately, I went back to bed. Yes, there was a killer on the loose, but everyone else Nina wanted me to investigate had gone back to sleep, I was exhausted, and it was my birthday. I wasn't particularly worried about the murderer bumping off other people in the few hours it would take me to rest up for the investigation. Lars Sjoberg seemed to be the prime target; the killer had made a concerted effort to get him and no one else.

My father wasn't in his sleep pod. I figured he must still be down in the medical bay, helping Chang take care of Lars.

Dad wasn't a doctor, but he had taken emergency medical training in preparation for coming to MBA. (All the adults had done this, but Dad had performed better on it than most—including Dr. Marquez.)

Mom and Violet were both crammed into my mother's sleep pod, which probably meant that Violet had experienced trouble getting back to sleep. She had nightmares sometimes, and the revelation that Lars Sjoberg had been poisoned wouldn't have helped that much. Thankfully, Violet seemed to be having a good dream at the moment. I heard her murmuring happily in her sleep, "Welcome to Atlantis. I am the dolphin queen."

Unfortunately, I had trouble getting back to sleep myself. Even though I was tired, I found myself plagued with questions about Lars's poisoning. If there wasn't supposed to be any cyanide at MBA, how had the killer gotten ahold of it? If they could have done the actual poisoning months before, how was I supposed to find any clues to who might have done it? And since everyone at MBA hated Lars, how was I supposed to narrow down the list of suspects? When I thought about it, I couldn't even rule out the members of Lars's own family. Sonja, Lily, and Patton were all vile people, and they probably had the biggest motive of all for bumping off Lars: his fortune. But there were plenty of other possible murderers to consider.

Finally, there was the question that bothered me most of

all: If I *did* get close to the killer in my investigation, would they come after me to protect their identity? It had happened before. For a while, I toyed with the idea of merely *telling* Nina that I was investigating, but not doing anything. After all, Nina, Chang, and my father were on the case already. If the killer managed to slip through their fingers and take out Lars, well . . . would that really be such a bad thing?

I ultimately decided to investigate, though. For a few reasons.

1) I might get in trouble for disobeying an order from Nina.

2) Letting someone get killed—even Lars Sjoberg—was wrong.

3) I didn't like the idea of there being another murderer loose at MBA. Even if they were only targeting Lars for now, what was to say that, if they got away with it, they wouldn't decide to go after more people who had rubbed them the wrong way?

So instead of dropping off to sleep, I tossed and turned. It didn't help that my sleep pod was cramped and my thin inflatable mattress pad smelled worse than lutefisk. While I was lying there, I tried projecting myself to earth via my thoughts, hoping to repeat the experience of going to Hapuna Beach. I had been trying to do this several times a day for the past month, with no success.

It didn't work this time either. I tried concentrating as hard as I could, then clearing my mind and thinking as little as possible, then blatantly wishing myself there. But I still remained at Moon Base Alpha.

So now, in addition to being concerned about the potential murder, I was also frustrated.

It was a long time before exhaustion finally won out and I drifted off to sleep.

I was out for a whole fifteen minutes before Violet woke me up.

In her defense, she was trying to be nice. She was singing "Happy Birthday" to me in Spanish, which she had recently learned in school. She wound up with a big finish at the top of her lungs and then exclaimed, "*Feliz cumpleaños*, big brother!"

"You couldn't have waited another hour to sing that?" I asked grumpily.

"Nope!" Violet proclaimed. "And I have a present for you!"

"Is it a trip back to earth?" I asked.

"I can't tell you what it is. It's a secret."

"Sorry for the early alarm," Mom told me. She was digging clothes for Violet out of our one bureau. "I kept her at bay for as long as I could. And besides, it was almost time for you to get up anyhow. You have school today."

That didn't make my morning any better. "Ugh," I

groaned. "We don't get a pass for having an emergency in the middle of the night?"

"No," Mom replied, then added conspiratorially, "I don't think NASA even *knows* about last night's events."

"Get up get up get up!" Violet urged. "You have to open your present!"

"All right. Keep your pajamas on." I slipped back out of my pod and dropped to the floor.

"Ta-da!" Violet held up a small present. We didn't have any wrapping paper at MBA—or much paper at all. Most of our reading material was electronic to cut down on the weight of our supplies. So the present had been wrapped in a few pages from our MBA residents' guide.

"Thanks," I said, taking the present from her.

"It's candy!" Violet announced, unable to keep her own secret any longer.

"Really?" I unwrapped the present to find that it was, indeed, a package of Skittles. Which wasn't a bad present at all.

Sure, back on earth a bag of candy would have been no big deal. But in the gastronomic desert that was MBA, any flavor at all was a cause for celebration. Hard candy was one of the few things that actually transferred well to space, although it still wasn't easy to come by, given that the closest grocery store was 250,000 miles away. Getting NASA to ship it up on a rocket would have taken quite a bit of advance planning.

"Thanks," I said again, giving Violet a hug. "This is awesome."

"Can I have some?" Violet asked.

"Now?" I asked. "We just got up."

"*You* just got up," Violet informed me. "I've been up for fifteen whole minutes."

"No candy until after dinner," Mom said, then gave me a wink behind Violet's back. Apparently, my birthday afforded me special candy privileges. Then Mom tossed Violet her clothes. "You haven't even had breakfast, kiddo. Get dressed."

Violet shrugged off her *Squirrel Force* pajamas and pulled her clothes on. I was already wearing mine. I had slept in them. Due to the lack of dirt, clothes didn't get very soiled in space, and due to the lack of washing machines at MBA, we were basically supposed to wear the same things over and over until they wore out.

While Violet was getting dressed, I spoke to my mother. "Thanks for the candy."

"That's not from us," she said. "It was all your sister's idea."

"But you arranged for delivery. . . ."

"Because Violet insisted on it. She thought this all up two months ago. Our present was the trip outside, which didn't last nearly as long as we'd hoped it would."

"It was amazing anyhow," I assured her. "Is Dad still down with Lars?"

Mom glanced at Violet, not wanting to discuss this in front of her, then lowered her voice. "He was there until around four in the morning. Then he went to clean off your space suits before anyone noticed them in the air lock. And after that, it was too late to go back to bed, so he just went to work in the science pod. He says the poisoning was an accident. A package of Lars's lutefisk got contaminated somehow."

Mom was telling me the fake story. Which meant that either Dad had given her the fake story as Nina had ordered him to—or Dad had disobeyed Nina's orders and told Mom the truth, but Mom was now lying to keep the truth from me.

Either way, Mom obviously didn't know I knew what had really happened.

"I'm dressed!" Violet announced, then did a twirl to prove that she did, in fact, have her clothes on. "Let's get breakfast! I'm starving!" She grabbed Mom's hand and dragged her out the door.

I snuck one Skittle from the bag, then tucked it into my mouth before following my family.

I was a big believer in savoring any decent food I got for as long as possible. On the rare occasions we got something special to eat at MBA—fresh fruit, a piece of candy, *anything* that hadn't been dehydrated—we had to make it last. If I had merely chewed up my Skittle, it would have been gone in less than a minute. Tucked into my lip, it might last half an hour. I knew the flavor had been completely fabricated in a lab in New Jersey, but I didn't care. It was delicious. A thousand times better than a dehydrated-and-reconstituted birthday cake would have been.

Outside our residence, things appeared to have returned to normal. From the catwalk I could see the other Moonies up and about. Dr. Goldstein and Dr. Iwanyi were heading into the mess hall with Kamoze. Dr. Janke was fiddling with something in the science pod. Dr. Howard was standing by the air lock, staring off into the distance, possibly thinking about something important—but just as likely zoning out.

Kira Howard was quietly slinking into the rec room, as though trying not to disturb whoever was inside.

This was completely lost on Violet. "Hi, Kira!" she yelled.

Kira spun around, shushed her, then continued into the rec room.

"Let's see what she's up to!" Violet announced, and then went down the stairs as fast as she could. She didn't exactly run, because stairs are hard to manage in low gravity, even after eight months of practice, but she did her best.

"Violet!" Mom shouted after her. "What about breakfast?"

"Not hungry!" Violet called back, even though she had announced she was starving only a minute before.

"I'll get her," I said, then hurried down the stairs after her.

"I'm going to go see your father," Mom called after me. "I'll meet you in the mess hall."

I probably could have caught Violet before she reached the bottom of the stairs, but I really wanted to know what Kira was up to as well. So I let my sister have a little room to run, and chased her toward the rec room.

I didn't quite make it there, though. I was about to enter it when I heard shouting from the medical bay. The door was closed, but whoever was shouting was loud enough to be heard from where I stood. It wasn't quite clear enough for me to make out *who* was doing the shouting, though.

Dr. Daphne Merritt walked past, her nose buried in an electronic manual. Whatever it was must have been awfully important, because normally Dr. Merritt would stop to talk, but today she barely gave me a glance. She also didn't seem interested in the shouting, which made me think that it had probably been going on for so long that it had become background noise.

I was interested in it, though, so I crept closer to the medical bay. Once I was directly outside the door, I could hear clearly enough to tell who was making all the racket inside:

Sonja Sjoberg.

That shouldn't have surprised me. If anyone was shouting at MBA, it was usually Lars or Sonja. Both operated under the misconception that the best way to get people to do something was to yell at them. Maybe that worked when they were home and surrounded by servants, but at MBA it generally made people *not* want to help them. However, the Sjobergs had completely failed to grasp this. Instead they just tended to shout louder.

"Lars needs to go back to earth!" Sonja was yelling. "And he needs to go back now! His health is at risk!"

"Not anymore," a second, much quieter voice answered. Nina Stack. "His condition has stabilized. Within a few hours he'll be back to normal."

"Back to normal?" Sonja shouted. "Someone tried to *kill* him! And they could try again, at any time! If that's not a risk to his life, I don't know what is!"

Obviously, Sonja had discovered the truth about what had happened. Or maybe she'd guessed it.

"We are working as hard as we can to find out who is behind this," Nina said.

Sonja gave a derisive snort, as though she didn't believe this. "Your own residents' guide states that if someone's health is at risk, then NASA is required to immediately send a rocket to bring them back to earth. Well I can't think of any greater risk to someone's health than having someone want to murder them!"

I had to admit, Sonja had a point. If we didn't catch the killer, there weren't many ways to protect Lars short of removing him from MBA altogether.

Only Nina didn't see it that way. "The rockets are reserved for *medical* emergencies only. This is a personal issue."

"A *personal* issue?" Sonja screamed. "He was poisoned! And for all we know, *all* his lutefisk could be poisoned!"

"Then I'd recommend not eating any more lutefisk. I can't requisition an emergency rocket for Lars at this time."

"Don't lie to me. If anyone else on this base had been poisoned, a rocket would already be on its way."

"Not only is that false, but I resent your implication. This is not my choice. I didn't say that I *wouldn't* requisition a rocket. I said I *can't* do it right now."

"Of course you can. You're the moon-base commander."

"That has nothing to do with it. But I assure you, it's not necessary anyhow. Whoever has done this to Lars will be caught."

"This is not—" Sonja began.

Nina quickly cut her off. "The longer you keep me here, the longer it will take to find the killer. So if you'll excuse me, we've wasted enough time as it is." Her footsteps started toward the door.

I hurried away. I didn't think Nina would want to discover that, instead of investigating anyone else, I was eavesdropping on *her*. And anyhow, if she saw me, she would want to know what I had found out, and I didn't want to admit that I had gone back to bed.

I ducked into the rec room and flattened myself up against the wall so Nina wouldn't see me. I heard the medical-bay door open and Nina storm through the base.

Why *couldn't* Nina requisition an emergency rocket? I wondered. Was that true, or was she merely making excuses so she wouldn't have to do it? Mounting a rescue mission would be expensive—launching a rocket cost billions of dollars—so it certainly wasn't something to take lightly. Only I had gotten the sense that Nina wasn't lying, which worried me. Was there a problem with the rockets back on earth? Or the launch facility? And if so, what would happen if we *really* had an emergency?

I could feel my heart rate rise as I thought about this, so I took some deep breaths and tried to calm down. There probably wasn't any issue with the rockets, I told myself. Nina was only lying to Sonja. There was no crisis . . . besides the attempted murder of her husband, of course.

As it was, I had plenty of other things to focus on.

Like what Kira Howard was up to in the rec room.

Excerpt from *The Official NASA Procedures for Contact with Intelligent Extraterrestrial Life* © National Aeronautics and Space Administration, Department of Extraterrestrial Affairs, 2029 (Classification Level AAA)

PHYSICAL MANIFESTATION

While the likelihood of an actual physical appearance of IEL on earth* without previous radio contact is regarded as highly unlikely, it cannot be ruled out. Therefore, NASA is constantly monitoring outer space in the immediate vicinity of our planet.** Should incoming IEL be detected, highly trained professionals will instantly be mobilized to ensure that, if they are not the primary contact with IEL, they will certainly be the secondary contact. Any untrained earthlings who might make primary contact with IEL are to immediately be placed under quarantine. (For more on this, please turn to the Quarantine section of this manual.)

---

* Or, as the case may be, the airspace and atmosphere around earth.
** Due to budgetary considerations and the enormity of space, NASA is unable to monitor the entire vicinity around earth all at once, but our scientists are doing their best.

6

RENEGADE UNICORNS

Lunar day 252
Breakfast time

In addition to Kira and Violet, Roddy Marquez was also in the rec room. This was no surprise. Roddy used the virtual-reality system every chance he got. It wasn't even rare to find him there before breakfast. Since school took place in the rec room, Roddy often got up early to score a few veeyar hours beforehand. He had a pair of hologoggles strapped over his eyes and sensogloves on his hands. Based on his movements, it appeared that he was playing a first-person shooter game. While the same moves probably looked cool inside the game, outside it Roddy looked bizarre, like a person who had found a snake in his pants.

Kira was crouched by the veeyar controls, about to jack her portable computer into the interface. Violet was beside her, watching gleefully.

"What are you—" I began, but Kira quickly hushed me.

Roddy froze in the midst of his game, as though he'd heard me, which was a surprise. The hologoggles had speakers built into them, and Roddy liked to play with the sound cranked to eleven. "Hello?" he asked. "Is anyone there?"

We all kept our mouths shut.

"Hello?" Roddy asked again. When there wasn't an answer, he resumed playing the game.

Kira hurried over to me with Violet and led us out of the rec room, into the hall where Roddy wouldn't hear us.

"What are you doing?" I asked.

"Getting Roddy off the veeyar system for once," Kira replied.

"Because he never shares it with anyone," Violet said angrily. "Especially me. Remember what he did the other day?"

"Yeah," I said. "I remember." Everyone at MBA knew what had happened. Kira called it the Rainbow Unicorn Incident. Violet and Inez Marquez had been dying to play Unicorn Fantasy, a new game that was a huge fad back on earth. (I wasn't very clear on the rules of the game, as I had never played it, but from what I could understand, you played a unicorn who could fix environmental disasters with the power of music and rainbows.) Roddy had staunchly refused to get off the system, though. For five hours. Finally, Violet and Inez had rebelled by tying his shoelaces together and then kicking him in the butt. Roddy had tried to chase them, tripped over his shoelaces, and face-planted on the floor. The problem was, he hadn't fully removed the hologoggles yet, so he ended up with two enormous welts around his eyes that made him look like an angry raccoon. The hologoggles had also been fractured. Luckily, Chang knew how to fix them, but he'd had to use duct tape, which meant they were now unwieldy and uncomfortable. There were only three other pairs of hologoggles on the base and it was unlikely that we'd get a replacement anytime soon. Even though Roddy had been the instigator, Violet and Inez had still gotten in trouble. (Most of the Moonies secretly sided with them, though. We had all had issues with Roddy hogging the veeyar system.)

It was possible to play veeyar games in our rooms, but those interfaces weren't nearly as good as the one in the main rec room. The games tended to glitch and stutter. So everyone wanted to use the main one—if we could ever get Roddy off it.

"So," Kira went on. "I've worked out a way to hack the system. I think I know how to get Roddy to stop playing."

"How?" I asked.

Kira smiled deviously. "Jack in and see."

"All right." I quickly returned to the rec room with the

girls, grabbed some hologoggles and sensogloves and pulled them on. "Hey, Roddy," I announced loudly, so he'd hear me over whatever he was playing. "I'm joining the game."

"I hope you do a better job than usual," Roddy replied churlishly. "This game's not easy. If you're gonna suck, you'll take me down with you."

Despite his attitude, Roddy was probably right. I wasn't very adept at first-person shooter games. But I jacked in anyhow.

There was a flash of light, and then I found myself standing on a strange planet, under attack by a horde of aliens. Often the extraterrestrial worlds Roddy chose were gorgeous, reminiscent of the most beautiful places on earth. This one wasn't. We were in the armpit of the universe, a planet that had apparently been used as a garbage dump by every other alien culture. Trash ranging from crashed spaceships to piles of smoldering metal scarred the entire landscape. I was up to my knees in some sort of foul, viscous sewage.

The aliens we were fighting weren't much more attractive. They seemed to be mostly composed of armor plating, spikes, and teeth. Instead of having weapons, they fired bolts of acid from various orifices on their body. I wasn't sure what the orifices were supposed to be. (To be honest, I didn't really want to think about it.)

Roddy's avatar was right beside me, a towering mountain

of muscle who looked nothing like Roddy at all. He was blasting aliens with machine guns the size of cannons.

I had never updated my avatar. It was simply me, and I was dwarfed by Roddy and the aliens. My gun looked like a peashooter.

"Get down!" Roddy yelled.

I had no choice but to dive into the sewage as an alien bombarded us with toxic bodily fluids. True, both the sewage and the alien were completely imaginary, but in the vee-yar system, they were both revoltingly realistic.

While I was submerged, Roddy shredded the alien with a burst of bullets, then took out the rest of the brigade as well. I resurfaced, dripping ooze, to find that the attack was over for the moment. We shifted into exploratory mode, slogging through the muck.

Roddy glared at the gun in my hand. "That piece of garbage won't do you any good against the Bosnakkian Blastbeetles. Why haven't you ever upgraded your weaponry?"

"Because I don't like playing this game."

"Then why are you even here?"

"I wanted to talk to you," I said. I wasn't merely stalling for Kira's sake; this was the truth. "About Lars Sjoberg."

"Why? Are you trying to figure out who poisoned him?"

"He wasn't poisoned," I lied. "His food got contaminated."

"Don't tell me you bought that load of crap from Nina."

"You don't think she's being honest with us?"

"Of course not. Someone's definitely trying to bump off Lars. Honestly, I'm surprised it's taken this long." It's hard to get a perfect read of someone's emotions by looking at their avatar, but I was pretty sure that Roddy was shifting into his smug know-it-all mode. After veeyar games, there was nothing Roddy liked better than sharing his opinions with you—whether you wanted him to or not.

Today, however, I wanted him to. "How do you think they did it?"

"They slipped cyanide into his food. Duh."

"Yeah, but . . ." I tensed as several eyeballs bobbed up from the goop around us. They weren't very large, but for all I knew, they were attached to something enormous and bloodthirsty beneath the surface.

"Relax," Roddy told me. "They're just Murkmoids. They can't do us any harm."

"You sure?"

Roddy blasted one of them out of the water. The others all shrieked and sank below the surface again. "Don't look harmful to me," he said, then continued onward.

I followed him, resuming my questioning. "As far as I know, there isn't any cyanide here at the base."

"Well, obviously there is, because someone poisoned Lars with it."

"I mean, there isn't *supposed* to be any. Because it's dangerous. So how did the killer get it?"

"Maybe they brought it up here without permission."

"You mean they snuck a poison into their personal supplies eight months ago just in case they wanted to kill someone while they were here?"

"Okay, maybe they made it up here. It's not too hard to make cyanide."

"It isn't?" I asked.

Roddy's avatar looked at me disdainfully. "Don't you know anything? Cyanide occurs naturally in . . ." He trailed off suddenly.

"In what?"

"Shhh!" Roddy warily cased the sewage around us.

The surface started to tremble.

"I've got a bad feeling about this," Roddy said.

Two more eyes emerged from the muck. They looked like the ones we had seen before, only these were the size of basketballs. Then the head emerged. And the rest of the body. The creature was the size of a ten-story building, and it was a hideous combination of tentacles and suckers, all of which had teeth on the edges.

"What is *that*?" I gasped.

"A Murkmoid."

"I thought you said they weren't dangerous."

"I didn't know they got so big!"

"And now you made it angry!" Even though I was only playing a game, it was realistic enough to frighten me.

Roddy blasted the Murkmoid with his gun. The alien didn't seem affected at all. Instead it seemed to merely absorb the bullets.

"Oh, crud," Roddy said. "It has projectile osmosis."

"What's that mean?"

"We should run." Roddy's avatar turned and fled.

I didn't bother. There was no way we could outrun the giant beast. Each of its steps would have been equal to a hundred of ours. The Murkmoid roared angrily, revealing a mouth full of serrated teeth tucked away beneath all the tentacles, then squelched toward me menacingly.

I cringed, ready to have my avatar flattened.

There was a sudden burst of upbeat, synthetic pop music, and a rainbow arced across the sky, turning the dull landscape into a kaleidoscope of color. The Murkmoid froze in midattack, understandably confused.

At the front of the rainbow, zooming toward us, was a flying unicorn. There did not appear to be any means of propulsion that allowed it to fly. But it was still flying, in violation of every known law of physics. As it got closer, I could see that Violet was riding on its back. Or, rather, it was Violet's avatar from Unicorn Fantasy, a warrior princess who was also a veterinarian. "Hi, guys!" Violet yelled.

"Hey!" Roddy yelled. "There's no unicorns allowed in this game!" He was so angry, he'd forgotten all about fleeing for his life.

Not that the giant Murkmoid was a danger any longer. It appeared completely incapacitated by the very presence of the unicorn. Violet circled it a few times on her flying unicorn, wrapping it in a rainbow, then cried, "Sparkle power!" A bolt of pink light shot from the unicorn's horn, zapping the tentacled beast, which promptly exploded into a cascade of flowers. Daisies and roses rained down around me.

"Kira!" Roddy roared. "I know you're behind this! What have you done to my game?"

There was another flash of light, and Kira appeared beside Violet, bobbing in the air astride her own flying unicorn. "I altered the source code to make a mash-up of our games," she said proudly. "Pretty cool, huh?"

"No, it's not cool!" Roddy yelled. "You've totally messed everything up!"

"I think it's fun!" Violet announced. She zipped around the landscape on her flying unicorn, turning our vile surroundings into beautiful things like fields of poppies and meadows full of rabbits.

"Fun?" Roddy spluttered. "What's fun about a bunch of stupid flying unicorns? That doesn't even make any sense!"

"Oh, and a mutant squid the size of a skyscraper is *totally* logical," Kira countered.

"Get out of my game," Roddy said angrily. "And reset it back to the way it was before."

"You mean, when you were about to get your butt kicked by the squid thingy?" Kira asked. "If it wasn't for us, you'd be dead right now."

"I was handling everything just fine," Roddy argued.

"You were running away like a chicken," Violet said, then imitated a chicken to get her point across. "Bock-bock-bock!"

Rather than debate this anymore, Roddy simply blasted Violet's unicorn. Thankfully, instead of turning into a gory pile of flesh, the unicorn died in an explosion of glitter.

Still, Violet wasn't pleased about this. "You jerkasaurus!" she shouted, still floating in the air. "You killed Sparkle-Bright!"

"Oh, that's the way you want to play?" Kira asked Roddy. "Fine. Let's play." Her unicorn fired a bolt of fuchsia light from its horn, hitting Roddy's avatar squarely in the chest. There was an explosion, and when the smoke cleared, Roddy's musclebound he-man had turned into a kitten. A light blue kitten with enormous eyes.

"Ooh!" Violet squealed. "He's adorable!"

"This is so uncool," the kitten groused. It was bizarre to

see something so cute speaking with Roddy's voice. "I was here first and you ruined my game. I'm telling Nina."

"Bye," Kira taunted, waving from her unicorn.

"Yeah. Bye!" Violet echoed.

The kitten suddenly vanished, meaning that Roddy had jacked out. Beyond the cloying synthetic unicorn music, I could heard Roddy in the real world, storming out of the rec room.

"Wow. That worked out better than I expected." Kira brought her unicorn in for a landing beside me. A rainbow ripple spread through the swamp, turning it into a gorgeous pond.

"It worked a little too well," I said. "Roddy was about to tell me something important."

"Like that he's the one who tried to kill Lars?" Kira asked.

I glanced at Violet to see if she was listening. Instead she was distracted creating a new unicorn. A pink one. With wings.

"No one tried to kill Lars," I said. "He was poisoned by contamination."

"Yeah, right," Kira said dismissively. "So what's the deal? Are you looking for the killer? Because I'll help."

I thought about saying no, but quickly decided against it. I didn't like the idea of lying to my friend, and the fact was, I *could* use some help. Even though I had solved some crimes at MBA before, I had never done it on my own. "Fine," I agreed. "But you can't tell Nina what we're up to."

"Like I'd ever tell Nina anything. What was Roddy's big lead?"

"He said it wasn't very hard to make cyanide. But he didn't get the chance to tell me how."

"That shouldn't be too much of a problem." Kira waved her hand and the world around us melted away.

"Hey!" Violet yelped. "I wasn't finished with my unicorn!"

"It's okay," Kira told her. "I only paused the game. We can get it back."

Around us, without the game running, the veeyar system reverted to the default mode, which was the classroom setting. This made sense, as we often used it for school. In the classroom mode we could perform virtual chemistry experiments under the watch of instructors back on earth, or work out virtual math problems in the air, or dissect virtual animals in biology.

"Computer," Kira said, "how do you make cyanide?"

I winced, unhappy that she'd asked this in front of Violet, because I knew what was coming next.

"What's cyanide?" Violet asked.

The computer quickly answered both questions, at once speaking in the standard, soothing female voice and writing the words for us in the air of the virtual classroom. "Cyanide is a poisonous chemical compound primarily used for the mining of gold and silver, although it also has some medical uses and can be used as a pesticide or an insecticide. It can be found naturally in many fruit seeds, such as cherry pits, peach pits and apple seeds."

Kira and I looked at one another, surprised. "There's cyanide in seeds?" I repeated.

"That's correct," the computer replied. "In addition to the ones I mentioned, it can also be found in the seeds of nectarines, plums, and apricots."

"But we don't have any seeds here," Kira told me. "Or much fruit at all. Not since those tangerines two months ago, when I first got here."

"Dr. Goldstein has apple seeds," Violet said. "Lots of them."

"She does?" I asked. "Where?"

"In the greenhouse," Violet replied.

That made sense. Dr. Goldstein was the lunar agriculture specialist. It was her job to maintain the greenhouse. Only . . .

"Dr. Goldstein isn't growing apples here," Kira pointed out.

"I know," Violet said, offended. "I'm not stupid. But she has seeds. Lots of them. I've seen them."

"How?" I asked.

"I just have," Violet replied. "I pay attention to things."

That was true. There had been many times when Violet noticed things that other people hadn't. In the past, I had made the mistake of discounting what Violet claimed was true, thinking she might be making things up, but now I had learned not to be so quick to do that. So had Kira.

"I think we ought to pay a visit to Dr. Goldstein," she said.

Excerpt from *The Official NASA Procedures for Contact with Intelligent Extraterrestrial Life* © National Aeronautics and Space Administration, Department of Extraterrestrial Affairs, 2029 (Classification Level AAA)

HOAXES AND MISUNDERSTANDINGS

In the case of any contact with IEL, you must be alert to the possibility that it is not true contact at all. In the great majority of cases, any reports of IEL will turn out to be false.* Sometimes, those who report IEL will be doing so as a hoax or jest, as they mistakenly believe such behavior is funny—although the far greater likelihood is that the reports will be in earnest, but will be cases of overzealousness. Therefore, it is paramount to respond to all potential cases of IEL with a healthy skepticism.**

---

* For reference, as of this writing, 100 percent of all reports of IEL have been false.

** The following have all been determined to *not* be actual manifestations of IEL and can thus be immediately discounted: the northern lights, lightning and other atmospheric phenomena, crop circles, earth mounds, large sinkholes, unusual rock formations, wind shears, icefalls, and Stonehenge.

SEEDS OF DOOM

Lunar day 252
Breakfast time

The greenhouse was located directly across from the mess hall, which allowed us to grab breakfast while casing the place. Normally, I wasn't a big fan of breakfast at MBA—or any meal there, really—but since I had already been awake for several hours, save for my brief nap, I was hungry enough to eat . . . well, space food. I made myself some reconstituted banana pancakes and a hot tea. (Since it's basically dried leaves and water, tea was one of the few things at MBA that didn't vary much from its earth version.)

In the mess, Dr. Iwanyi sat at a table with Kamoze, while most of the Brahmaputra-Marquez family was at another.

Only Roddy was missing, probably off making his case to Nina, as he'd threatened. None of the other adults were there; they were all at their workstations already. The entire Sjoberg family was absent as well. Lars had been released from the medical bay, and now all the Swedes were holed up in their suite, as usual.

Mom and Dad were seated at one of the big tables, almost done eating. They obviously expected Violet and me to sit with them, so we did, and Kira joined us, as her father was nowhere to be seen.

"Don't tell Mom and Dad about the apple seeds," I warned Violet on our way to the table. "It's a secret."

"Okay," Violet said, through a mouthful of blueberry muffin-like substance. She seemed very excited to have a secret with Kira and me.

"What took you so long to get here?" Mom asked as we sat down. "You guys get lost?"

"We can't get lost in here, Mom," Violet replied, missing the joke. "It's way too small. We were playing a prank on Roddy with Kira."

"Oh?" Mom arched an eyebrow. "What sort of prank?"

"We attacked him with unicorns and sparkle power!" Violet exclaimed, then launched into an explanation of what we'd done.

While Kira helped her tell the story—leaving out the

part about our investigation—I observed the greenhouse from my seat. The room was glass on two sides and stretched all the way to the top of MBA, where it had a glass roof as well. (An extremely thick, meteor-proof glass roof, for safety's sake.) For our first six months, the greenhouse hadn't been very green at all; the plants hadn't been growing nearly as well as we had hoped. However, Dr. Goldstein had recently had some breakthroughs. Even though the Sjobergs had greedily raided the greenhouse four weeks earlier, the plants had rebounded nicely: There were clumps of red strawberries and quite a few cherry tomatoes on the vine. The sugar snap peas were doing particularly well. In the low lunar gravity, they had rocketed up the stay wires toward the skylight, creating a curtain of greenery along the glass. Behind it, I could see Dr. Goldstein tending to her garden.

"Sorry our catch this morning got cut short," Dad whispered to me. Kira and Violet were so busy telling Mom their story that he felt it was safe to say this without being overheard.

"It's okay," I assured him. "Thanks for even taking me out."

"So you know, I took care of our space suits. Got all the dust off and moved them into the lockers."

"Thanks."

Dad hesitated a moment, as though he wasn't completely

convinced he wanted to say the next thing, but then went with it. "While I was in the air lock at four thirty in the morning, I saw you coming out of Nina's quarters."

I gagged a bit on my pancakes. Partly caught off guard by Dad's statement. Partly because I had hit a poorly rehydrated chunk of banana.

"Want to tell me what you were doing in there?" Dad pressed.

I glanced back at the girls. They were still telling their story. Violet was being extremely animated, acting out her part, as well as that of the Murkmoid and the unicorns. She had attracted the attention of everyone else in the mess hall.

"Nina told me what really happened with Lars," I confided to Dad. "That it wasn't an accident."

Dad's eyes widened in surprise, then narrowed as he realized what was going on. "Did she ask you to help investigate this?"

"Yes," I admitted.

"I can't believe she would do that," Dad said angrily. "I know you've solved some crimes here, but you're only thirteen years old—and that's only as of today. Whoever did this is dangerous. I don't want you getting involved. Chang and I can handle it on our . . ." Dad trailed off as he put two and two together. "Oh, crud. She suspects Chang or I might have done it."

"She only mentioned Chang."

"Well, she wouldn't have told you that she suspects your own father. Even Nina is human enough to realize that wouldn't go over well."

Violet wrapped up her story with a grand reenactment of the Murkmoid's death, dramatically collapsing to the floor. All the Moonies in the mess hall applauded.

I considered asking Dad if *he* thought Chang could have done it, but I was pretty sure he would be upset at me for even thinking it—and while I waffled on the issue, Dad got up from the table.

"I'm going to take care of this right now," he said, then started toward Nina's residence.

"Where are you going?" Mom asked, startled by Dad's sudden departure.

"To talk to Nina," Dad replied, and then hurried on without an explanation.

Violet took her seat at the table and dug into her muffin again. She seemed a bit winded from the exertion of telling her story.

Mom's watch pinged, signaling she had received a message. She glanced at it, then stood herself. "I have a call from earth in a few minutes," she told us. "I need to prepare for it. Dash and Kira, can I trust you two to get Violet and yourselves to school on time?"

"Of course," Kira agreed. "Although, it *is* Dash's birthday. Maybe letting him get to school late would be a nice present . . . ?"

"No," Mom said curtly. "Your teachers take a great deal of time to prepare your lessons, and if you three show up late, that's disrespectful. So please be on time today."

"We will," I said, fully intending to keep my word.

"Hug first," Violet announced, opening her arms wide.

Mom hugged her tightly, then gave me a peck on the cheek and hurried off toward the science pod.

Her behavior struck me as odd. Mom had calls with earth all the time, but she seemed unusually uptight about this one—as well as being unusually concerned about when we got to school. Quite often, when Mom was in charge of getting Violet to class, they rolled in a few minutes late, even though we only lived thirty seconds away from school.

Still, I might not have really noticed this if it hadn't been the latest in a string of odd behavior by adults that morning.

Or if all the other adults in the mess hadn't got up to leave at the exact same time.

At the other tables, Drs. Iwanyi, Marquez, and Brahmaputra-Marquez were all saying good-bye to their children and heading off to the science pod as well, which made me think that Mom wasn't the only one who had just received an important message. In addition, they were all very insistent that the kids had to be in school on time. Dr. Iwanyi asked Cesar Marquez to make sure Kamoze got there, then rapped on the glass of the greenhouse to get his wife's attention and pointed to his watch. Dr. Goldstein quickly scrubbed some soil off her hands, exited the greenhouse, and headed to the science pod with her husband.

"Do you get the sense that something strange is going on here?" I asked Kira.

"Stranger than Lars Sjoberg being poisoned?" she replied.

"In addition to Lars being poisoned," I said. "Has your father been acting weird lately?"

"My father is *always* acting weird."

"Well, weirder than usual."

"I honestly can't imagine what that would be like." Kira watched Dr. Goldstein and Dr. Iwanyi disappear into the science pod. Now that there were no more adults around, she snapped to her feet and started for the greenhouse.

"What are you doing?" I asked, starting after her.

"What do you think I'm doing?" Kira answered. "I'm looking for apple seeds."

"Yeah," Violet chimed in, tailing us. "We're looking for apple seeds."

"We're not going to get a better chance than this," Kira said. "All the adults are probably going to be on that call for a while."

Before I could even start to argue that my father didn't want me investigating anymore, Kira already had the door open and was inside the greenhouse. Violet followed her, so I went in too.

I hadn't been in the greenhouse in a few weeks, as it was supposed to be off-limits to kids. The moment I stepped inside, I was overwhelmed. There wasn't a great deal of greenery, but I still hadn't been around this much of it since I'd been back on earth. Everything was wonderful and intoxicating: the smell of flowers and the soil, the variety of colors in the flowers and fruits, the mere sense of being surrounded by living things. It made me realize how sterile and drab the rest of Moon Base Alpha was.

It also made me more homesick than ever. I found myself longing for the earth, missing the great grass fields and thick rain forests of Hawaii.

Violet and Kira seemed equally awestruck. They froze in their tracks, taking in the sights and smelling the air. "This is so cosmic!" Violet exclaimed. "It's like being in a terrarium!"

A sudden knocking at the glass snapped us all back to reality. Cesar Marquez was glaring at us through the window. Behind him, Kamoze and Inez were still finishing their breakfasts.

"What are you doing in there?" Cesar demanded. "Stealing food?"

Kira put a finger to her lips, signaling him to be quiet before the adults heard, then pointed toward the door.

Cesar stormed inside, leaving Kamoze and Inez in the mess hall. "This food is for everyone," he informed us. "Not just you." He seemed completely unmoved by the experience of being around all the plants.

"We're not stealing it, you dodo," Violet told him. "We're only looking for apple seeds."

"I'm no dodo," Cesar responded, then frowned in confusion. "What do you want apple seeds for?"

"It's a school project," Kira lied. "We're studying the life cycle of the apple tree."

"Really?" Cesar asked, now sounding upset. "I don't get to do anything cool like that. I just have to do algebra all the time. Like that's ever going to come in handy."

"Uh, Cesar?" I said. "This whole moon base wouldn't exist without algebra."

"Yeah, right," Cesar said, as if I were trying to trick him.

Kira and Violet were now moving through the greenhouse, on the hunt for the apple seeds. Luckily, Dr. Goldstein was intensely organized. (Or perhaps MBA guidelines had stipulated an extremely organized system. Space travel often requires such anal-retentiveness.) The plants were all growing in raised beds: tables with deep pockets for soil in the top. Underneath the beds were storage units full of drawers of various sizes. Each was neatly labeled to indicate what was inside: gardening implements, fertilizer, spare parts for the irrigation system, and . . .

"What's excrement?" Violet asked.

Kira, Cesar, and I all looked to the large storage unit where she was pointing. Sure enough, there was a nice, clear label on it: EXCREMENT. Cesar started laughing.

"It's poop," I said.

Cesar laughed even harder.

"Poop?" Violet repeated. "What kind of poop?"

"Probably ours," Kira replied.

Violet's face contorted in disgust. "Ooh! Gross! Why's it in *here*?"

"To help the plants grow," I explained. "The soil on the moon is really lousy—"

"It's not soil at all," Kira interrupted, continuing to search the greenhouse. "Moon dust is really mostly silica, which is a kind of glass created by meteor impacts."

"It is?" Cesar asked, astonished.

"You've been on the moon eight months," Kira said. "Haven't you learned *anything* about it?"

"I know it's old," Cesar said defensively. "Like, millions of years old."

"Try billions, you nimrod," Kira muttered under her breath.

"Anyhow," I said quickly, before Cesar could take offense, "plants don't grow in silica. So we had to bring soil from earth. Only soil is really heavy. And it still needs some fertilizer. I guess Dr. Goldstein realized we were creating an awful lot of fertilizer ourselves."

Cesar couldn't help himself. He opened the storage unit, then wrinkled his nose in disgust. "That psycho put all our poop in bags."

The rest of us peered into the storage bin. Sure enough, all of our poop was bagged. There were dozens of small opaque white plastic sacks. Each was helpfully labeled MBA HUMAN EXCREMENT and stamped with a date.

"Dr. Goldstein didn't bag all our poop like this," Kira informed Cesar. "The space toilet does that."

"Why?" Cesar asked, still disgusted.

"I guess so we can bring it back in here and use it on the plants," Kira said. "And, possibly, because if it wasn't bagged, it might contaminate the moon."

"Or stink," I suggested.

I had never seen what happened to our poop after it disappeared into the toilet. The bags were all packed full, then sealed tight (thankfully). There was a plastic zipper built into each, similar to that on a ziplock bag, so that it could be reopened, probably for ease of getting the contents out to mix with the plants.

Violet poked one experimentally. It appeared firm under her touch, indicating that the water had been removed (and almost certainly recycled into our water supply). "Why do they have to say 'excrement'?" she asked. "Why not just say 'poop'?"

"Maybe because 'excrement' sounds more scientific?" I guessed. I really had no idea.

"Or maybe because everyone at NASA has excrement for brains," Cesar said, and Violet giggled.

I picked up one of the bags, just to check it out. Although it was small enough to fit in a pocket of my cargo shorts, it was packed pretty solid. It probably had dozens of dehydrated poops crammed inside, meaning it represented the digested meals of multiple Moonies. (The toilet system simply filled the bags with poop, then automatically sealed the old ones and slotted fresh ones into place.) And yet, without the water, it didn't weigh that much, only about two pounds.

"Here we go!" Kira exclaimed triumphantly. "Seeds!" At the far end of the greenhouse from the entrance, beneath a planting bed full of snap-pea vines and tomato plants, was a storage unit filled with long, flat, shallow drawers. The top one was labeled FRUITS while the bottom two were labeled VEGETABLES.

I replaced the bag of poop, then joined Kira as she slid the top drawer open.

There were thousands of seeds inside, possibly tens of thousands, organized by type in airtight containers, each of which had been labeled as well. Many represented fruits Dr. Goldstein hadn't even tried growing yet. Perhaps she hadn't had the time or space; perhaps they were being stored for the larger greenhouse that would be part of Moon Base Beta. There were seeds for watermelons, cantaloupes, strawberries, kiwis, mangoes, papayas, guavas, grapes, lemons, limes, kumquats, tomatoes, and cucumbers. (Dr. Goldstein, being a botanist, had put the last two where they belonged scientifically, instead of with the vegetables.)

"Here we go," Kira said. "Apples." She grabbed the container out of the drawer.

Cesar started laughing when he saw it. "Looks like you're gonna have to do a different science project."

The container was empty. All the apple seeds were gone.

TRANSLATION

Translation of an incoming communication from IEL will probably not be easy. Consider that there are thousands of human languages on our own planet, most of which are impossible for the speaker of another language to understand.* The task of translating these communications should be directed to NASA's Alien Communication Office, which is staffed by many distinguished mathematicians and linguists who have had extensive training in interpreting potential alien communication.

DO NOT, under any circumstances, attempt to formulate a response or communicate with the IEL on your own. Until their language is properly understood, even the slightest gesture or inflection, no matter how innocuous, could be considered threatening or hostile.

---

* Not to mention the hundreds of thousands of forms of nonhuman communication. Whether or not these qualify as language, the fact stands that it is extremely difficult to communicate between species on our planet.

BAD NEWS

Lunar day 252
Right after breakfast

"We have to tell Nina," I said, exiting the green-house. "Right away."

"Nina?" Cesar asked, following me with Kira and Violet. "She's not gonna care about your dumb science project."

Kira didn't bother trying to explain what was really going on to Cesar. Instead she said, "I think telling Nina is a mistake."

"Yeah," Violet said. "Telling Nina is a mistake."

"Nina ordered me to tell her about anything important immediately," I said. "Well, this is important."

"No it's not," Cesar said. "It's just a bunch of stupid seeds."

I stopped suddenly, having noticed something highly unusual.

The doors to the science pod were closed.

It was the first time the doors had been closed in the eight months I had been at MBA. I had known they *could* be closed: If there was an emergency, there were several areas at MBA that could be sealed off from the rest of the base, and the science pod was one of them. But the doors had been open for so long, I had forgotten they even existed. It was unsettling to see them closed, kind of like walking into your house and finding a room missing. It made MBA feel even smaller and more claustrophobic than before.

"Why's the pod closed off?" Kira asked, echoing my thoughts.

"Mom said she had a call with earth this morning," I said. "Maybe everyone else is on it too."

"What kind of call would all the adults have to be on?" Cesar asked.

"Maybe they're asking for more apple seeds," Violet suggested.

Kira walked up to the doors and pressed her ear against them. She listened a few seconds, then frowned. "I can't hear anything. These are totally soundproof."

That made sense. The science-pod doors had to be thick and sturdy, because they needed to hold up in emergency situations. Unlike the walls of our residences, which were so cheap and thin that I could currently hear my father and Nina arguing in Nina's room on the other side of the base. I couldn't hear them well enough to make out exactly what they were saying, but I could guess: My father was berating Nina for bringing me into the murder investigation, and Nina was annoyed that this was keeping them off their important call with NASA.

I started toward Nina's residence again. Kira bounded after me. "Whoa! You seriously shouldn't tell Nina about this yet."

"Why not?" I demanded.

Kira gave Cesar a wary glance. Obviously, she didn't feel comfortable discussing this in front of him. So she lied to throw him off track. "Like Cesar said, she's not going to care. And besides, we all have to get to school. Class is about to start." She looked to Cesar. "Didn't you promise that you were going to get Inez and Kamoze there?"

"Maybe," Cesar said. There was a decent chance he would have blown this off—Cesar wasn't very good about getting *himself* to school on time—but then Lily and Patton Sjoberg came around the far side of the greenhouse, heading for the mess.

I was surprised to see them up and about. They should have been awake at this time most days, since they were supposed to go to school with us, but the Sjobergs often skipped their classes, arguing that they were on vacation—and besides, they didn't really have to learn anything, because they were going to inherit a huge fortune no matter what. But today, in addition to their general hatred of school and early mornings, their father had nearly died. That seemed like a better excuse than usual to skip school.

Patton looked haggard, like he hadn't been able to go back to sleep, while Lily looked surprisingly put-together. She had her hair done up and makeup on, and she beamed when she saw Cesar. (Another thing that I—and everyone else at MBA—knew due to our thin walls was that Lily had a big crush on Cesar.) "Good morning!" she crooned, like it was a totally normal day. "How's it going, Cesar?"

"Okay," Cesar said, heading back into the mess to talk to her. "How's your dad?"

"Better," Lily said. "He's still a little loopy, but he'll live."

Patton sat down heavily at a table, glowering. He didn't seem that pleased by the idea of his father surviving.

Then he noticed me and paled a bit. A month before, when Patton had been trying to beat me up, Zan had rescued me by appearing to him as a terrifying space snake. She had literally scared the pee out of Patton. Ever since, he had been extremely skittish around me, worried that I could summon the snake again whenever I wanted. His family insisted (correctly) that space snakes didn't exist and thought Patton was being crazy—but since Patton had actually *seen* a space snake and they hadn't, he stuck to his story, no matter how much they ridiculed him. In the meantime, I was enjoying his fear of me to the fullest. It had kept him from bullying me—or anyone else—for weeks.

I gave him a friendly little wave. Even that made him flinch in fright.

While Cesar was distracted by the Sjobergs, Kira and I slipped away. Violet followed us.

With most of the adults inside the science pod, it was a lot easier to find privacy at MBA than usual. No one was in the control room or the robotics center. The staging area by the air lock was completely empty. We stopped there, though we still took care to keep our voices low.

"What if Nina's the one who poisoned Lars?" Kira asked.

I looked at Violet. I wasn't thrilled about having this conversation in front of her, but now that Kira had begun it, I knew there was no other option. Violet was obviously fascinated, and any attempt to ditch her now would probably result in her throwing a fit.

"Nina asked me to help look for the killer," I said. "Why would she do that if she *was* the killer?"

"To divert attention from herself," Kira said.

"Yeah," Violet echoed. "To revert detention from herself."

"And this way," Kira went on, "she could use you to help shift the blame to someone else."

I thought about my conversation with Nina. "She did tell me to keep an eye on Chang."

"Chang?" Violet asked, way too loud. "He would never poison anyone! He's too nice."

Behind Violet's back, Kira rolled her eyes, indicating she didn't believe Chang was such a saint. But this still didn't change her thoughts about Nina. "There! You see? Anyone else?"

"Actually, she told me to keep an eye on *everyone* else."

"Even me?" Violet asked, startled. "I wouldn't poison anyone. Even Roddy, and he's a jerk."

"Everyone except you," I corrected.

"Inez wouldn't poison anyone either," Violet said. "And neither would Kamoze."

"Okay. I won't investigate them."

"And Mom and Dad."

"Of course."

"Think about it," Kira told me, before Violet could list any more people. "Nina has as much reason to hate Lars as anyone here. More, maybe. He's been a problem for her since the day he got here, and I know he's threatened to destroy her career when he gets back to earth. So what if she couldn't take it anymore? She poisons him, then sets out to pin it on Chang. Or someone else. Then she brings you in to back up her side of the story."

I mulled that over. It wasn't completely implausible. "How could she make me back her up?"

"She's running the investigation, right? So she controls all the evidence. She asked you to come directly to her with anything you found out. Well, if it's evidence against her, she can ditch it. And maybe she can even plant some evidence against someone else."

"But Nina *wouldn't* poison Lars," Violet said. "Poisoning someone is wrong—and Nina's the moon-base commander."

"So?" Kira asked. "Nina has broken the rules before. Like last month, when she went missing. . . ."

"But she was manipulated into that," I countered.

"Big deal," Kira said. "She still did it. She's not as strait-laced as she'd like us all to think she is. Plus, the woman came out of the military. So she's been trained to kill people. That's what the military does. And she's weird. She's one of the weirdest people here—and this place is chock-full of wackos. Think about how cold and detached she is. That's the classic profile for a psycho killer."

I thought about it some more. I had spent a lot more time alone with Nina than Kira had. It hadn't been enjoyable, but I'd done it. So I'd had a bit more of a glimpse of the person beneath the icy exterior than Kira had. "I don't think she's a psycho killer," I said finally.

"Fine," Kira said, obviously annoyed I hadn't agreed with her. "Then who do *you* think tried to kill Lars?"

"It *could* have been Chang," I pointed out, then started ticking names off my fingers. "Or Dr. Goldstein. She was the one with access to the apple seeds, and now they're gone. Or Dr. Iwanyi. Or Dr. Balnikov. Or pretty much anyone here. Including the whole Sjoberg family."

"Patton and Lily?" Violet asked innocently. "But they're Lars's children."

"I don't think they like him very much," I explained. "Patton certainly doesn't. Lars treats him like crud. And they have more to gain from Lars's death than anyone else here. Trillions of dollars, maybe."

"Would Mrs. Sjoberg get that much if Lars died too?" Violet asked.

"Probably," I said.

"Then I think *she* did it," Violet proclaimed. "She's mean and her face is all weird."

I returned my attention to Kira. "That's an awful lot of potential suspects."

"It is," Kira agreed. "But that doesn't mean Nina *didn't* do it. Which means that reporting everything you find to her is a bad idea."

"Why?" Violet asked.

"Because keeping things to ourselves gives us an edge,"

Kira explained. "If we don't tell Nina we know about the missing seeds, then she doesn't know we know about the missing seeds. If she knows we know, then she can get rid of the evidence that she took them. But if she doesn't know we know, then maybe she drops her guard and then we can bust her. Understand?"

"No," Violet said.

Kira sighed. "Then just trust me. I know what I'm talking about here. If there's anyone we should be investigating, it's Nina. She's definitely been hiding something lately."

It seemed to me that *everyone* had been hiding something lately, but I didn't say it. Nothing I said was going to change Kira's mind. And there was a decent chance she was right. "What do you want to do?"

Kira put a finger to her lips, beckoned us to follow her, and started up the stairs toward Nina's residence.

For once, Violet took the hint and stayed silent. School was about to begin, and we should have been in the rec room, but suddenly this seemed much more important than English class.

We crept up to the catwalk. Now that we were right outside Nina's door, we could hear her and my father arguing inside much more clearly.

But Kira didn't stop there. Instead she led us past Nina's door and to that of our own residence.

I realized what she was up to and used my thumbprint to unlock the door. We slipped inside and headed right for our sleep pods, which were aligned along the wall to Nina's room. We each picked one—Violet and I took our own pods, while Kira took Mom's—then climbed inside and got as close to the wall as we could.

We could now hear Dad and Nina's conversation almost as clearly as if we had been in Nina's residence ourselves. Both were angry, speaking louder than they might have done otherwise. I wondered if both were assuming everyone else was in the science pod or at school.

". . . and you have put my son's life in danger yet again," Dad was saying.

"He won't end up in danger if he doesn't do anything stupid," Nina argued.

"You can't guarantee that! Remember what happened to him the last time there was a murderer on the loose? Garth Grisan nearly killed him with the robot arm!"

"Last time Dashiell was investigating behind my back, sneaking around without authorization. This time I can keep an eye on him."

"You can't do that twenty-four hours a day! How could you even *think* about something like this without talking to me or his mother first?"

"As I'm sure you're aware, I have more than enough

trouble to deal with right now. So do you and Chang and every other adult here. And that was *before* we had another killer on the loose. Dashiell is smart, and he was available, so I utilized him."

"You *utilized* him?" Dad repeated. "He's my son, not an appliance! Can you even imagine what you would feel like if someone put a child of yours in harm's way like this?"

"The way you risked his life with that stunt on the surface this morning?" Nina asked pointedly.

"There was virtually no risk to that. We were being careful. . . ."

"Well, I'm being just as careful with this investigation. End of story. We've wasted enough time as it is. We're supposed to be on that call with everyone else and I have ten thousand things I have to take care of before ten-hundred hours tomorrow." The sound of Nina's footsteps could be heard, heading for the door.

Dad didn't follow her, though. "What's it even matter, Nina?" he asked. "With everything else that's going on right now, is finding Lars's killer really so important that you have to drag Dashiell into it? Is it worth putting his life at risk like this?"

"The lives of everyone on this base are already at risk," Nina said curtly. "I'm doing everything I can to protect all of them."

I stiffened, disturbed by this statement, and whacked my head on the ceiling of my sleep pod.

I heard the door open in Nina's residence. She seemed to be waiting for my father to leave with her.

Kira, Violet, and I quickly clambered out of the sleep pods and ran for our own door. Without discussing it, we had all come to the same conclusion at once: There was no point in hiding the fact that we'd been eavesdropping. Whatever was going on was too important. We raced out the door, right as Dad and Nina exited Nina's residence.

Dad and Nina both froze on the catwalk, startled by our sudden appearance.

"What's going on?" I asked, before they could tell us we were supposed to be in school.

"Yeah," Kira agreed. "What's with all the secrecy?"

Nina narrowed her eyes at us angrily. It looked like she was going to chew us out.

Only Dad spoke up before she could. "The moon base is in trouble," he said. "We need to evacuate."

Excerpt from *The Official NASA Procedures for Contact with Intelligent Extraterrestrial Life* © National Aeronautics and Space Administration, Department of Extraterrestrial Affairs, 2029 (Classification Level AAA)

SECRECY

If you are party to primary or secondary contact with IEL, it is imperative that secrecy be maintained. Once the press—and thus, the public—finds out about the existence of the IEL, the responses will be immediate and very difficult to control. Therefore, all interhuman communication will be limited to members of the primary and secondary contact teams and NASA's Department of Extraterrestrial Affairs. No one will be allowed to contact anyone outside this circle—even family members—until the IEL can be properly assessed. Anyone who violates this directive is guilty of breaking federal law and will be immediately removed from the project and incarcerated.

SYSTEM FAILURE

Lunar day 252

T minus 24 hours to evacuation

"Something's wrong with the air-recycling sys-tem," Mom said. "It's not providing as much oxygen for us as it should."

Now that the cat was out of the bag, Nina had pulled her from the call with NASA in the science pod so she and Dad could break the news to Violet and me. We were all in our residence, seated on our InflatiCubes. Kira and Dr. Howard were in their residence next door.

Since none of the other kids had caught on to what was happening, they were all still in school. Although I was pretty sure their parents were going to have to tell them the truth soon. The chances of Violet keeping the secret were awfully slim.

The call with NASA, it turned out, had been about emergency procedures to shut down the moon base.

"Why isn't the system making oxygen?" Violet asked.

"It's making *some*," Dad corrected. "Just not quite as much as it should. We don't know why. If we did, we could fix it."

"We've been *trying* to fix it," Mom said. "For two weeks now."

"And you didn't tell us?" I failed to keep the annoyance out of my voice.

"There was a lot of debate about that," Mom said.

"A *lot*," Dad emphasized.

"But it was ultimately decided that it would be the best for all the children here if we didn't tell them," Mom said. "So you wouldn't panic. Or stress out."

"'It was decided'?" I repeated. "Meaning it wasn't your decision?"

"There was no way some families could tell their kids and others couldn't," Dad explained. "Because if some kids knew, they would definitely tell the other kids. And Dr. Marquez felt that children might not be able to handle this."

"Dr. Marquez is a quack," I said.

"He's the moon-base psychiatrist," Mom said sternly,

although behind her back Dad made a face to indicate he agreed with me. "NASA put him here to deal with things like this, so they listened to his opinion. However . . ." She glanced at Dad, then looked back to us. "It was never something we were comfortable with."

"The point is," Dad said, "we spent two weeks trying everything we could to fix the system—or even to figure out what's wrong with it. But we couldn't, and the oxygen levels have kept dropping."

"Not by much," Mom said reassuringly. "Only fractions of a percentage. However, if that continues, the air here will eventually become too weak to support humans."

"But *we're* humans," Violet said worriedly.

"We're going to be fine." Mom quickly moved to Violet's InflatiCube and put an arm around her shoulders. "Once NASA realized there was potential danger, an evacuation plan was immediately put into place. Rockets have already launched from earth to get us. The first two will be here tomorrow."

"They've already launched?" I asked. "How is that possible? It wasn't on the news. And no one texted me or anything." I was thinking specifically of Riley Bock, who had become a space fanatic since I was selected as a Moonie. She was always begging me for the latest updates. If rockets had left for the moon, she would have mentioned it. And if she had somehow missed it, at least one of the millions of other MBA fans back on earth would have said something.

"No one back on earth knows," Dad said. "Not unless they work for NASA. The agency has been doing everything they can to keep this secret until we all get home safely."

"But they launched *two rockets*," I said. "You'd think people would notice something like that."

"NASA claimed they were merely satellite launches," Mom said. "Satellites launch all the time. The people who live around the Kennedy Space Center don't give them a second thought."

"And they're going to be here tomorrow?" Violet asked. Her concern over the depleted oxygen had already given way to excitement. "All of us are going home tomorrow?"

Mom and Dad didn't answer that right away. I realized why they were hesitating. "Wait," I said. "Only two rockets are coming? Each of those only holds eight people, and that includes the pilots."

"Right," Dad said. "We can't all leave in the first wave. Some people will have to stay behind for the next two rockets."

"For how long?" I asked.

"Another week," Mom replied.

"So we might have to wait here?" Violet asked, growing worried again. "Without oxygen?"

Mom tightened her arm around Violet. "No. The families

with young children are going to be the first to leave."

"We are?" Violet asked.

"NASA considers children's safety their number one priority," Dad said. "Our family will go with Kamoze and his parents on one rocket, while the Marquez family will go with Kira and her father on the other."

I was quite sure that our priority had less to do with NASA's concern for our safety than it did with NASA's concern about the agency's image. It would look pretty bad if they allowed grown-ups without children to return to earth before children. Especially if something went wrong at MBA in the interim and the children died. I didn't want to bring that up in front of Violet, though. Instead I said, "And the Sjobergs are okay with waiting?"

Mom and Dad looked to each other awkwardly, then back to Violet and me. "The Sjobergs don't know what's going on," Mom confided.

"They don't?" I asked. "They're going to have a cow when they find out."

"They're going to have *four* cows," Violet agreed.

"That's why they haven't been told," Dad said. "Although there is nothing they can do about this. Part of the contract they signed to come up here stated this emergency-return system very clearly. No matter how much they complain, they'll have to wait."

"We're simply hoping to cut down the amount of time in which they *can* complain," Mom said.

"So when are they going to be told?" I asked, then thought to add, "When were you going to tell *us*?"

"Tonight," Dad answered. "We didn't want to alarm anyone until we had to."

"And you sent us to *school*?" I chided. "On our last full day on the moon? My birthday?"

"The idea was to keep you distracted," Dad said. "Although we all felt you should be aware that your final evening here would be your final evening. So you could say good-bye to the place."

"That's why you took me outside this morning?" I asked.

"Yes," Dad said. "It seemed like a shame to let you come all this way and never get the chance to play catch on the lunar surface. Plus, we didn't have a present for you."

"What about me?" Violet asked angrily. "I never got to play catch on the lunar surface! Or do gymnastics. Or anything."

"You'll get some time out there tomorrow," Mom told her. "On the way to the rocket. Maybe you can do some cartwheels then."

"Okay!" Violet said, her anger instantly gone.

Dad stood suddenly. "That reminds me, Vee. We need to check your space suit to make sure it still fits you nice and tight. We should probably do that right now."

Violet leaped to her feet, already excited about the next day. "Do you think I'll be the first person to ever do cartwheels on the lunar surface?"

"I think Neil Armstrong might have done a few," Dad replied. "And a round-off."

"Daddy," Violet said sourly. "You're lying."

"Maybe," Dad admitted, and then they slipped out the door, leaving only Mom and me in the room.

"I'm sorry we didn't tell you earlier," Mom said. "Believe me, we wanted to. We didn't like keeping this a secret."

"It's okay," I assured her. Then, since Violet wasn't around, I asked, "Is it really safe here, with the oxygen levels dropping?"

"We should be okay until tomorrow," Mom said. "And even the people who have to wait for the next rockets will be fine. After all, over half the other humans will be gone. So they won't be depleting the oxygen as quickly. In fact, they might even end up with *more* oxygen after we leave."

"But they still all have to evacuate? One or two people couldn't stay behind and keep the base going?"

"Why do you ask?"

I looked around our residence again. "It just seems like a shame. Abandoning this base after so much work."

"Leaving a skeleton crew behind has been discussed. But NASA has decided it's not worth the risk. What if the oxygen levels dropped to dangerous levels and it became too late to mount a rescue mission?" Mom walked to our single, small bureau and began taking the clothes out of it, already starting to pack for the trip home. "Space travel is hard, Dash. Harder than all of us hoped it would be. I know we have these dreams of leaving our galaxy and even visiting other planets someday. But that really might not be possible. Even if we could build a rocket that could travel that far—or go warp speed—our bodies might not be able to handle it. We are acutely evolved for our own planet. Except for that tiny little spot, the rest of the universe is absolutely toxic for us."

I found myself thinking about the conversations I'd had with Zan. She had indicated this was the case for species other than humans as well, though she'd never been specific about her own. When I had showed her space movies like *Star Wars* and *Star Trek*, she had always pointed out how ludicrous it was that every planet the heroes visited had the exact same atmosphere and gravity as earth. She had originally found this hilarious, believing it to be a joke.

Although it now occurred to me that, no matter how much I had prodded Zan, she had never admitted whether or not any species could actually travel between planets.

"Besides," Mom went on, "just because we abandon this place doesn't mean it's a failure. We made it eight months— and we could still come back."

"We?" I asked, worry creeping into my voice.

"I mean other people could come back," Mom corrected. "Different lunarnauts. Once NASA determines what's going wrong here and how to correct it, we could send some people back up to repair the base and get it going again. But I promise you, our family won't be coming. We've already done our time on this rock."

I sighed, relieved, then asked, "Have there been any side effects of having the oxygen drop?"

Mom paused in the midst of cleaning out the bureau, like I'd caught her off guard.

"There have," I pressed. "Haven't there?"

"Possibly," Mom agreed. "It's nothing severe. . . . But even a slight decrease in the amount of oxygen can have effects on people. Physically, it can be a bit harder to do exercise. Our hearts might beat a bit faster. We might find that we feel short of breath on occasion."

I thought back to the past few days. "I haven't felt anything like that."

"Well, you're young. Some of the adults have had issues. And then there's the psychological effects, which might even be stronger. Loss of concentration. Lapses in judgement. Increased irritability."

"Sounds like the Sjobergs have had oxygen deprivation since they got here." I was only joking, but as I thought about the last few weeks, I realized that the effects of oxygen depletion had been evident. My fellow Moonies had definitely been more irritable with one another. I had chalked that up to being trapped together in a relatively small moon base, but oxygen deprivation seemed to be an even better explanation. I also realized that *I* had been more irritable, especially with Violet.

"If you think the Sjobergs have been bad so far," Mom said, "wait until they find out they don't have priority on the rockets home."

I imagined what Lars Sjoberg's reaction to that would be. He had been clamoring to return to earth for weeks, but there had never been available seats on a rocket for him and his family. Now two empty rockets were going to arrive, and he *still* wouldn't have seats on them. He would go ballistic. "I feel sorry for everyone who gets stuck here with them after we're gone."

"No kidding. Someone might end up dead." The moment the words were out of her mouth, Mom gasped. "Oh my. That was a poor choice of words. I wasn't even thinking about the poisoning. I was just . . ." She looked at me. "Your father says you know the truth."

"I know someone did it on purpose."

"I don't think you should investigate. No matter what Nina says. In a little more than a day, we're going to be gone from here. The last thing you need to do is put yourself in danger."

"You don't have to worry about that," I said. "I'm playing it safe as can be until I get on that rocket tomorrow."

Mom smiled, then returned to packing. It didn't look as though it would take her very long. We hadn't been allowed to bring much to Moon Base Alpha to begin with.

I probably should have helped her, but I was still processing everything I had just learned. MBA was losing oxygen. It was potentially dangerous, which was scary, but because of it we were evacuating. I would be leaving the moon soon, more than two years before I was supposed to. The news was so incredible, it didn't seem real. . . .

And yet I also felt a pang of regret. It wasn't like I wanted to stay, but at the same time, the way it was all ending seemed wrong. Like we'd failed.

Plus, there was still a murderer on the loose.

I wondered if that could have had anything to do with the loss of oxygen. If a slight drop in oxygen ramped up people's irritability and impaired their judgment, then maybe someone who normally would have never considered murder might have suddenly done so. Or taken a risk when they wouldn't have otherwise.

Or maybe it was the upcoming evacuation that had forced someone's hand. Lars Sjoberg had sworn that he would destroy the lives of a lot of his fellow Moonies. All that had stopped him from doing it already was that his lines of communication with earth had been cut. But once he got back to earth, there would be little to stop him from trying. It was possible that someone—if not multiple people—didn't want to give him the chance.

Once half of us evacuated the next day, we would be abandoning the crime scene, possibly forever. There was a better than 50-percent chance that the killer was heading back to earth—fourteen of the twenty-five Moonies would be on the first wave home—and even a possibility that the killer would be on my rocket with me. After all, Dr. Goldstein had been the one with the apple seeds, and now they were gone. And Dr. Goldstein had proven herself somewhat conniving before. Or maybe Dr. Iwanyi had done it; he hadn't liked Lars either.

On the other hand, there was an almost 50-percent chance that the killer would be stuck back on MBA with Lars. Which might give them another chance to kill him—or give Lars a chance to get revenge.

Whatever the case, it seemed like there were still a lot of scenarios in which something could go wrong.

As it turned out, things were going to get far worse than I had ever imagined.

Excerpt from *The Official NASA Procedures for Contact with Intelligent Extraterrestrial Life* © National Aeronautics and Space Administration, Department of Extraterrestrial Affairs, 2029 (Classification Level AAA)

ESTABLISHMENT OF A SECURE PERIMETER

In the case of physical manifestation of IEL, a perimeter around the affected area must be immediately established to keep distance between the IEL and the public, thereby minimizing the threat of accidental contact and potential ensuing panic and/or large-scale public gatherings. The simplest way to do this is to declare that there has been a gas leak or other equivalent disaster,* then evacuate any locals "for reasons of their own safety." Use your federal powers to enlist the local police, but of course do not tell them the true reasons for establishment of the perimeter. The actual size of the perimeter will most likely be based on the size of the area of physical manifestation, though as a rule it is good to give yourself a half mile of distance on all sides.

---

* Other disaster options include (but are not limited to) downed power lines, brush fires, flooding, and rogue grizzly bears.

SERIOUS GAPS IN INTELLECT

Lunar day 252

T minus 22 hours to evacuation

Once word got out that we were leaving Moon Base Alpha, school was canceled for the day. The adults all realized that we kids wouldn't be able to concentrate on our classes—and that we could be better used helping with the evacuation procedures.

It didn't take long to pack our own things for evacuation, but prepping the rest of MBA was a great deal of work. Lots of delicate scientific equipment had to be carefully packed, while other experiments had to be configured to continue running while we were gone. Since the second wave of rockets would only be a week behind the first, we also had to begin prepping all the remaining equipment for "hibernation mode," and there was a great deal of equipment: evaporators, rehydrators, air-circulation systems, maintenance robots. Most of us had our hands full helping out.

Meanwhile, Roddy Marquez was spending his last day on the moon the way he'd spent every one of the 251 days before it: playing veeyar games. Now that we didn't have school, the rec room was wide open.

Although I was worried about the depleted oxygen, overall I was happier than I'd been in weeks. Months, maybe. I had been expecting to spend another twenty-eight months on the moon. Now, in only a day, I would be leaving. Suddenly, all the things that had made life miserable on the moon didn't seem so bad, because I wouldn't have to experience them much longer. My lunch of rehydrated pepperoni calzone may have been lousy, but at least it was probably my *last* lunch of rehydrated pepperoni calzone. A visit to the space toilet was far less awful knowing that I would only have to visit it a few more times.

Assuming the evacuation went off properly.

I had lived on the moon long enough to know that things there rarely worked out exactly as planned. I could only hope that this would be an exception, that the rockets would arrive on time, that there wouldn't be any malfunctions, and that nothing would get worse with our air supply before we left.

I had just polished off that hopefully-the-last pepperoni calzone when Zan appeared. I was in the mess hall, putting my garbage in the recycler for what was almost the last time.

Zan instantly gleaned that I was in a far better mood than usual from reading my emotions. "What's going on?" she asked.

"We're evacuating the moon tomorrow," I told her, doing my best not to say it out loud.

"Why?" Zan asked, understandably surprised.

I glanced around the mess hall, which was a bigger hive of activity than usual. "Let's talk about this in my residence," I said. I could see Violet helping my parents in the science pod, so I figured our room would be peaceful for once.

"All right," Zan said.

I quickly dumped my used food packets in the recycler, then hurried through the base to our room, and told Zan everything I knew about the evacuation along the way.

"I can't believe you're going," she said, once I'd closed the door behind us. "This must be quite a present for your birthday." While she sounded happy, there was something I couldn't quite read beneath the surface. The interface of our emotions went both ways when we were in contact, although I wasn't quite as adept at reading hers as she was at reading mine.

"Is something wrong?" I asked her.

"It's nothing to be concerned about. You might not have enjoyed being here, but this moon base is special to me. It is the only place I have ever communicated with humans."

"But that doesn't mean you can't contact me when I'm back on earth, right?"

"I have had contact with life on earth before."

"Hold on. I thought Dr. Holtz was the first human you ever spoke to."

"Who said I could only speak to humans?"

I sat down on an InflatiCube, surprised. "You've communicated with life that wasn't human?"

"There are millions of different life forms on earth, Dashiell."

"Yes, but most of them aren't very good at conversation."

"That's true," Zan admitted. "However, I felt it was worth trying to understand them when weighing the fate of your planet. After all, their lives hang in the balance too. I don't talk to them, exactly, but I *can* experience what they do."

"And what do they experience?"

"It varies. Your elephants and dolphins have an astonishing array of emotions. In fact, they feel some things even more strongly than you do. Whereas a wildebeest doesn't seem to have much on its mind except grass."

"You've been inside the mind of a wildebeest?"

"Yes. And moose and honeybees and tiger sharks and sea

otters and dozens of other animals. I must admit, the otters were quite fun."

"Did the animals understand what you were?"

"Even less than you do."

Something about that statement struck me as a bit insulting. "Zan, are you saying that I *don't* understand what you are?"

"That's correct."

"Well, that's not my fault! You've barely told me anything about yourself!"

"I know. And as I promised you, I am going to try to rectify that. That's why I have come to you again today."

"Really?" My annoyance quickly gave way to excitement. Zan sensed this. "However, I have to warn you, I still won't be able to answer everything you want to know about me."

"Why not?"

"Because you won't understand it."

"You can't even try?"

"It wouldn't be worth our time."

I wondered if I should feel insulted by this, too. "Is this because I haven't been able to figure out how to transmit my thoughts the way you do?"

"It's more complicated than that."

"What do you mean?"

Zan sat down across from me and looked directly into

my eyes. Her eyes were so blue I almost felt lost in them. "Have you ever heard of Fermi's paradox?"

"Sure. The idea is that if there are hundreds of millions of planets in our galaxy, then the probability is that at least one of them should have intelligent life. So Fermi wondered why we hadn't heard from anyone yet." This was the sort of thing that got discussed quite often at mealtimes at MBA. Obviously, I had a whole new perspective on it lately.

"Exactly. Dr. Holtz told me about it. The truth is, there are actually *billions* of planets in our galaxy, and thousands of them have intelligent life. So I suppose the question for you is: Why have none of us contacted you until now?"

"When we first met, you said that was because you didn't know we were around until recently. That you hadn't noticed us yet."

"That wasn't quite honest of me. The truth is, many alien civilizations have known about you for much of the past thousand years. In fact, some of them even tried to contact you. But you couldn't comprehend them."

"Why not?"

"Because our civilizations are far too advanced compared to yours. Imagine a colony of ants trying to understand what a rocket ship is."

I *definitely* felt insulted now. "And humans are the ants in this scenario?"

"Please don't take offense. We know you are smarter than ants are. But compared to us . . ."

"We're as dumb as ants."

"Let's just say that you're operating on a different plane of understanding from ours. So when attempts to contact you were made, you didn't have any idea what they were."

"Maybe that was the case a few thousand years ago. But we're smarter now. I mean, *I* understand you."

"Yes, but . . . that has less to do with your species getting smarter than, well . . ." Zan shifted uncomfortably. "I have figured out how to communicate on your level."

"You mean you've figured out how to talk down to us? Like humans figuring out how to communicate with ants?"

"Yes."

I frowned at this, disturbed by the thought of being so dumb. "Is that why the other civilizations aren't so concerned about whether or not we wipe ourselves out? Because we're just like a bunch of ants to them?"

Zan dodged my question. Instead she said, "You wanted answers, Dashiell. This is part of the reason I have been hesitant to share them with you. If this conversation is disturbing to you, we can stop it."

"No!" I said, more sharply than I'd expected. I took a moment to gather my thoughts. "It's just a lot to get my head around."

"I expected as much. And you are better prepared for it than most people would be. Even though Dr. Holtz was excited to reveal my existence, he had some grave concerns about how humanity would handle it."

"Not as grave as Garth Grisan," I said sourly. Garth had killed Dr. Holtz to keep Zan's existence a secret.

"Oh, Dr. Holtz had many of the same worries as Garth," Zan replied. "That's why he didn't want to tell the entire earth at once. He felt that the revelation could have a dangerous effect."

"No, it wouldn't," I said. "Not if you came in peace."

"Dr. Holtz told me a story once. The tale of a tribe in your Amazon rain forest that didn't encounter the rest of civilization until relatively recently. They were what you would think of as primitive: only a few hundred people with Stone Age technology. However, since they didn't know about the rest of the world, they thought they were the pinnacle of human achievement.

"One day, two Western explorers stumbled into their village. The tribesmen recognized that the explorers had different technology than they did, but they still considered the men far inferior to them. After all, the tribe was far better suited to its habitat than the explorers were, and the explorers needed all sorts of silly clothing and gadgets to survive. The explorers offered to take some of the tribesmen to see their civilization, and the two bravest tribesmen agreed. So they went off down the river. The tribesmen expected that everyone they encountered would be lesser than they were. Within a few hours, they had traveled farther than anyone from the tribe had ever gone before in their history.

"In a day's time, they reached a small town, and the tribesmen were startled to see that this town had far more people than they even knew had existed on earth. They were overwhelmed by everything the townspeople had: so much food, so many boats, so much technology. And then they came to a larger town, and a larger town, and a larger town, until, eventually, they arrived at the great city at the mouth of the Amazon, with millions of people and skyscrapers and cars and ships the size of mountains. By this time, the poor tribesmen were catatonic with shock. Because their entire view of the world had been overturned. They had gone from being the most important, advanced people on earth to an insignificant, irrelevant little group. It was a tremendous blow to their mental states—and they never recovered from it. One died within a few weeks, while the other went insane."

I thought about that for a while. "That might not happen with us. Humanity has prepared itself for the possibility of alien life. Lots of the world is excited about it."

"I have seen what you have imagined alien life to be. The

spaceships and creatures of your movies and TV shows. As you know, I have found those ridiculous. But I haven't quite let you know *how* ridiculous. The spaceships you envision are merely rudimentary modifications to your airplanes. To travel from planet to planet requires technology you aren't even close to understanding. It requires spacecraft that would, well . . . blow your minds."

"And you can't even *try* to explain this to us?"

"Not really."

"But you actually have this technology? You can travel between planets at warp speed and stuff like that?"

"There are some civilizations that have mastered inter-planetary travel. Although, once again, it doesn't work with warp speed or anything like you have imagined."

I noticed that she hadn't quite answered my question. "Can *your* civilization do it?"

"Our technology is not quite as advanced as some civilizations', but we understand the concepts behind interplane-tary travel. However, it would be ludicrous for us to attempt such a thing. We couldn't possibly travel anywhere else."

"Why not?"

"Because my species isn't terrestrial."

I took a moment to process that, failing to hide my surprise. "You live in water?"

"Yes. Just as most life on your own planet does. In fact,

on both our planets, life first evolved in the water. On my planet, it just so happened that the most intelligent life forms stayed there."

"So you can't build spaceships because they would need to hold all the water," I concluded. "And that's too great a weight to fly with. Plus, if you got to a planet without water, you wouldn't be able to get around."

"That's correct. Luckily, we evolved some adaptations to our aquatic environment that gave us other ways to travel across space. For example, we needed to develop another way to communicate besides voice, and that eventually led to our telepathic abilities."

I was glad I was sitting down. I was so amazed by all these revelations, my knees had gone wobbly. It had never occurred to me that there might be a hyperintelligent aquatic species on some other planet. "So, are you like some sort of really smart fish?"

Zan smiled, amused, then said, "Perhaps I should just show you what I look like."

"You mean it?" I asked excitedly. "Right now?"

"I think the time has come," Zan replied.

And then she changed.

One moment, she was a human being. The next, she wasn't.

I admit, I had been slightly worried that she would turn

out to be some sort of hideous sea creature. A lot of aquatic life on earth is disturbing to look at: anglerfish, hagfish, wolf eels, sea cucumbers. But Zan wasn't anything like that.

She was like nothing I had ever imagined.

In the most basic sense, she was like an enormous jellyfish, but there were major differences. For starters, her skin—or whatever her surface was called—was a gorgeous color that was completely new to me, a kind of luminescent pink, like the color of a sky during a sunset, only better. From within the large bulb that would be the body of a jellyfish, there was a glow that seemed to indicate an immense brain at work inside, while all around the bulb were hundreds of little blue dots. Since these were the same color as Zan's eyes when she showed herself to me, I figured that they were her eyes now as well, although they obviously weren't anything like my eyes. A dozen long, tubelike tentacles extended from her body.

She wavered in the air in front of me, as though she was bobbing in water that I couldn't see, her tentacles and body rippling.

She was definitely alien, absolutely nothing like a human being at all—or any of the humanoid beings that showed up in all our movies. And yet . . .

"Zan," I said. "You're beautiful."

Zan's color shifted to a crimson red. "Thank you," she

said, actually sounding flattered. "Would you like me to stay this way . . . or would it be easier if I returned to human form?"

"No offense, but human form would be easier."

"I understand." Zan was instantly human again. "How's this?"

"Better," I said, although this was a slight lie. It was now hard not to think of Zan as some sort of enormous gelatinous polyp. "Thanks for showing me your real form."

"I'm glad you liked it. I expect you must have many questions."

"Yes." In fact, I had so many, I had almost no idea where to start. "Are you carbon-based? Like life on earth?"

"I am. And so is most of life in the universe. Although beyond that, our bodies are constructed quite differently."

"So those tentacle things. Are those arms?"

"Yes. Although we can also use them to sense the world in various ways. And we eat through them."

"How?"

"We catch food and then absorb it through special organs. It is far more efficient than your need to shift food from your hands to your mouths in order to consume it."

"What do you eat?"

"Aquatic creatures. I suspect you would find them disgusting. The truth is, we don't make as big a deal out of eating as you humans do. Cooking is one of the things I find so fascinating about your culture."

"If you evolved the ability to communicate telepathically, do you think that's why I can't do it?"

"But you *did* do it, Dashiell. When you appeared to Riley back on earth."

"Yes, but you were kind of helping me then, weren't you? I could feel you inside my head when it happened."

"I was there with you, but *you* were the one who jumped. I will admit, I was skeptical that you could do it until that moment. I am not anymore. You have the power to do it again."

"Then why can't I?"

"Well, it's not easy. Even for me. And I suspect that, to do it with any regularity, you will need to train your mind to work in a very different way than it's used to."

"Is this one of those things that's going to be way too complicated for an ant like me to understand?"

"You're not an ant. But yes, it might be too complicated. There are things that evolve besides our bodies. Ways of thinking evolve too. Ways of understanding the universe. For example, you see a limited part of the color spectrum and hear a limited part of the aural spectrum, but other animals can see colors that you can't or hear sounds that you can't."

"Like how bees can see infrared and dogs can hear high notes?"

"Exactly. And those limitations shape your perspective of the world. Well, there are other, more complicated forms of perception too. Like your concept of distance."

I cocked my head, trying to understand. "You mean different species can perceive distance differently?"

"Yes. And what you think of as a massive distance between two planets may not appear the same to a different creature."

"That doesn't make any sense."

"There was a time when people would have said that Einstein's theory of relativity didn't make any sense. And a time before that when people thought it was heresy to say that the earth revolved around the sun. Right now, you have barely begun to scratch the surface of what the universe is truly like. Although some human scientists are beginning to theorize that what I am saying about distance might be true. Including at least one scientist on your moon base."

"Who?"

"Dr. Brahmaputra-Marquez. She is really quite brilliant."

And yet she still married Dr. Marquez, I thought. "So your planet really isn't hundreds of light years away?"

"Well, it still takes hundreds of years for light to travel from one to the other, but that is only one way to perceive distance. Has it ever occurred to you that our conversations take place without any gaps in time even though we are on different planets?"

I winced, feeling like an idiot. Because it hadn't occurred to me. When I spoke to people back on earth over the Com-Links, there was always a slight delay in transmission, because it took a few seconds for the sound to cover the distance to the moon. But this had never happened when I talked to Zan, even though we were light years apart. "I guess I figured thought moved faster than light or something."

"No. It can simply travel in ways that light can't."

I rubbed my temples. My head was starting to throb. Talking to Zan was always mentally taxing, but the complexity of this conversation was taking an additional toll on me.

"Are you all right, Dashiell?"

"Yes. I'm just trying to comprehend everything."

"It may take time."

"Right," I agreed, although I was wondering if I would *ever* understand this, even if I had the rest of my life to do it. "This secret that you have that could save humanity. . . . Is there a chance that, even if you tell me what it is, humanity won't understand it?"

"I suppose. Although I have faith in you, Dashiell."

"Does that mean you're going to share it?"

Zan pursed her lips. "I'm afraid I still haven't decided."

I was about to press her on the issue, but before I could, Violet walked into the room. She froze upon seeing me, surprised.

"Hey," I said. "Could you give me a little privacy? I was about to call Riley. . . ."

"No, you weren't," Violet said matter-of-factly. "I know you're talking to Zan."

I sighed. A few weeks before, Violet had caught me talking to Zan, so I'd had to pretend that I had an imaginary friend. "I'm not," I argued. "Zan doesn't exist."

"Sure she does," Violet said. "I can see her." Then, to my surprise, she looked right at Zan and said, "Hi!"

After which, to my even greater surprise, Zan looked right back at her and said, "Hello, Violet. It's nice to see you again."

Excerpt from *The Official NASA Procedures for Contact with Intelligent Extraterrestrial Life* © National Aeronautics and Space Administration, Department of Extraterrestrial Affairs, 2029 (Classification Level AAA)

QUARANTINE

Once a perimeter has been established, it is paramount that no one inside the perimeter be allowed to leave it for a period of at least forty-eight hours. (Including the IEL.) Any life form coming to earth from another planet will very likely be carrying potentially infectious or dangerous agents—or may *be* a potentially infectious or dangerous agent itself.* To this end, it is important to establish a quarantine area to prevent any potential spread of such agents into the general populace. As quickly as possible, DEXA will deliver mobile quarantine units (MQUs), which have comfortable living quarters and high-pressure showers. Until the MQUs arrive, those who have made primary contact will need to improvise, using local buildings if feasible.**

Any non-NASA personnel who may have been engaged in primary contact must be quarantined as well, although they should not be told the true reasons for this. Instead a fabrication should be given, explaining (calmly yet firmly) that this is for their own personal health and safety. (For example, one might insinuate that there is a severe danger of radiation poisoning or exposure to toxic chemicals that

---

* Such agents may include (but are not limited to): viruses, bacteria, mutated genes, and allergens.
** If there are no local buildings anywhere nearby, tents or lean-tos will suffice.

must be dealt with immediately). DEXA will also dispatch trained medical personnel as quickly as possible. NO ONE IS TO LEAVE THE QUARANTINE AREA UNTIL CLEARED BY TRAINED DEXA PERSONNEL.

STRONG ACCUSATIONS

Lunar day 252

T minus 21 hours to evacuation

"You can see Zan?" I asked Violet.

"Duh," Violet said. "She's right here with us."

"I know she is," I said. "But I didn't know *you* knew. I, uh . . ." After a day of startling revelations, I was surprised how much this was throwing me. "How long have you known each other?"

"For a few weeks," Zan answered. "Once Violet stumbled upon you and me talking to each other, I felt I should present myself to her."

"And you didn't tell me?" I asked.

"It was our little secret," Zan said.

I looked to Violet. "You've never been able to keep a secret in your life!"

"Yes, I have," Violet said. "I keep secrets all the time. I didn't tell you that I ate your Skittles today."

"You ate my Skittles?" I asked.

Violet flushed red, embarrassed. "Not all of them. And we're going home soon, so it doesn't matter."

Normally, I would have been upset by this, but there were more pressing issues at the moment. I turned to Zan. "Have you two been talking regularly?"

"About as often as you and I have been talking," Zan replied.

"Why?"

"Because I'm awesome!" Violet exclaimed.

"I thought she was an interesting representative of humanity," Zan replied. "Given that you are closely related, your dispositions are surprisingly different."

"No kidding," I said.

"I showed Zan how I can burp the alphabet," Violet said proudly.

"Great," I muttered. "That's exactly what humanity needs to prove its worth to the universe."

"Zan was very impressed," Violet told me.

"I'll bet." I turned to Zan, expecting her to back me up. Instead she shrugged apologetically.

"It might not have been a Beethoven symphony," she said, "But it did require some talent."

There was a knock at the door. "Dashiell!" Nina called from outside. "I need to talk to you. Now."

I looked at Violet and put a finger to my lips, hoping to make Nina think we weren't there. Violet nodded understanding.

"I know you're in there," Nina said. "I heard you talking through the wall. If you don't come out on your own, I will drag you out."

"All right," I said. "I'm coming." I turned to Zan and spoke in my thoughts. "Please stay here. I'll try to make this quick."

"I'll do what I can," Zan replied.

As I headed for the door, Violet turned her attention to Zan and said, "What would you like to learn about today? Turtles?"

"That sounds lovely," Zan said.

I wasn't sure why, but I felt upset that Zan had been secretly talking to Violet. A mixture of jealousy and betrayal. Which was odd, because up until that point I had felt like being the *only* person to stand trial for humanity was a burden. And even though my conversation with Zan had been taxing, I was still annoyed with both Violet and Nina for interrupting it.

So I was in a pretty bad mood when I stepped out onto the catwalk. It didn't get any better when Nina ordered, "In my office. Now." She pointed to her open door.

I walked into her residence. Nina followed me in and shut the door behind us.

I didn't sit down on the InflatiCube. I didn't want Nina to think I'd be staying a long time.

She didn't sit either. "Have you learned anything of importance in this investigation?"

"I thought my father told you he didn't want me to investigate."

"He did. That doesn't mean that I agree with him. So, have you learned anything?"

"Yes," I said. I figured avoiding any arguments with Nina was the fastest way to get back to my conversation with Zan.

"Well . . . ?"

"Cyanide can be made from apple seeds. Dr. Goldstein had some apple seeds in the greenhouse, but now they're all gone."

It was hard to read Nina's face, but it seemed as if this might have been news to her. "Do you think Dr. Goldstein made the poison?"

"Not necessarily. Anyone could have gotten the seeds. They weren't locked up or anything."

"I asked you to come to me with any information you learned right away. Why didn't you do that?"

"I forgot," I admitted.

"You mean, you got too carried away eavesdropping on *me*."

"There was also the fact that we're evacuating the base tomorrow because the oxygen is leaking out and we all might die otherwise. That was a little distracting."

Nina obviously didn't appreciate my sarcasm. "I'm aware that Kira has suggested that *I* might be the killer," she said coldly. "I can assure you that I'm not. Lars Sjoberg may be a constant problem for me, but that doesn't mean he deserves to die."

I noticed that she hadn't offered any alibi. She seemed to simply expect me to take her at her word. Still, I didn't want to challenge her on it. If she actually *was* the killer, it seemed like a bad idea to confront her by myself in her locked room. As Kira had said, Nina had probably been trained to kill. "All right," I said. "I'm sorry that we even thought it was you." I started for the door.

"We're not done here, Dashiell."

I froze, not liking the tone in Nina's voice. "We're not?"

"There is a killer on the loose in this base, and I still need your help to find them."

"But my father—"

"Your father is not in charge here. I am." Nina strode over to her SlimScreen table. "I need you to break into Chang's room and look for evidence."

"What?" I gasped. "Why?"

"Because I have further suspicions that he might be the killer." Nina brought up a video file on the SlimScreen. "This is from last night, in the mess hall." The footage was from one of the many security cameras mounted inside the base. This one was up in the ceiling of the mess hall, giving an angle down toward the food-storage area. It was time-stamped at the bottom: 00:24:35. Twenty-four minutes after midnight.

There was no one in the mess hall, which made sense, given that it was the middle of the night. Then Chang entered. It was easy to recognize him, given the Mohawk and the tattoos. He glanced around furtively, as though worried about being seen.

"I thought you said it was pointless to comb through all the footage from the food-storage areas," I said.

"I changed my mind. I didn't think it would be likely, but then I found *this*."

In the footage, Chang rifled through hundreds of packets of food, as though looking for something specific. Due to the angle of the camera, it was hard to see exactly what he was doing; his body blocked most of the drawer. Finally he stood again, clutching a packet of food. He took it to the rehydrator.

"He wasn't doing anything strange," I said. "He was only getting some food for himself."

"Chang knows there are cameras in the mess hall," Nina

pointed out. "If he poisoned the lutefisk and left without taking any food, he'd look guilty."

"He just looks *hungry* to me," I pointed out.

"That's the same storage unit the lutefisk is kept in." Nina closed the video file and immediately opened a second one, which had been recorded by the exact same camera. It was from the same angle, although now the time stamp said 02:01:05. "An hour and a half later, Lars came down to get some of it," Nina said.

Sure enough, Lars Sjoberg entered the mess and went directly to the same food-storage unit. He opened it, and quickly searched through it until he found a package of dehydrated lutefisk.

Nina froze the image. "That's what he was poisoned by."

"Why was Lars Sjoberg eating lutefisk at two o'clock in the morning?" I asked.

"I don't know. Maybe he had a craving."

"For lutefisk?"

"Yes! The man likes lutefisk. I don't know why. I think it tastes like paint thinner. But it doesn't matter *why* Lars ate it. What matters is that Chang was fiddling around in the storage unit shortly beforehand."

"Even if he *was* trying to poison Lars, there's no way he could have guaranteed that he'd poison the package Lars was about to eat."

"I'm well aware of that."

"And that footage doesn't even show Chang poisoning the food. There's no proof he did it at all."

"Obviously. If there *was* proof, I'd have arrested Chang already. That's what I need *you* for. Chang's activity last night was suspicious enough to warrant further investigation. And you're going to do it for me."

"Why me?"

"Because he won't suspect you. This afternoon, we have a great deal of work to do closing down the science pod. All the adults are expected to be there—but not you. So while I keep Chang distracted, you will go into his room and see what you can find."

"No." I said the word so forcefully, I surprised myself.

It seemed to surprise Nina, too. "I'm the moon-base commander, Dashiell."

"It's wrong," I told her.

"I decide what is right and wrong here. Not you."

I started for the door again. "My parents will think it's wrong too. I can tell them about this right now—"

"And I can bump your family off the rocket tomorrow and make you wait for the next ones."

I froze once more, my hand only inches from the knob, then turned back to Nina.

Given what she had just said, I had expected that she

would have an angry look on her face, or maybe an evil one. Instead she was calm as could be, which was somehow even worse. This was simply business to her.

"As you know," she said, "the Sjobergs are going to be very upset when they learn they aren't going back tomorrow. It would certainly make *my* life much easier to let them leave earlier. No one at NASA would question the decision."

"They wouldn't think that you were jeopardizing our lives by keeping us here longer?"

"*Someone* has to stay."

I considered the implications of that. Although the second wave of rockets was only a week away, I didn't want to wait any longer than I had to for a ride home. Neither did my parents, I was sure. But it was Violet who really clinched the deal for me. I thought about what her reaction would be if she found out we'd been bumped from the first rocket. Violet was joyful enough to bounce back from most things, but a delay in our trip back to earth would be different. More importantly, it was *dangerous* to stay longer at MBA. The oxygen system was failing. Every extra day we remained at the base was another chance to die.

I couldn't do that to Violet.

Besides, all I had to do in exchange was poke around Chang's room for a bit, looking for evidence that probably wasn't even there. Even though Nina had her suspicions, I figured Chang hadn't been doing anything wrong. If I didn't find anything incriminating, that would prove it.

"All right," I said.

The look on Nina's face didn't change. She simply gave a curt nod. "Very good. Of course, you are not to tell your parents about this. If you do, I'll bump you from the flight tomorrow anyhow."

"I figured as much."

"You can ask Kira to help you, if you'd like. I'm guessing you were going to do that anyway."

I hadn't actually decided to do that, but the thought had certainly crossed my mind.

Suddenly there was a howl of rage outside the room. It sounded like it had come from the other side of MBA, but was loud enough to echo throughout the base. "Niiiiiiinnn-nnaaaaaaa!!!!"

There was only one person at MBA who ever made a sound like that: Lars Sjoberg.

Now Nina finally showed some emotion. She looked to the ceiling in exasperation. "He must have found out about the evacuation schedule. Just what I need right now."

"Niiiiiiiinnnnnaaaaaaa!!!!" Lars roared again.

"You're dismissed," Nina told me. She smoothed out her uniform with her hands, as if girding herself for having to deal with Lars.

I hurried out of her residence as fast as I could. As I stepped through the door, I saw that Lars was already out of his room, storming down the catwalk toward Nina's office. It was the first time I'd seen him since he'd recovered from his poisoning, although it was hard to tell if the cyanide had taken any toll on him, given his current enraged condition. His face was as red as the blast from a booster rocket. Sonja, Patton, and Lily followed him, like leaves caught in the wake of a passing car.

"You!" Lars exclaimed when he saw me, pointing a stubby finger accusingly. "Your family is behind this! I know it!"

I didn't stick around to argue. I simply ducked through the door of my residence and slammed it behind me.

Sadly, Zan was no longer there, waiting for me.

Instead, Dr. Goldstein was.

Excerpt from *The Official NASA Procedures for Contact with Intelligent Extraterrestrial Life* © National Aeronautics and Space Administration, Department of Extraterrestrial Affairs, 2029 (Classification Level AAA)

ALIEN APPEARANCE

It is important to note that the IEL may look radically different than we expect. Years of Hollywood movies and other mass entertainments have conditioned us to believe that any IEL will look something like us, with bipedal body structure and an obvious head, among other traits. This will probably not be the case. Although the basics of chemistry indicate that any IEL will most likely be carbon-based, as we are, there are an infinite number of possible body forms an IEL might have, any one of which might be startling, unsettling or even frightening to observe.* DO NOT JUDGE THE IEL BASED UPON ITS PHYSICAL APPEARANCE. Keep in mind that, even if an IEL appears hideous to us, that is based upon our own species-centric experience, and we might look equally as hideous to it.

---

* A simple consideration of the myriad body forms on our own planet indicates that an IEL could look like anything, from an octopus to a beetle to a mold spore.

HONEST-TO-GOD FOOD

Lunar day 252

T minus 20 hours to evacuation

"It's such a shame," Dr. Goldstein said.

We were no longer in my residence, even though that was where she had been waiting for me. (Violet had let her in, but had then gone off to find my parents.) It had been impossible to have a conversation with Lars raging in Nina's residence next door. Lars had been shouting so loud, the walls had actually trembled.

So we were now in the greenhouse. This gave us some privacy to talk—and it also allowed me to help Dr. Goldstein get things prepared for the evacuation. All the plants she had worked so hard to grow now had to be composted in hopes that, should MBA come back online, there would be usable soil to restart the greenhouse once again.

There was a plus side to this, however: All the fruits and vegetables that she had grown were going to be served up with dinner that night.

"What's a shame?" I asked.

Dr. Goldstein waved to the plants around her. "Eight months of work right down the tubes. I was finally getting the hang of this . . . and now it's all going to waste." She grasped a strawberry plant by the stalk, but hesitated before uprooting it. She looked like a woman who had been asked to put down her pet dog.

It occurred to me that Dr. Goldstein probably loved her plants as much as most people love their animals. She had spent hours each day for the past few months nurturing them, tending to them, struggling to keep them alive. There were some insects at MBA that had been brought up to see how life on the moon would affect them—ants and bees and earthworms—but they were locked away in terrariums and no one had really considered them pets. Even so, the ones that had survived would get to live: They were coming back to earth with us so their vitals could be studied. The plants all had to die.

"Do you want me to do that?" I asked.

Dr. Goldstein looked at me, startled, as if perhaps she

had been so upset, she had forgotten that I was there. "Yes," she said thankfully. "If you wouldn't mind."

So I went to work uprooting the plants while Dr. Goldstein harvested the vegetables. She started with the snap peas, twisting each pod off the vine and plunking it in a small bowl.

On the other side of the glass walls, the base was humming with activity. I could still hear Lars Sjoberg raging. Everyone else was doing their best to ignore it, though now and then I noticed someone glancing toward Nina's residence, either feeling sorry for Nina or fed up with Lars.

"I didn't poison him," Dr. Goldstein said.

I turned to her, surprised. She had said it so quietly, I wasn't sure if she had even meant for it to be out loud.

"Lars?" I asked, then winced at my own stupidity. It wasn't like there were any other poisoning victims at MBA.

"Yes." Dr. Goldstein didn't look at me. She stayed focused on her peas. "I know you found out about the apple seeds."

"How?"

"After the Sjobergs got in here last month and ate all the strawberries, I rigged up a sensor system. Now when someone enters the greenhouse, I get an alert. And then I can check the camera feeds."

"Wouldn't it have been easier to just put a lock on the door?"

"That isn't my decision to make. This greenhouse is communal property for everyone at MBA. I only grow the plants." Dr. Goldstein plunked a few more peas in the bowl. "I watched all the footage of you in here. I thought you might have been trying to eat something without permission at first—but you didn't. It took me a while to figure out what you'd been up to."

I glanced up toward the top of the greenhouse door. Sure enough, there was a security camera there. It would have offered a decent view of us inside the room, although, like most of the cameras at MBA, it probably didn't record sound. Otherwise, Dr. Goldstein would have known what we were doing right away.

"I didn't even know the seeds were gone until after *you* noticed," Dr. Goldstein said.

"You didn't?"

"I have thousands of seeds in here. It never occurred to me that anyone would steal them."

"Even after you heard that Lars had been poisoned?"

"I didn't know that it had been done on purpose. Nina said it was an accident." Dr. Goldstein snapped off a few more peas. "It wasn't until you found the seeds were missing that I realized what must have really happened."

I uprooted the last of the strawberry plants and laid it on the pile with the rest. There was something awful about the sight of it. It reminded me of the horrible moment in *The Lorax* where the very last of the truffula trees has been cut down. "So you knew cyanide could be made with apple seeds."

"Of course. Plants are my specialty. That's why I collected the apple seeds in the first place."

I looked to her, surprised. "Not for growing apples?"

"Dashiell, apple trees are enormous. I couldn't possibly grow one to full fruiting height in here."

"I thought maybe you knew how to do a dwarf version. . . ."

"Cyanide, properly handled, is a very effective pesticide."

"But we don't have any pests in the base. It's supposed to be sterile."

"That doesn't mean it will stay that way. No matter how hard we try, there's always a chance something will get through. Especially when you're dealing with organic matter." Dr. Goldstein's gaze dropped to the packs of poop she had stored under the planting table, as though they might be a breeding ground for trouble. "I figured it paid to be prepared." She pointed to the plants I'd laid out. "Why don't you pluck the strawberries off those?" Then she lowered her voice conspiratorially. "If one or two went missing, I'd never notice."

"Really?" I asked, unable to control my excitement.

"I understand it's your birthday."

I looked over the strawberries. It had been eight months since I'd had one, given that the Sjobergs had devoured the last crop. As much as I wanted one, I had conflicting emotions. It seemed wrong to take one for myself before everyone else got to share. Plus, I wondered if Dr. Goldstein was trying to distract me from the topic at hand—or buy my trust.

"It's no big deal," Dr. Goldstein urged. "Soon enough, all of us will be back on earth again with as many strawberries as we can eat."

There was a beautiful, perfectly ripe strawberry lying atop the pile of plants. I couldn't resist it anymore. I picked it up, relishing even the feel of it, then held it up to my nose and inhaled. It smelled incredible.

And it tasted even better.

I had to turn my back to the greenhouse windows so no one would see that I was getting special treatment. My first bite was small, but loaded with flavor. I had forgotten how amazing food could taste.

"When was the last time you checked to make sure the apple seeds were here?" I asked.

Dr. Goldstein grew a bit flustered, as though this question made her uncomfortable. "I honestly don't know. Like I said, it never occurred to me that anyone might take them. The fruits, definitely. But not the seeds. Someone might have taken them as much as two months ago."

"Which was before you put the sensor on the greenhouse door."

"Yes."

Which meant that pretty much anyone on the base could have stolen the seeds and not been noticed. Assuming they had planned the crime well ahead of time.

"What about more recently?" I asked. "Since you've been monitoring the door, have you seen anyone sneak in here?"

"Oh, Dashiell, I've seen practically *everyone* on this base sneak in here."

I almost gagged on my next small bite of strawberry in surprise. "Everyone?"

"This is a very special place at Moon Base Alpha. It might not be very much like earth, but it's the closest thing we have. Quite often, when it's late at night, and someone thinks they're the only one awake, they'll come in here. Usually on the way back from the bathroom."

I thought back to the feeling I'd had when I'd first entered the greenhouse earlier that day. If I had known about that sensation before, I probably would have been sneaking into the greenhouse every chance I got.

"Did you ever notice anyone doing anything suspicious?" I asked.

"Well, quite a few people snuck a little something to eat."

"Really? Who?"

"Again, pretty much everyone. Even Nina has raided this place. And your own parents."

"They did?"

"They came together. And they only took a cherry tomato between them. I'm sure they thought no one would miss it. But I know every single fruit and vegetable in this place."

"You didn't see anyone fiddling around with the seeds?"

"No, but I did see some people who came in here and didn't eat anything."

"Like who?"

Dr. Goldstein looked out the windows warily, as though worried someone might be watching us. No one was, though. Even so, she still lowered her voice. "Dr. Janke and Dr. Brahmaputra-Marquez both did."

"Together?"

"No, at separate times. More than a week apart, in fact. And both spent quite some time in here. Now, they may have simply been enjoying the sensation of being in this room, but then, they might have swiped the seeds as well."

I wasn't aware of either Dr. Janke or Dr. Brahmaputra-Marquez having a major grudge against Lars, but then, like everyone else at MBA, they probably hated the man. I wondered if that would be enough to drive someone to murder, especially in a place where tensions were running high and oxygen was running low.

In addition, Dr. Brahmaputra-Marquez definitely had issues with Patton and Lily, who had been terrible to Roddy. I wondered if, perhaps, she'd poisoned the lutefisk to take out one of them, not realizing that Lars was the only one who ate it.

"And then there's Lily Sjoberg," Dr. Goldstein said.

"She came in here and didn't eat anything?"

"Yes. Unlike her brother. That pig Patton has gobbled up so much of my food that I've had to get Nina to intervene."

"How so?"

"She told Lars that if Patton ate anything else in here without permission, she'd put Patton in charge of acquiring the human fertilizer from the composter. That seems to have done the trick. But as for Lily . . . She comes in here quite a lot, late at night, and just sits among the plants."

That didn't sound much like Lily to me, but then, even though I'd been cooped up with Lily at MBA for several months, I had to admit I didn't know much about her at all. She had never wanted much to do with me and had barely spoken to me unless she had to. So maybe she *had* come into the greenhouse simply to experience the wonders of life.

Or maybe she had it in for her father.

"And there's Chang."

"Chang?"

"Yes. He was rooting around in here for a few minutes

about a week ago. I figured he must have been looking for something to eat, but when I checked in the morning, not a single fruit or vegetable was missing."

"And you're sure you would have noticed?"

"This isn't a very big greenhouse, and I'm in it at least eight hours a day. I know every last edible morsel in here."

Through the wall I heard a commotion in the rec room. People were starting to raise their voices, though it was too muffled for me to make out who was speaking, or what they were saying. I figured it was probably someone yelling at Roddy for hogging the veeyar system again.

I took one last bite of strawberry, wondering about Chang.

Chang had been poking around in the greenhouse. Now the apple seeds had gone missing. And if anyone was smart enough to know how to make cyanide from apple seeds, it was Chang.

Chang had been rummaging through the food storage the night before. Shortly afterward, Lars Sjoberg had been poisoned.

In the rec room, the voices were getting louder and angrier. I could now make two of them out: Patton and Lily Sjoberg. I did my best to ignore them. If Roddy had run afoul of the Sjoberg twins again, that was his problem. I had wound up in too much trouble defending him against them before.

And besides, I had other things to think about:

No one had a grudge against Lars Sjoberg like Chang Kowalski. As much as I hated to think that Chang might have poisoned Lars, he was an awfully good suspect.

Therefore, it made sense that someone ought to search his room for evidence. And thanks to Nina, that person was me.

There was a shriek from the rec room. A shriek I knew all too well. The Sjobergs weren't picking on Roddy.

They were picking on Violet.

Chang's room would have to wait. I had to face the Sjobergs first.

Excerpt from *The Official NASA Procedures for Contact with Intelligent Extraterrestrial Life* © National Aeronautics and Space Administration, Department of Extraterrestrial Affairs, 2029 (Classification Level AAA)

POTENTIAL HOSTILITY

There is much debate about whether any IEL that purposefully makes contact with earth will come in peace, but for our own safety, the possibility of hostile alien contact should certainly not be ruled out.* Anyone present for contact with IEL must remain constantly vigilant and on guard. At the same time, it is important to not appear outwardly hostile to any IEL. Weapons, while recommended, should remain sheathed or holstered. And given the likely intelligence of any IEL that initiates communication with us and/or travels to our planet, it must be assumed that they have weaponry that is far more advanced than ours. In fact, their weapons may not even look like weapons, so be alert and attuned to any potential danger at all times.

In addition, the IEL itself might be dangerous, armed with biological weapons such as venom or razor-sharp teeth—or perhaps something we can't even imagine yet. Should the IEL behave in any way that appears hostile or threatening (e.g., growling, tensing up, bristling, or merely exuding an aura of menace), it might be best to keep your guard up.

---

* Unfortunately, there are some factions within our government who believe that the *only* reasons for IEL to approach our planet would be hostile ones, but it is the belief of NASA that all intelligent life should be presumed peaceful until proven otherwise.

PLAN B

Lunar day 252

T minus 19.5 hours to evacuation

When I entered the rec room, things were bad.
Violet was cowering in a corner, defiantly holding a set of
hologoggles, while Patton advanced on her menacingly. Patton's face was as red as his father's had been, and there was
rage in his eyes.

Kira was yelling at Patton to leave Violet alone, while
Lily was cheering him on. Kira looked terrified. Lily looked
disturbingly excited, like a spectator at a dogfight.

"Patton!" I yelled. "Stop!"

Patton froze in his tracks and whirled toward me. The
blood drained from his face in fright. He instantly went

from red to white, like he'd been bleached. He'd apparently been so angry with Violet that he'd forgotten all about the space snakes.

"Don't call the snakes on me!" he pleaded, then pointed accusingly at Violet. "She started it! She kicked me!"

"He deserved it!" Violet argued. "Kira and I were in here, playing Unicorn Fantasy, and then they came in and tried to boot us off."

"We asked nicely," Patton protested.

"Like heck you did," Kira said, then looked to me. "They tried to take the goggles right off us. Violet was only defending herself."

"Yeah, you big jerk!" Violet screamed at Patton. "I hate you!"

Patton seethed with rage and spun toward Violet, his fists clenched.

"Don't you dare touch her!" I yelled. It surprised me how forceful I sounded.

Patton backed down, torn between his anger at Violet and his fear of me.

However, Lily Sjoberg grew even more excited, as though she had been anticipating this moment. "Or what?" she asked me tauntingly. "Are you going to call your space snakes on us?"

"Lily . . . ," Patton said weakly. "Don't . . ."

"Oh, give it a rest, you moron," Lily told him. "There's no such thing as space snakes."

"Yes, there is!" Violet said. "And if you don't back off, Dash will call one here and it will swallow you whole and then barf up your bones."

She was probably trying to be helpful, but her threat made the space snakes sound even more ridiculous than usual. If anything, this encouraged Lily.

"All right, then," she said confidently. "Call them, Dashiell. I'm not afraid of them." She came toward me, smiling cruelly, enjoying this. I thought back to what I had just learned about her, how she snuck into the greenhouse at night to sit among the plants. Even if she was the kind of person who took time to contemplate the wonders of life now and then, she was still a bad person. She was cruel and mean and as big a bully as her brother. Bigger, maybe.

I looked around the room, hoping Zan might make a sudden appearance. Maybe she could present herself to Lily as something even *more* hideous than what she'd shown Patton, scaring the pee out of her, too, and then the Sjobergs would finally leave the rest of us alone once and for all.

Only Zan didn't show herself. We were on our own.

"You *should* be afraid of them," I said, although the threat sounded hollow, even to me. "Don't tempt me."

"You mean I shouldn't try to hurt you?" Lily continued

toward me, her wicked smile growing bigger. "Even though you cost us our ComLink privileges. . . ."

"I didn't cost you those," I protested. "You're the ones who broke the rules here."

"And you're the one who ratted us out to Nina!" Lily snapped. "The whole time we've been at this base, you have been constantly causing trouble for us."

"Me?" I asked, backing away. "You've been bullying me and everyone else since you got here!"

"Because everyone here has been horrible to us," Lily said. "But *you* . . . You have been the worst. You even tricked my poor brother into believing in these stupid snakes. He's been a wreck because of you!" Lily's eyes narrowed into little angry slits. "So now I think I *am* going to tempt you. Because I need to prove to Patton once and for all that you're a liar and a fool."

"My brother isn't a liar!" Violet shouted. "Show them, Dashiell! Call those snakes!"

I glanced outside the rec room, looking for an adult or two who might be walking past, someone who could come to my aid. To my dismay, the only adult I could see was Sonja Sjoberg, and Sonja wasn't going to be any help at all. Instead she was standing in the doorway, watching everything transpire with glee, her overinflated lips curled into a frightening grin.

Just my luck. Normally, I couldn't do anything at MBA without an adult stumbling onto me, and now when I needed one, there was no one to be seen but the dragon queen.

Lily was now looming over me. She was a head taller than me and built like her brother, big and broad-shouldered. I had never considered fighting a girl, but I figured that Lily could probably wipe the floor with me. "What do I have to do to see these snakes?" she taunted. "This?" She poked me hard in the chest with a sharpened fingernail.

Patton cringed, as though Lily had made the worst mistake of her life.

But of course, no snakes appeared. Because I couldn't conjure them up. All I could do was make a final desperate bluff. "Trust me, Lily, you really don't want to do this."

"Oh, I do," she said. "I really do want to see them. What if I do this?" She shoved me backward with an open palm.

"Lily! Stop!" Kira yelled.

But Lily kept on coming. She was grinning broadly now, pleased that she'd called my bluff. Behind her, even Patton seemed to grasp what was going on.

"Hey!" he growled. "There aren't any snakes, are there? You tricked me!"

"Of course he tricked you, you idiot!" Lily shouted. "The snakes don't exist. This twerp can't defend himself against us. Which means it's payback time."

Now Patton grinned cruelly as well. His hands clenched into fists and he stormed toward me. It seemed that he'd spent the last month building up hatred for me, and now it was all about to come flooding out.

"No!" Kira yelled. "Patton! Don't!"

I tried to run, but Lily was already on me. She grabbed my arm hard enough to bruise it and held me there.

Out in the hallway, Sonja Sjoberg was watching intently, enjoying every second of this.

Patton was almost on top of me, fire in his eyes.

So I resorted to plan B. Maybe no adults were going to come to my rescue. And maybe Zan wasn't, either. But Lily had been wrong about one thing: I still had ways to defend myself. I had figured there was a good chance my space-snake bluff wasn't going to hold up, so before leaving the greenhouse, I had swiped something in case of emergency:

Two bags of grade-A Moon Base Alpha human excrement.

They were crammed into the pockets of my cargo shorts. I whipped out one of the opaque white packets and held it up, clutching the plastic zipper like the pin on a grenade. "Don't make me use this," I warned.

Patton paused long enough to read the label. Unfortunately, he had no idea what "excrement'" meant. Instead of being concerned, he laughed. "Oooh. Excrement," he taunted. "I'm soooo scared." And then he lunged at me.

So I had no choice but to rip the bag open and cram it in his face.

Now Patton discovered what excrement was.

Since the poop had had most of the water sucked out of it, it didn't splatter all over him. Instead it was more like a thick wad of extremely disgusting dirt. It smeared his pale face brown and got into his eyes and his nose. And since Patton was laughing as he attacked, the biggest portion of it went straight into his mouth.

He reared back, screaming in disgust. Or *trying* to scream in disgust. It was hard to scream with a mouth full of dehydrated human feces. Instead of words, he could only make guttural screeches. Then he collapsed to his knees, gagging and retching.

Lily Sjoberg had released my arm to give her brother the chance to pummel me. Now, she reached for me again, determined to avenge his honor. I quickly skirted away from her.

"You're dead!" she yelled at me, slashing with her nails. "I'm going to kill you!"

"Dash, shut her up, will you?" Kira asked.

"Gladly," I said, then pulled a second packet of excrement from my other pocket and tore it open.

Lily's eyes went wide as she realized I was more prepared

than she'd expected. But instead of backing off, she slashed at me again.

I dodged her and then slammed the second bag into her face.

Lily might have been a little bit smarter than Patton, but she still hadn't been smart enough to keep her mouth closed while attacking me. In fact, she'd had hers open quite wide, as she'd been screaming some sort of Swedish war cry. The moment she got a mouthful of space poop, however, she abandoned her attack and dropped to the floor beside her brother. Now both Sjobergs were gagging and retching in unison.

Violet burst into laughter. "You guys just ate excrement! And excrement is poop! So you ate poop! Serves you right!"

A banshee wail echoed through the room. It was so unearthly, for a moment I thought we might be under alien attack, but then I realized it was coming from Sonja Sjoberg. She was staring in horror at her children as they writhed on the floor, spitting and hacking up poop. Then she turned on me. Her wail became more of a shriek and she charged.

I didn't have any more bags of excrement.

I didn't need them, though. Sonja had only taken a few steps when Kira lashed out a foot and tripped her. In the low gravity, Sonja went flying. I dove out of the way as she soared past me and smacked face-first into the wall. There was a faint crunch, and then she grabbed her face, howling. It appeared that her surgically sculpted nose had been broken. "My nose!" she cried. "My nose!" Although due to the damage, it sounded more like "By doze! By doze!"

Violet kept on laughing. "This is way better than Unicorn Fantasy," she announced.

"What on earth happened here?" Dr. Janke stood at the doorway to the rec room, gaping at the Sjobergs. *Now* an adult had shown up.

Sonja pointed at me accusingly. "He boke by doze! And he bade by babies eat excrebent!"

Dr. Janke looked at her curiously. "I'm sorry. Was that Swedish?"

Kira immediately came to my defense. "They attacked Dash first! He was defending himself."

"He made Patton and Lily swallow poop!" Violet said, then burst into laughter again.

"He did?" Dr. Janke asked. It looked as though he was on the verge of laughing himself. "That's unfortunate."

Patton finally appeared to have coughed up most of the poop that had gone in his mouth. He staggered to his feet, trying to claw brown gunk off his tongue, and started for the door.

"Batton!" Sonja yelled at him, then pointed at me. "Kill him!"

"I'll do it later," Patton whined. "I have to wash my mouth out." And then he scurried out the door.

"Me too!" Lily gasped, and then she raced out after him.

Sonja let out a scream of frustration, as though she was upset that her children had opted to rinse the excrement from their mouths instead of causing me bodily harm. She fixed me with a hard stare and threatened, "Dis isn't over. You will bay for dis." She pointed to her damaged nose, then stormed out of the room.

"They won't *really* try to kill you," Dr. Janke told me, trying to be supportive, although it sounded as if he wasn't quite so sure of this. "They're just very upset right now."

"Look at it this way," Kira said. "Even if they *do* want you dead, we're leaving tomorrow. You only have to watch your back for one more day, and then you'll be in the clear."

Assuming the rockets actually get here on time, I thought. *Or they don't blow up while landing. Or the oxygen doesn't all leak out of the base.*

I didn't say any of that out loud, because I didn't want to upset Violet. But the fact was, things rarely worked out exactly as planned in outer space. The only thing you could really count on was that you couldn't count on anything. And even if things did work out, and the rockets came right when they were supposed to, that was still hours away: easily long enough for the Sjobergs to try to get their revenge.

Plus, Nina was still blackmailing me into helping her hunt for a killer, sending me into Chang's room to hunt for evidence against him and then who knew what else. It seemed there were plenty of ways *that* could go wrong as well.

Overall, it was shaping up to be a pretty lousy birthday.

Excerpt from *The Official NASA Procedures for Contact with Intelligent Extraterrestrial Life* © National Aeronautics and Space Administration, Department of Extraterrestrial Affairs, 2029 (Classification Level AAA)

SPACECRAFT

It should be noted that there is a significant chance that our primary contact might not be with the physical IEL itself, but merely with the craft by which they have traveled here. This might take the form of the craft merely passing through our solar system, or hovering in our atmosphere, or perhaps (sadly) crashing into our planet and leaving no survivors. It is also quite possible that primary contact will be through probes sent here, rather than craft bearing actual IEL. Once again, given our limited knowledge of the universe, there are most likely an infinite variety of possible craft that could appear. Whatever the case, the craft should be assessed carefully. DEXA will send engineering and military specialists for this exact purpose. Wait for them to get to the scene. They will be there as soon as humanly possible. DO NOT APPROACH THE CRAFT OR ENGAGE IT IN ANY WAY UNTIL DEXA HAS FORMULATED A PLAN FOR THIS.

ILLEGAL ENTRY

Lunar day 252

T minus 16 hours to evacuation

I got the message from Nina shortly before din-nertime:

DIVERSIONARY TACTICS UNDERWAY. LOCKING MECHANISM DISMANTLED. INITIATE PROCEDURES IMMEDIATELY.

Which I figured was Nina-speak for "I'm distracting Chang. His door is open. Go break into his room."

I was helping my parents pack up their experiments in the science pod at the time. (I was no longer allowed to help Dr. Goldstein since I had swiped excrement from the greenhouse and used it on the Sjobergs, even though most of the other Moonies were secretly thrilled I had done this.) Kira was helping with Dr. Iwanyi's experiments nearby. No one was keeping an eye on us, though. They all had a hundred other things to do. So all I had to do was say, "Kira, want to take a break?"

"Sure!" she said, trying to tamp down her enthusiasm. Kira loved going places that were supposed to be off-limits to her. When I'd approached her with Nina's plan earlier, all I'd had to say to convince her to break into Chang's room with me was, "Want to help me break into—" She had exclaimed, "Yes!" before I'd even said where, let alone launched into an explanation of *why* we were doing it.

Kira set down the equipment she was packing, and we hurried through the base.

I knew our mission was taking place much later than Nina had hoped; a lot of unexpected things had happened to me that day. Thankfully, Nina hadn't come looking for me yet; she'd had her hands full as well. In addition to her standard duties of running the moon base and overseeing the evacuation, she now had to deal with the Sjoberg excrement incident. Lars had already been furious about not getting first dibs on an evacuation rocket. When he learned that his children had been smeared with space poop, he went nuclear. He had raged so violently that I thought he might collapse from a heart attack, negating the whole point of investigating his attempted murder. He had been particularly enraged at me, because his wife and children all claimed that Patton and Lily had been merely minding their own business in the rec room when I had entered and attacked them out of the blue.

So Nina had been forced to take statements from everyone involved and then compare what we claimed against the security footage from the rec room, which of course proved the Sjobergs were lying through their poop-stained teeth. This reinforced Nina's insistence that the Sjobergs didn't deserve any priority for seats on the rockets home, which only angered Lars Sjoberg even more. He claimed I had obviously doctored the footage (as if I even knew how to do such a thing, or could manage it on such short notice) and that I had been a constant menace to his family. He also warned that, once he got back to earth, he was going to sue NASA for every penny it was worth as well as make life miserable for Nina and everyone else from MBA.

Which probably left most of the other Moonies wishing that whoever had poisoned Lars the night before had done a better job of it.

At least, that was what *I* was wishing. I knew it wasn't right to wish someone dead, but on the other hand, Lars Sjoberg seemed to want the exact same thing for me. Eventually, he stopped shouting at Nina and me and retired to his residence, but he continued to rage in there for a long time afterward. And even once that had stopped, there had been periodic bursts of what I assumed were Swedish obscenities from behind his door all afternoon.

Meanwhile, Patton and Lily Sjoberg had used up most of the base's remaining toothpaste supply brushing and rebrushing their teeth.

Chang's residence was located almost directly below the Sjobergs' suite, right across from the rec room. Through the open rec-room door, I could see Violet, Inez, and Kamoze in there, but they couldn't see me, as they all had holo-goggles on. Now that Patton and Lily had been vanquished and Roddy had been roped into helping his mother pack for evacuation, the little kids were all free to use the veeyar system. They were galloping around while Violet kept yelling things like "Blast them with sparkle power!"

"Looks like they're playing that unicorns-versus-aliens mash-up you created," I told Kira.

"It's more fun than I expected," Kira said. "You should try it."

"Boom!" Violet yelled. "Nice work, GlitterWings!"

Kira and I waited while Dr. Balnikov carried some equipment past and Dr. Marquez wandered by aimlessly before the coast was clear. Then we tried Chang's door.

As Nina had promised, it wasn't locked.

Normally, all our doors had electronic locks that could

only be opened by the people who lived in those rooms, but Chang's clicked open when I turned the knob. We quickly slipped inside.

"How do you think Nina managed that?" I asked, keeping my voice low.

"She must have the ability to override any lock in the base," Kira said confidently. "Makes sense that the moon-base commander would be able to do that."

"So Nina could come into our rooms any time she wants?"

"Maybe. I wouldn't get too worked up about it. After tomorrow, it's not going to matter anymore."

Kira and I cased the room. It didn't look like it would take long to search. To begin with, it was significantly smaller than our room, as it was designed for only one person. There was only a single sleep pod built into the far wall, with a cheap chest of drawers, a SlimScreen table, and an Inflati-Cube. There was no window. It was small, square, and drab. Like living in a walk-in closet. It occurred to me that Chang didn't spend much time in his room. Now I knew why.

If Chang *had* hidden evidence, there was almost no place to hide it.

"I'll take the drawers," Kira said quickly, before I could claim them myself. "You take everything else." She made a beeline for the spindly bureau.

Since Chang wasn't evacuating the next day, he hadn't packed anything yet. Not that any of us had much to pack.

I wandered over to his SlimScreen table. It was in sleep mode, the screen saver a rotating collage of photos. They were all of people who looked a good deal like Chang, so I figured they were family. There were parents, grandparents, people about Chang's age who were probably siblings or cousins, and some nieces and nephews.

A clarinet lay atop the table: one of the few personal items Chang had brought. In addition to being a genius, Chang was also a gifted musician. Dad said he could play the piano, too, but it was impossible to bring a piano into space—or even a keyboard, really. Both were too big and heavy. So the clarinet had come instead. Occasionally Chang treated us to performances at night.

I gingerly picked the clarinet up and shook it. Nothing rattled inside. I peered into the bell at the end and didn't see anything jammed up into it.

"You should take that apart," Kira said. She had already gone through the first drawer of the bureau.

"There's nothing in it."

"Well, make sure."

"What do you think? Chang had a bunch of leftover cyanide, so he jammed it into his prized clarinet?"

"Maybe."

I examined the clarinet closely. There were multiple parts to it, but I wasn't quite sure how they all fit together. "If you want to take this apart, be my guest. But I'm not doing it. If I break this, Chang will kill me."

"Scaredy-cat," Kira taunted. But I noticed that *she* didn't rush to touch the clarinet either.

I set it back down, drew my fingers across the SlimScreen, and got an ENTER PASSWORD command. I had no idea what Chang's password would be, so I abandoned the SlimScreen altogether and checked out the sleep pod.

Chang's pod looked exactly like mine. Same crummy, smelly sleep pad. Same rumpled sheets. It was even the same size, despite the fact that Chang was much bigger than me. To him, it must have felt even more like a coffin than mine did.

I lifted the pad and rapped my knuckles on the area beneath it, trying to see if there was a hidden compartment. I would have considered this ridiculous if Kira and I hadn't found just such a hidden compartment under Nina's pad a few weeks before. I didn't find anything, though.

"Hmm," Kira said, like she'd come across something interesting.

I hurried over. "What is it?"

"These were under his shorts." Kira held up a few pressed flowers. They were all small and pink.

I recognized them immediately. "They're from the pea plants in the greenhouse."

"Why would Chang have flowers in his drawers?" Kira asked suspiciously.

"To remind himself of earth?" I suggested. "To have a little color in this crummy room?"

"Then why are they hidden?"

"Maybe he had them out when they were alive, and then they started to die, so he pressed them and tucked them away."

"Whatever the case, it shows he's been stealing things from the greenhouse. And that's where the apple seeds were."

"That doesn't mean he stole the seeds, though. In fact, it makes him even *less* suspicious."

"How's that?"

"Dr. Goldstein was wondering what Chang was doing in the greenhouse. Now we know."

"I suppose." Kira sighed, like this was disappointing. Then she slid the drawer shut. "There's nothing else in here. Just a bunch of clothes."

"Looks like Chang's clean," I said, pleased by the thought of it. "Let's get out of here before he comes back."

I started for the door. As I did, my watch buzzed.

It was a message from Nina, in red capital letters to indicate how urgent it was: ABORT!

Unfortunately, Kira hadn't followed me to the door. Instead she was standing in the middle of the room, looking all around, as if trying to spot any other possible hiding places.

"Kira!" I exclaimed. "Nina wants us to leave. Now!"

Kira sighed, like I was being overly dramatic, then turned to go and banged into the SlimScreen table. The clarinet wobbled and rolled off.

Kira lunged for it, but it glanced off her fingers and clattered to the floor. A few pieces of metal popped off and skittered under the table.

"Aw, great," I muttered.

Kira dropped to her knees to pick the pieces up.

"Forget those!" I hissed. "There's no time!"

"If we leave them, Chang will know someone was in here!"

"So? He won't know it was us!"

Kira ignored me, sliding on her belly under the table to get the clarinet parts.

"I'm going," I told her. I had already ended up in enough trouble that day. If she wanted to be there when Chang got back, that was her problem.

Only, as I was reaching for the doorknob, Kira gave a gasp of surprise.

Despite my best survival instincts, I turned back around. "What?"

Kira reached up and pulled something off the underside of the SlimScreen table. Something that had been taped there.

It was a syringe. Inside it was the remains of a slight bit of golden liquid.

I had no idea how to recognize cyanide, but I knew that it had been injected into Lars Sjoberg's lutefisk. So a hidden syringe was awfully incriminating.

Before I could even say anything, though, the door opened, and Chang Kowalski entered the room.

Excerpt from *The Official NASA Procedures for Contact with Intelligent Extraterrestrial Life* © National Aeronautics and Space Administration, Department of Extraterrestrial Affairs, 2029 (Classification Level AAA)

RESPONSE

Once DEXA has been activated, our experts will immediately assess the messages from and/or physical presence of the IEL to determine the appropriate response. THIS MAY TAKE TIME. In an event of this magnitude, it is extremely important to not rush our response. Once the appropriate response has been determined, it will be up to officials from DEXA—and only officials from DEXA—to deliver it. The response may be delivered in a variety of ways (e.g., mathematical signals, music, light patterns) based upon the method of primary contact from the IEL. Once again, DO NOT ENGAGE THE IEL UNLESS AUTHORIZED TO DO SO BY DEXA. Any unauthorized communication is a federal offense.

RATIONAL ARGUMENTS

Lunar day 252

T minus 15.5 hours to evacuation

Chang didn't seem very surprised to see us. "I *knew* Nina was up to something," he grumbled. "How on earth did she rope you two into this?"

"She blackmailed Dash," Kira said. She had already moved the syringe behind her back so that Chang wouldn't see it.

"With what?" Chang asked.

"My family's seats on the rocket tomorrow," I admitted. "She said she could give them to the Sjobergs instead of us."

Chang looked surprised, then sighed. "Man, I knew that woman could be cold, but . . . blackmailing kids to do her dirty work? That's absolute zero."

"It is," Kira said. "Maybe you should go give her a piece of your mind."

She said it a little too quickly. Chang didn't bite. Instead, he looked at her skeptically. "What do you have behind your back?"

"Nothing," Kira said. Again, way too quickly.

"That is one pathetic acting job," Chang informed her. "Do yourself a favor and just—"

To Kira's surprise, he didn't finish the sentence. Instead he sprang across the room, moving with startling speed for someone so big. He caught her arm, spun her around, and pried the syringe from her grasp in the space of a single second.

I tried to bolt from the room—though I wasn't abandoning Kira. I was hoping to get help.

But once again, Chang moved faster than I could. He caught my arm and yanked me backward, throwing me into Kira, then stood between us and the door, blocking our escape.

Then he held up the syringe. When he'd grabbed it from Kira, the protective cap had come off, leaving the needle exposed. Chang looked at it curiously. "Where did you get this?"

"Where do you think?" Kira said defiantly. "Under your SlimScreen."

"Really?" I had expected Chang to be angry, if not downright dangerous. Instead he seemed amused. "Do you have any idea what this is?"

"It's a syringe with cyanide in it," Kira said.

"Yes," Chang admitted. "But it's also the most blatant piece of planted evidence I've ever seen in my life." To our surprise, he started laughing. As though we'd found a rubber chicken in his room, rather than a syringe full of poison.

Kira and I shared a wary look, wondering if Chang was trying to trick us somehow.

"You mean you didn't put that there?" Kira asked.

"Of course I didn't put it there!" Chang exclaimed. "If I was actually going to go through all the trouble to poison Lars Sjoberg, why would I keep the syringe in my room? Especially when there are thousands of other places on this base to hide it? For that matter, why would I keep it at all? To have a memento of the time I tried to kill someone?"

Kira and I shared another look. The argument certainly made sense.

"It's not like it would have been hard to get rid of," Chang went on. "There's a hundred separate waste receptacles here. Or I could have planted the syringe in someone else's room. Or if I *really* wanted to ditch it, I could have taken it outside after everyone else was asleep and thrown it into a field of moon dust. No one would find it for a thousand years. There are only two reasons someone would leave a syringe with cyanide in it taped to the bottom of a table in their room:

"One: They're an idiot. And I am not an idiot."

"Two: I'm being set up by the *real* killer."

I could actually think of a third reason: Chang hadn't had time to get rid of the syringe. After all, if he had only poisoned the lutefisk the night before, this made at least a little sense. He certainly couldn't have left the base with it, because he knew my father was taking me outside for my birthday catch. (In fact, he was the *only* person besides my family who'd known that.) So he'd hidden it in his room, which was admittedly stupid—but everyone, even geniuses, made mistakes. And now that we'd caught him red-handed, he was simply emphasizing how stupid it was to throw us off.

I didn't say any of this to Chang, though. Because I didn't want his good mood to shift to an angry one.

Also, it wasn't a great theory. As Chang had pointed out, even if he couldn't take the syringe outside, he could have tossed it in the garbage or planted it somewhere else.

Chang was now scrutinizing the syringe. "Looks like there's only two prints on this besides the ones I've just made, and I'm guessing they're yours, Kira. Whoever planted it here would have certainly wiped it clean, although we can check." He tapped the plunger so a tiny bead of the fluid inside formed at the tip of the needle, then gave it a smell. "And that's definitely cyanide."

"Okay," I agreed. "Let's get it to Nina."

Chang held up a hand. "Not so fast. I want to know why Nina was so convinced that I was the murderer that she sent you in here scrounging for evidence."

"Well, you've threatened to kill Lars before," Kira said.

"So has almost everyone else here," Chang pointed out. "So why me?" His gaze shifted my way.

I thought about keeping what Nina had told me a secret, then decided against it. After all, Nina had blackmailed me into searching Chang's room. For all I knew, *she* was the one who had planted the syringe.

"She has footage of you poking around in the food-storage area last night," I said. "The same place where the lutefisk is kept."

"Oh," Chang said, not so amused anymore. "I wasn't poisoning Lars's lutefisk."

"Then what were you doing?" Kira asked accusingly.

"I was getting some rassolnik," Chang said.

"Rassolnik?" Kira and I repeated.

"It's a traditional soup made from pickles, barley, and kidneys."

"Pickles and kidneys?" I repeated. "That sounds even worse than lutefisk."

"It is," Chang said, making a face. "But Viktor likes it. It's a Russian thing."

"Dr. Balnikov?" Kira asked. "Why were you getting him food at midnight?"

"Because I was on my way to his room," Chang replied. "And it seemed like a nice thing to do."

Kira and I stared at Chang, trying to make sense of that. Then we looked at each other. Then we looked back at Chang.

"Are you and Dr. Balnikov a couple?" Kira asked.

"Sort of," Chang admitted. "It's been kind of difficult to start a relationship up here."

Suddenly a lot of things made sense. I had known Chang was gay, although it had never been a big deal. I knew lots of gay people back on earth. I had always felt a little bad for Chang—and all the other single people at MBA—because they didn't have significant others there with them, but it had never seemed to bother any of them: They had known they were going to be single for three years when they agreed to come to the moon.

I hadn't known Dr. Balnikov was gay, though. That was a surprise—along with the revelation that he and Chang were seeing each other.

Kira seemed only moderately surprised herself. "Why's it difficult to start a relationship?" she asked.

"There are actually rules against it," Chang explained.

"You're not allowed to date here?" I asked, far more

astonished by this than the fact that Chang and Viktor were dating at all.

Chang explained, "NASA believes that if you start a relationship, and then it falls apart, it could cause stress in the work environment up here."

"That's stupid," Kira pronounced.

"Yes," Chang agreed. "Forcing people to stay single for three years isn't exactly a cure for stress. And it's not as if any of the married couples here couldn't break up."

"I'm surprised the Marquezes are still together," Kira said.

"Me too," I added. Dr. Brahmaputra-Marquez and Dr. Marquez argued a lot. They tried to keep it quiet, but it still came through the walls. But then, *all* the couples argued at times. Even my parents. Living at MBA was already stressful without NASA interfering in people's personal lives.

"Anyhow," Chang said, "stupid rule or not, Nina is still determined to enforce it."

"That figures," Kira grumbled. "Seeing as she's a machine and all."

"Which means Viktor and I have had to see each other on the sly," Chang continued. "Though even without the NASA rules, we still might have had to keep this a secret. Sadly, Viktor has never felt he could be as open with his homosexuality as I am."

I wondered if this was because Viktor was from Russia.

I had heard that, in some countries, being gay wasn't as accepted as it was in America. Although my parents had also told me that when they were kids, America hadn't been completely understanding of homosexuality either. Back then, gay people hadn't even been allowed to get married. That all seemed like ancient history, even though I knew there were plenty of people in America who still had a problem with it.

"So the flowers in your drawers were from him?" I asked.

Chang seemed caught off guard for a moment, surprised we knew about the flowers, then figured out why. "Guess you guys were snooping through my stuff. Yes, they're from him. There's not much in the way of gifts to bring each other up here. The occasional flower. Some Russian soup—even if it's disgusting. We're not even allowed to have wine at this base. Although even if it was allowed, I'm sure NASA would find a way to make that crummy too."

"You've brought him flowers too?" I pressed.

"Sure. A couple times."

Which definitely explained what Chang had been doing in the greenhouse on occasion. And why he'd been sneaking around the moon base late at night.

Assuming he was telling the truth. It could all be a cover story, although it would be relatively easy to confirm with Dr. Balnikov.

"Aw, man!" Chang exclaimed suddenly. "What happened to my clarinet?"

Kira's cheeks turned pink. "I . . . uh . . . kind of knocked it over."

Chang knelt beside the table, looked over the instrument, then heaved a sigh of relief. "Whew. It's not too bad. I can fix this." He then gave Kira a hard stare. "Although if I couldn't, you'd be in serious trouble. It's very hard to get replacement clarinet parts on the moon."

"Sorry," Kira said. "It was an accident."

Chang started putting the clarinet back together, fitting the metal bits that had come off with speed and precision.

I asked, "So it was just a coincidence that that disgusting soup and the lutefisk were in the same storage bin last night?"

"Yes," Chang said, but then something occurred to him. "Or maybe it wasn't." He looked to me. "Did Nina tell you *why* she had footage of me last night?"

"She went through the security feeds," I said. "Although that *was* kind of weird, because when I suggested it to her earlier, she said it would be pointless, because someone could have poisoned the lutefisk weeks ago. But then, when she called me in later, she said she'd changed her mind and decided to look at the footage after all."

"I'm betting someone tipped her off," Chang said.

"Probably the killer themselves. They saw *me* going through the food. And once Lars ended up eating the poisoned lutefisk, they saw it was the perfect opportunity to frame me. So they snuck the syringe in here and called Nina."

"But how'd they get the syringe in here?" I asked. "Your door was locked."

"*You* got in here," Chang pointed out. "So obviously the security system isn't that secure."

"Wait a minute!" Kira exclaimed. "Nina's the one who unlocked your door for us. That means *she* could have accessed your room whenever she wanted. So maybe *she* framed you."

Chang paused in the process of repairing his clarinet to consider that. "Maybe," he agreed. "But anyone with a decent knowledge of computers could hack the locking system. The tech on this base is ancient compared to what we have on earth."

I knew that was true as well. One of the many problems with building bases in outer space was that by the time you figured out how to make all your tech strong enough to handle the rigors of operating outside earth, it was already several years out of date.

I asked, "Hacking the system still wouldn't be *easy*, though, would it? Whoever did it would have to be pretty smart."

"I suppose," Chang said thoughtfully. "Although whoever tried to frame me made some pretty dumb mistakes."

"Like what?" Kira asked.

"Well, like I pointed out before, leaving that syringe in my room was a pretty lame frame job." Chang replaced the last piece of his clarinet and carefully placed the instrument back on his SlimScreen table. "But there's also the fact that they tried to frame *me* at all."

"Why's that dumb?" I asked.

"Because I'm *me*," Chang replied. "I have the highest IQ of anyone on the moon by far. That's been documented." The way he said it didn't come across as a boast. He was merely stating facts. I'd seen the reports: Chang had the same IQ as Albert Einstein.

"If I were actually going to poison Lars like this," Chang went on, "do you think I'd be so stupid as to let myself be recorded on the cameras while injecting the poison into the lutefisk? Do you think I'd wipe my fingerprints off the syringe with the poison in it and then keep it in my room? And, honestly, if I was going to poison Lars, I would have done it *right*. He'd actually be dead right now. But whoever did this screwed up and didn't put enough poison in the lutefisk to kill him. So instead of a dead Lars Sjoberg, we have a Lars Sjoberg who's even more of a raging bunghole than he was yesterday." Chang was getting worked up as he said this. His amusement had faded, and he was starting to show traces of his temper. "Frankly, I find it offensive that Nina would even consider that I'd done such a crummy job of murdering someone. And you can feel free to tell her that when you bring that syringe to her."

"You don't want to tell her yourself?" Kira asked.

"I have better things to do," Chang said curtly. Then he offered me the syringe, holding only the plunger between his fingers. "Careful not to get your prints on this, or Nina will think *you* murdered Lars too."

I took the syringe from him, holding it the same way he did, so only the tiniest bit of my thumb and forefinger touched it. As I did, my watch buzzed.

It was an urgent message from my parents: COME TO THE MESS HALL ASAP!!!!

Good grief, I thought. *What now?*

Excerpt from *The Official NASA Procedures for Contact with Intelligent Extraterrestrial Life* © National Aeronautics and Space Administration, Department of Extraterrestrial Affairs, 2029 (Classification Level AAA)

CONTACT OUTSIDE OF US BORDERS

Given that the United States occupies less than 7 percent of the earth's total land mass (and less than 2 percent of the earth's surface, period) there is obviously a large statistical chance that primary contact with IEL will occur outside the borders of the United States. In fact, given that oceans cover 70 percent of the earth, there is a great chance that IEL will make contact over an ocean at first.* DEXA is extremely prepared for this scenario, and will work with foreign governments to facilitate the first meeting with IEL no matter where it happens. If you happen to be in another country when primary contact first occurs (for purposes of US government work, or even if you are on a fortuitously timed vacation there), proceed with the steps in this manual as if you were still in the United States. The arrival of IEL will have repercussions for the entire world and must be handled correctly. Thus, international boundaries are a secondary concern.

---

* If they have spent any time studying us, IEL ought to certainly recognize that humans are the dominant species on the planet and approach on land, though there is always the chance that their first contact will be accidental—a crash landing, perhaps. But given that they will doubtlessly be a different species from us, there are certainly reasons they might choose to approach the oceans first. For all we know, they might try to make primary contact with dolphins.

FREEZE-DRIED MILK SOLIDS

Lunar day 252

T minus 14 hours to evacuation

"What's up?" Kira asked as we hurried out of Chang's residence.

Chang didn't follow us. He stayed back in his room. Maybe he really had other things to do, as he'd claimed, though I had the sense that he was so annoyed at Nina, he didn't want to see *anyone* else for a bit.

"Another emergency," I said. "In the mess hall."

From Chang's door we could see the mess through the corner of the greenhouse. To my surprise, no one seemed to be there. In fact, there didn't seem to be anyone anywhere in the base. The corridors along the residences were completely empty, as was the rec room across the hall: For once, no one was using the veeyar system. Obviously, everyone could have been on the side of the base I couldn't see, where the science pod and the bathrooms and the maintenance offices were—or they could have been in their residences—but I couldn't hear any voices, either, which was unusual.

I wondered if there had been a new problem with the oxygen system, and everyone had passed out from hypoxia.

Kira looked concerned as well. "C'mon," she said, and we ran toward the mess. It didn't take long to get there. Only a few bounds down the corridor. As we rounded the greenhouse, it became evident that the mess was completely empty—even though my parents had just asked me to come there. The science pod and the gym were empty too.

Which was very, very unsettling.

If everyone had collapsed from hypoxia, there should have at least been some bodies around.

I swung back around toward the greenhouse.

At which point, almost all our fellow Moonies leaped out from where they'd been crouched at the base of the wall, hidden from view, and screamed, "Surprise!"

Under different circumstances, the surprise party would have been a very lovely effort on everyone's part. They had curled pages from the residents' guide into conical party hats and decorated them festively. They had inflated surgical gloves to make balloons (although with all the fingers sticking out, they looked more like cow udders). They had even made confetti, which Violet and the other kids flung in the air.

Unfortunately, it wasn't the best day for a surprise party. I was already on edge, worried about oxygen leaks and killers on the loose. So when everyone jumped out and startled me, I screamed in terror.

So did Kira, who was equally on edge. Both of us leaped several feet in the air, given the low gravity. And I lost my grip on the syringe I'd been holding.

It flew into the batch of inflated surgical gloves Roddy Marquez was holding and pierced three in one shot. They all exploded with a series of loud bangs, frightening Inez Marquez, who started bawling.

The syringe itself ended up jabbed in Cesar's thigh, where it stuck like a dart in a bull's eye.

Turns out, Cesar had a fear of needles. He made a surprisingly high-pitched shriek and then passed out, nearly taking Kamoze Iwanyi down with him.

This stopped the celebration dead. All the Moonies had been about to burst into "Happy Birthday to You," but no one got past the first syllable.

Except Violet, who obliviously kept singing. And when

Violet sang "Happy Birthday," she did it as operatically as possible.

The only Moonies who weren't there were the Sjobergs (naturally), Chang (obviously), and Nina (who had probably never celebrated anything in her life). Dr. Brahmaputra-Marquez quickly ran to Cesar's side to check on him and gasped when she saw the syringe. "Why were you carrying this?" she asked me accusingly.

"Chang found it in his residence," I said, deciding it wasn't time to go into the whole story. "It might, uh . . . still have a little cyanide in it."

"What?!" Dr. Marquez gasped.

"The killer planted it on Chang," Kira said quickly. "To frame him for killing Lars."

In all the commotion, she had forgotten that a lot of Moonies hadn't been told that the poisoning wasn't an accident. Particularly the children. This revelation was enough to stop even Violet in the midst of her song.

"Someone killed Lars?" Inez yelped, then started crying even louder.

"Actually, they only *tried* to kill him," Kira said quickly, which didn't help much.

"We should get Cesar to the medical bay right away," Dr. Brahmaputra-Marquez said.

Although he was only a teenager, Cesar was still one of

the biggest Moonies. Even so, Dr. Balnikov handled him easily. He picked Cesar up, cradled him in his arms, and hustled him off with his mother. Dr. Marquez followed along. "Do you think I can help?" he asked meekly.

"I doubt it," Dr. Brahmaputra-Marquez said. "He needs a *real* doctor."

"But I *am* a real doctor," Dr. Marquez protested. "You're just an astrophysicist!"

"Then tend to Inez, for Pete's sake," Dr. Brahmaputra-Marquez told him. Inez Marquez was still crying, having been ignored in the uproar over Cesar. In fact, a fragment of one of the surgical gloves was still draped over her head, like a little latex yarmulke.

It occurred to me that the syringe was an important piece of evidence, but given that it was still stuck in Cesar's leg, it seemed like bad manners to ask for it back at the moment.

In any event, my parents had now come to my side. They were terribly upset and embarrassed about how badly the surprise party had worked out.

"I am so sorry," Mom said, hugging me tightly. "We all thought this would be a *nice* surprise. Your birthday hasn't gone the way we'd hoped, and so . . ."

"We didn't mean to frighten you like that," Dad put in.

"It's all right," I said. "Really. I'm sorry I ruined everything."

Close by, Dr. Howard was comforting Kira as well, one

of his rare moments of emotional engagement. He wasn't hugging her, though. They were just talking things through.

"It's not ruined," Mom assured me. "We only got off on the wrong foot. But we still put together a wonderful birthday meal for you."

It turned out they had. At least, they had put together the best birthday meal possible, given that it was made almost entirely of space food.

First and foremost, Dr. Goldstein had harvested everything that remained from the greenhouse. When the produce was divvied up, it didn't amount to very much per person: six pea pods, five cherry tomatoes, three strawberries, a few slices of cucumber, and a smattering of bell pepper. But it still was much more fresh food than any of us had eaten in months.

Then all the kids were allowed to pick whatever we wanted to eat from the food storage. Since NASA had sent a year's worth of space food per person and we weren't about to haul it all back, there was plenty for everyone. (True, the rest would be left in storage in case MBA got going again, as it had a shelf life of five hundred years, but certainly no one was going to need it for a while.) I didn't have a favorite food so much as foods I didn't hate quite as much as the others, but once again, it made a difference. I opted for two servings of shrimp cocktail.

Finally, there was cake and ice cream. Or cakelike substance sprinkled with globules of freeze-dried, gelatin-coated milk solids. Since we weren't allowed to have open flames, we couldn't have any candles, so Mom and Violet had made candle cut-outs. But I appreciated the effort everyone had gone to. For a little while, I actually forgot about the threat of our diminishing oxygen supply and being blackmailed to track down Lars Sjoberg's killer.

Chang arrived not far into dinner and joined the party. If he was still upset at Nina, he didn't show it. Nina and the Sjobergs never showed, but that was probably for the best.

All in all, it was the best meal I'd had at MBA in a long time.

At least until Dr. Brahmaputra-Marquez returned from the medical bay. She came directly to where I was sitting with my family, Kira, and Dr. Howard. We were all having a good time, polishing off our desserts. Dr. Howard was even engaged for once, discussing an idea he'd had to improve the quality of space ice cream by amping up the viscosity in the compression process (or something like that; I was having trouble understanding it) while Violet was wrapping up her fifth rendition of "Happy Birthday," this time in pig latin.

"I'm sorry to interrupt the party," Dr. Brahmaputra-Marquez said. "But I have some questions about that syringe."

"Is Cesar all right?" Mom asked.

"It appears so," Dr. Brahmaputra-Marquez replied. "There was very little poison in the syringe to begin with—although it *was* cyanide. Not enough ended up in Cesar's leg to be dangerous, but we still gave him the full complement of antidotes, just to be safe. We also gave Cesar a mild sedative. He has a slight fear of needles."

"Really?" Kira said, with mock sincerity. "I didn't notice."

I observed Dr. Balnikov, across the room, returning from the medical bay himself. He sat down at a table with Chang, Dr. Merritt, and Dr. Janke. He and Chang both put on a show of simply being coworkers, not betraying the slightest hint of their relationship.

I also noticed Dr. Marquez was glaring at his wife. Possibly he was unhappy that she had come directly to us and not to her own family. Or maybe he was still smarting from her insult about his medical abilities earlier. Or maybe things were just strained in their relationship.

"Anyhow," Dr. Brahmaputra-Marquez said, "I need some clarity on *where* the syringe came from. You said the killer planted it on Chang?"

"Yes," I said. "They left it in his room. To make it look like he'd tried to poison Lars."

"And how did *you* get it?" Dr. Brahmaputra-Marquez asked.

"Chang gave it to us to give to Nina," I explained.

Dr. Brahmaputra-Marquez glanced across the mess at Chang, then lowered her voice. "Then how do you know for sure that it was planted in Chang's room?"

Violet gave a gasp of surprise. "You think Chang could be the mmmmpphhtthhh?" She didn't get the last word out, because Mom had slapped her hand over Violet's mouth before she could announce it to the entire mess hall.

"Sorry, sweetie," Mom told her. "But you have to watch what you say out loud in front of everyone. If Dr. Brahmaputra-Marquez thinks Chang might be the killer, that's our secret. Understand?"

Violet nodded that she did. So Mom took her hand off Violet's mouth.

Violet immediately announced, way too loud, "I wasn't going to say Dr. B thought Chang was the *killer*. I was only going to say that she mmmmpphhtthhh." This time it was Dad who slapped his hand over her mouth.

We all glanced furtively over toward Chang to see if he'd heard. And since we all did it at the same time, it wasn't very furtive at all.

Chang had heard, of course. He gave Dr. Brahmaputra-Marquez a nice, mock-friendly wave, which made Dr. Brahmaputra-Marquez shrink in embarrassment.

"Perhaps you shouldn't have brought this up in front of Violet," Dad told her pointedly.

"Or at our son's birthday dinner," Mom added, even more pointedly.

"I'm sorry," Dr. Brahmaputra-Marquez apologized, "but this is important. Chang has a big grudge against Lars Sjoberg and the intelligence to create cyanide—"

"Honestly, that describes almost every person on this base," Dr. Howard observed. "Including myself."

"Chang is also known to have a temper," Dr. Brahmaputra-Marquez went on. "He and Lars have come to blows on many occasions."

"I guess that's why the killer framed him, then," Kira said. "If *I* was going to frame anyone for murdering Lars, I'd pick Chang too."

Dr. Brahmaputra-Marquez gave her a wary look. "How can you be so sure he was framed? If the syringe was in his room, that seems like a lot of evidence against him."

It seemed to me that Dr. Brahmaputra-Marquez was pressing us quite hard to admit that Chang might be guilty. However, instead of making me question Chang, her insistence made me grow suspicious of Dr. Brahmaputra-Marquez herself. I wondered if *she* had been the one who put the syringe in Chang's room, and now she was panicking because it hadn't implicated him as strongly as she'd hoped.

Or maybe she was trying to protect someone else in her family. Perhaps Dr. Marquez had been behind the attempted murder: As a doctor, even a bad one, he probably knew *something* about cyanide. And I could imagine him making the lame attempt to frame Chang.

Or maybe Roddy had done it. If anyone in that family knew how to get past the computer systems and unlock Chang's door, it was Roddy. Roddy didn't have as big a grudge against Lars as he did against Patton, who'd bullied him relentlessly at MBA, but . . .

Once again, it occurred to me that Lars Sjoberg might not have been the definite target for the poison. Yes, he was the only one who ever ate NASA lutefisk, but perhaps not everyone knew that. The killer might have been targeting Patton Sjoberg instead. Or Lily. Or Sonja. After all, the lutefisk was a Swedish delicacy, and the Sjobergs were the only Swedes at MBA.

If Roddy had been targeting Lars—or Patton—it made sense that he might have gotten the dosage for the poison wrong. After all, Roddy was only a kid. Maybe he underestimated how much he would need for a man as big as Lars. Or maybe he simply didn't make enough.

I suddenly felt guilty for considering Roddy as a murderer. After all, he was my age. It didn't make sense that a kid would have done something so horrible. But then, nothing about this case made sense. I found myself growing annoyed at Nina for dragging me into the investigation—and at Dr.

Brahmaputra-Marquez for bringing it up again in the middle of my birthday dinner.

To my side, Kira was finishing up her defense of why Chang had obviously been framed, which had probably been a recitation of all Chang's reasons. (I'd been too distracted with my own thoughts to pay attention to it.) She must have done a good job, because everyone else at the table appeared convinced—except Dr. Brahmaputra-Marquez.

"Consider this," Dr. Brahmaputra-Marquez proposed. "What if Chang was the killer, so to deflect attention from himself, he faked a lousy job of framing himself?"

"Ilina," Dr. Howard said, "don't take this the wrong way, but that's an idiotic theory."

Dr. Howard wasn't that adept at interpersonal relationships.

Dr. Brahmaputra-Marquez recoiled, offended. "How am I not supposed to take that the wrong way?"

Dr. Howard didn't even bother to respond to this. Instead he said, "Chang isn't any more of a suspect than anyone else here. Placing the murder weapon in his own room would be far more likely to draw attention to himself, rather than deflect it, as evidenced by the fact that we are discussing his possible guilt right now. Ergo, framing himself—or simply keeping the syringe at all—would be moronic. And Chang is not moronic."

"Fine," Dr. Brahmaputra-Marquez said bitterly. "If you're so smart, why don't *you* tell me who poisoned Lars Sjoberg?"

"To be honest, I haven't given it much thought," Dr. Howard said.

"You haven't?" Violet asked, surprised. Dad had finally removed his hand from her mouth. "I've been thinking about it plenty."

"Really?" Mom asked, unable to hide her amusement.

"Yes," Violet said. "I think Sonja Sjoberg did it."

"Why?" I asked.

"Because she's mean," Violet said. "Mean mean mean mean mean. The meanest person I've ever met. She even has a mean face. Like this." Violet scrunched her face up into what was actually a decent imitation of Sonja's permanent scowl. "Also, she hates her husband."

This last bit caught everyone at the table by surprise.

"How do you know that?" Dad asked.

"Well," Violet explained, "one day Inez and I were pretending to be unicorns on the catwalk outside the Sjobergs' room, and I heard Sonja screaming something in Swedish over and over and over at Lars. It was like 'ya haw-tar day' but more Swedishy. And Inez and I were wondering what it meant. So I asked the base computer to translate it, and the base computer said she was saying, 'I hate you.'"

We all looked to one another, impressed.

"That's some good detective work," Dr. Brahmaputra-Marquez said.

"Duh," Violet replied. "I'm a good detective. I helped find Nina when she went missing."

"You did," I admitted.

"I'm not surprised Sonja hates him," Kira said. "Everyone says she only married Lars for his money."

"Who's 'everyone'?" Dad asked.

"*Everyone,*" Kira repeated. "Like all the gossip sites and shows and everything. I mean, the guy looks like a toad. And Sonja was a model. She used to be beautiful before she let all those doctors mess up her face. So she probably never even liked the guy. Only it didn't matter, because they had fifteen houses and each one of them was enormous, so they probably never even had to see each other. But then Lars booked this trip up here, and instead of it turning out to be amazing, Sonja ended up cooped up in a tiny room with Lars and their dimwit kids for three months. Maybe she couldn't take it anymore."

"I've heard many times that money is the number one motive for murder," Mom said. "With Lars gone, Sonja inherits billions."

"If I had billions of dollars, I'd give it all away to charity," Violet pronounced. "Although I'd build myself a castle first. And a safari park. And genetically engineer a unicorn."

"Oooh!" Dr. Brahmaputra-Marquez cooed. "That's a great idea! Unicorns are beautiful."

This struck me as odd. It wasn't unusual for Violet to say something like this, but Dr. Brahmaputra-Marquez didn't strike me as the unicorn type.

"They are," Violet agreed. "Did you know that they poop rainbows?"

That seemed odd as well, even for Violet. Although, now that she had mentioned it, I couldn't get the image of unicorns pooping rainbows out of my head. It was as though I had lost control of some part of my mind.

It seemed to be affecting my vision, too. Because Violet's skin had changed color slightly. She was looking a little more blue than usual.

So was Dr. Brahmaputra-Marquez. It was hard to tell, given her dark skin, but there was definitely something bluish around her lips.

"Oh my God," Mom gasped. She suddenly seemed extremely concerned, as did Dad. Both of them were checking their pulses.

At the next table over, Dr. Marquez suddenly squawked in alarm. "Inez? What's wrong?"

Inez was slumping at his side and babbling incoherently.

"We're getting hypoxic," Dad announced. "The oxygen levels must be dropping."

At which point alarms went off throughout MBA. Then the voice of the base computer rang out through the halls, informing us that there was a major emergency. The oxygen system was severely compromised.

We all needed to evacuate immediately.

Excerpt from *The Official NASA Procedures for Contact with Intelligent Extraterrestrial Life* © National Aeronautics and Space Administration, Department of Extraterrestrial Affairs, 2029 (Classification Level AAA)

MILITARY PRESENCE

Sadly, we cannot rule out the possibility, no matter how disturbing, that IEL will come here for hostile reasons rather than peaceful ones. Thus, any response to their arrival mandates the activation of US armed forces. DEXA has worked at length with the US military to form an IEL Action Plan (IELAP), which will be initiated immediately upon the first sign of primary contact. Rest assured, the military's presence will only be a precautionary measure, rather than an aggressive one. The IELAP clearly states that the military is to respond only with defensive action, and therefore cannot attack, assault, strike, or provoke the IEL (or their craft) in any way without provocation.*

---

* For further details, anyone with level AAA security clearance is allowed to consult the official IEL Action Plan.

CRISIS MODE

Lunar day 252

T minus ten minutes to emergency evacuation

We had all rehearsed evacuation procedures many times. NASA mandated that we had to do it once a month, and Nina occasionally threw in a bonus fake emergency just to keep us on our toes.

We never *really* evacuated, as that was considered too dangerous, but we at least went through the motions so we would know where to go and what to do and what everyone's job was.

Unfortunately, there'd been no way to completely prep for an actual emergency, because the circumstances of an actual emergency were very different. We always *knew* that the rehearsals were rehearsals, and that if we screwed up, we wouldn't die. But now it was real, and that created a very different mind-set. No matter how much we had practiced not panicking, most of us were now on the edge of panic. And to make matters worse, since our oxygen levels were already low, none of us were thinking as clearly as we should have been.

Some people, like Mom and Dad and Chang, appeared to be thinking more clearly than others, but they were working at it, almost willing themselves to fight off hypoxia long enough to function.

Others, like Dr. Brahmaputra-Marquez, succumbed too quickly. She was laughing giddily and talking to an imaginary kangaroo.

To my surprise, Dr. Marquez turned out to be one of the competent people. Seeing that his wife was in trouble forced him to step up his game. He tended to Dr. Brahmaputra-Marquez while also helping Roddy and Inez. Inez was probably doing the worst of anyone, but at least she was still conscious and able to follow directions.

Cesar Marquez may have been the calmest of everyone—although that was probably the result of the sedative his mother had given him. He emerged from the medical bay looking serene and well-rested (although possibly a bit spaced out). "We're evacuating?" he asked. "Cool. Sounds like fun."

The first order of business was to get oxygen. Emergency canisters of it were bolted to the walls throughout MBA, the same way that fire extinguishers are everywhere in buildings back on earth. Those adults who still had their faculties grabbed the canisters as quickly as they could . . . while still taking care not to go *too* quickly. Anyone who moved too fast would increase their heart rate and breathing speed, which would only make them more hypoxic.

The canisters all had transparent face masks to fit over the user's nose and mouth, and these were connected to the oxygen supply by tubes. They looked very much like the face masks that drop down on an airplane if the cabin depressurizes. The procedures for using them were the same as on an airplane as well: Mom, Dad, and Chang each took a few breaths off their canisters first, making sure that *their* minds were thinking straight before turning their attention to helping everyone else.

Meanwhile, I led Violet toward the air-lock staging area, knowing our parents would meet us there with the oxygen. There wasn't any time to spare waiting around for them. I was trying to soothe Violet and keep her from getting scared, although she was too looped out to really grasp what was going on. Instead *I* was ending up getting scared, because she was acting even sillier than usual. "Know what else I'd like besides a unicorn?" she asked. "Some dinosaurs. The ones that are all gray and fuzzy and adorable with huge ears."

"Uh, Violet," I said, "I think those are koalas."

"Right! Koalas! That's what I want!"

Nina came rushing down from her residence, toting the emergency canister from her room, the mask already strapped to her face. Because of this, she was completely clearheaded and began barking orders. I didn't really grasp what she said, though, because it was all highly technical, I wasn't in the best frame of mind, and none of it was directed at me anyhow. "Chang, placate the orbital dingus flange! Stephen and Rose, diffuse the bicaudal ventricles! Daphne, oscillate the flammable terrapins!"

Or something like that.

The Sjobergs burst from their residence like a herd of spooked cattle, shoving one another out of the way and all yelling that they ought to be first to evacuate. Although they had two emergency canisters in their suite, they hadn't remembered to bring either one.

Through it all, the sirens kept wailing and the base computer continued calmly announcing that we needed to evacuate immediately. Whoever had programmed this had probably expected that it would be soothing, but it had the opposite effect, like someone repeatedly reminding you that you only had a few minutes left on a math test when you were trying to focus on the test itself.

Mom raced over to Violet and me with her oxygen canister. She clapped the mask over my nose and mouth before

I could even protest that Violet should have it first.

My first breath of oxygen had a startling effect. My head cleared almost instantly, as though a cloud had evaporated inside my skull. I immediately grasped exactly what I had to do next and how to do it. After a few more breaths, we forced the mask onto Violet's face. I saw clarity return to her eyes within only a few seconds.

"Both of you, suit up to go outside," Mom said. "I have to stay back here to fix the system."

"What?" Violet asked worriedly. "Why?"

"Because it has to be done and I know how to do it," Mom said. "Your father is coming outside with you, but he has to work on the problem out there, so I need you two to stick together." She shifted her focus to Violet. "Your brother is in charge. Stay close to him and do what he says, all right?"

Normally, Violet might have protested, but now she grasped that this was important and that she had to listen. "All right."

Mom said, "It's a good thing your father checked your suit with you today, so we know it still fits."

"It does," Violet agreed. "Though it's a little tight. I've grown two inches since we got here!"

"Two inches? My goodness. Your grandparents won't even recognize you when we get home." Mom's tone was light and easygoing, but I knew it was all an act to keep Violet calm.

It worked like a charm, though. Violet didn't seem very worried, despite everything that was going on, and even I felt a bit more relaxed myself. "Now, even though this is an emergency," Mom continued, "we still have plenty of time to evacuate. You don't need to rush putting your suits on. Let's take it easy and not make any mistakes. I'll stay with you until you get into the air lock to make sure everything is done right."

I opened the space-suit storage and started removing our gear. Mom stayed close by with the emergency oxygen, helping us out and giving us breaths from the mask so that our minds stayed clear.

Kira was a few feet away, getting her suit while her father helped her.

Someone suddenly shoved me from behind. "Out of the way, idiot!" Patton Sjoberg snarled. He snatched his own suit from storage, nearly clocking Violet in the head with his helmet.

"*You* watch it, you big bully!" Violet shouted.

Patton sneered at her, and I got the sense that, if he hadn't been in such a hurry to get out of the base, he would have shoved her down just to make her cry. Then he set about putting his suit on.

Nearby, none of the other Sjobergs were behaving much better. They were rudely jostling people aside—mostly children—in order to grab their suits, as if the rest of us were merely objects that had gotten in their way. Since the Sjobergs had skipped many of the emergency meetings, they were at a loss as to how to put their suits on properly. Lily was trying to put her boots on the wrong feet, even though they were very clearly labeled LEFT and RIGHT, while Sonja was putting her suit on backward. Given their rude disregard for the rest of us, I wouldn't have been surprised if no one bothered to help them suit up, but Nina came to their rescue. "Listen up!" she ordered them. "I'm going to show you how to get your suits on properly. Now pay close attention—or you will die."

The Sjobergs all clammed up and actually listened as she explained what to do.

I held out Violet's suit for her and she clambered into it.

Dad came along. He had a large red tool kit marked EMERGENCY in five languages. "Everything all right here?" he asked us calmly, as though we were merely packing the car for a day at the beach.

"We're good," I told him.

"Great," he said. "I'm going to suit up. Don't go out without me." Then he went off to retrieve his own space suit.

Dr. Marquez had given Dr. Brahmaputra-Marquez oxygen, so she now appeared to have regained her senses and was ordering her children around like a drill sergeant. Cesar and Inez were already halfway suited up, although Roddy was having trouble. He was obviously fighting panic, and his refusal to work out over the past few months was coming back to haunt him. He barely had the strength to support his heavy suit.

I knelt and started to snap Violet's boots onto her feet.

"I can handle that, Dash," Mom said. "It's time for you to get ready yourself."

So I got back to my feet and climbed into my own suit.

Even though Mom was letting me have puffs of oxygen when I needed them, the chaos and the stress of the evacuation were wearing on me. It probably didn't help that, except for a brief nap, I'd been awake since two a.m. I had to focus so closely on suiting up and not making mistakes that I stopped noticing what was going on around me. It was as though the periphery of my range of sight had slipped away. My vision was tunneling slightly due to the lack of oxygen. I was vaguely aware that, despite Nina's insistence that the Sjobergs double- and triple-check to make sure that their suits were on safely, they had completely ignored this in their rush to get outside. Additionally, Chang made an announcement that, to speed the evacuation, some people ought to come to the emergency backup air lock in the gym with him, but I didn't notice who actually went. When everyone was wearing matching space suits, it was very hard to grasp who was who.

Eventually I got my suit on properly. And Mom got Violet into hers. It was so heavy, it was difficult for Violet to move around in it, even though she'd been doing her exercises.

A group of five people passed into the main air lock and shut the door behind them, preparing to go outside. Because they were suited up, I had no idea which five people it was.

I clamped the helmet down over my suit and locked it into place. The clamor of the alarms faded, and the suit's oxygen system activated. Now my clarity of mind wouldn't be yo-yoing as my oxygen level rose and fell, which was a relief.

Mom locked Violet's helmet into place as well, which gave Violet a steady oxygen supply too. Mom could now affix the mask from her emergency canister over her face and breath easy for the first time since the emergency had begun.

"You each have at least five hours of oxygen in your tanks," Mom told us. She had to yell so that we could hear her through our helmets. "Although it will last up to twice as long if you don't overexert yourselves and focus on breathing slowly. That means no goofing around out there. Stay close to the base, keep within sight of each other, and take the time to enjoy the view."

"How's *your* oxygen?" I asked.

"Fine," Mom said, pointing to the indicator on her canister. It was well into the green "safe" zone. "And there are plenty more of these. We're going to get this problem fixed long before you need to come back in. Now, let's put you guys on radio channel seventeen so you can communicate with me and each other."

Violet and I switched to channel 17. "Can you hear me?" I asked her.

"I can!" Violet exclaimed. "Hi, Dashiell!"

"Great!" Mom shouted, then plucked a radio from her belt and spoke to us through it. "Now let's do your safety checks."

Another group of Moonies stepped into the air lock. The first group had already headed out onto the surface. Along with Dad, who was currently snapping his helmet on, we were the only people in suits left inside the base. Either we were being poky, or everyone else wasn't exercising as much caution with suiting up as we were.

Dad clicked to channel 17 and we all went through our safety checks. There no longer seemed to be such a big hurry, as we were in our suits with our own personal oxygen supplies, so even if the oxygen in the base suddenly disappeared, we'd be okay.

For the next few hours, at least.

Eventually Dad and Mom pronounced that our suits were on properly. Mom gave us each a kiss on our helmets, warned us once again to stay together, and then headed off to deal with the oxygen crisis.

Dad, Violet, and I stepped into the air lock and shut the door behind us. The chamber depressurized, and then the indicator light turned green, signaling that it was safe to head outside. We opened the outer door and stepped onto the surface.

Even though I had been outside less than twenty-four hours earlier, everything felt very different this time. The lunar surface itself looked exactly the same, since the slow rotation of the moon meant the sun was still up—and would be for days to come—but everything else was different. On my previous venture outside, Dad had been in charge, looking after me. This time, I was the one with responsibility, taking care of Violet, which added a whole extra level of stress to the anxiety I already felt.

And this time, it was crowded. Before, Dad and I had had the whole moon to ourselves. Now there were people everywhere. Obviously, the actual number of Moonies outside was small, given the size of the moon itself, but still, no matter where I looked, there was someone in a space suit. With the reflective visors down on their helmets, I couldn't tell who anyone was. Everyone looked exactly the same. The only exceptions were Violet, Kamoze, and Inez, who were so much smaller than everyone else that they looked like dwarf astronauts.

"I'm heading to the other side of the base to the oxygen regulators," Dad informed Violet and me over channel 17. "Both of you stay here, close to everyone else. The moment we get this fixed, you'll be able to head back inside. Since you're the youngest, you ought to have priority."

"Okay," I replied.

"Gotcha," Violet said. "Have fun!"

Dad laughed. "I'll do my best," he said, then waved good-bye and bounded toward the northern side of the base.

The sound of his breathing cut out from my radio, which meant he had switched to a different radio channel, probably so he could talk to Mom and Chang about the repairs without Violet and me interrupting.

I watched him disappear behind the rover garage, then turned back to Violet.

She was gone.

I had a moment of panic, then spotted her running across the lunar surface. Or doing her best to run across the lunar surface, which wasn't very good at all. After months in low gravity without her space suit, she had completely forgotten how to move with additional weight. She only made it ten steps before she stumbled and fell onto her stomach.

"Oof!" she cried, then tried to get up and failed at that, too. Instead she could only wiggle her arms and legs around uselessly, like a turtle flipped on its back. "Dash! Help! I'm stuck!"

Even though she had only gone ten steps, those were ten low-gravity steps, which had still carried her a good distance from the air lock. She lay on the ground in the direction Dad and I had gone to play catch, away from the small crowd by the base.

I took my time heading over to her, partly because any time she was on her stomach was time she wasn't running off somewhere else, and partly because the sight of her writhing around was kind of funny. "Didn't Dad just tell you to stay close?"

"I *am* close," Violet protested.

"You were running away."

"I was trying to have fun. Dad didn't say we couldn't have fun."

"You're welcome to have fun out here. But you have to be careful."

"I *was* being careful."

"No, you weren't. You can't just run off. You have to stay with me. And you have to go slowly at first until you get the hang of things. You don't want to make a mistake out here." I knelt down to help Violet back to her feet. . .

And froze, struck by a thought.

We didn't want to make mistakes on the surface, because mistakes could be deadly.

And yet Lars Sjoberg had survived for the opposite reason. Whoever had tried to kill him had made a mistake.

"Dash!" Violet yelped. "Why aren't you helping me?"

"Sorry," I said, returning my attention to her. Her little arms and legs were windmilling wildly. "I was thinking about something."

"What?"

"Chang said that if he had wanted to kill Lars, he wouldn't have made any mistakes. But whoever actually tried to kill Lars got it wrong. They didn't use the right amount of poison."

"So?"

I couldn't simply grab on to Violet's suit and haul her to her feet. My thick gloves made it hard to get a purchase most places, and I didn't want to use one of the many tubes coming from the back of the suit. They controlled things like her air supply and temperature regulation; if I accidentally pulled one of those free, Violet would be in serious trouble. Instead I needed Violet's help to get her to her feet again. I needed to roll her onto her back, as that would make it easier for her to hold on to me. So I wiggled my arms into the moon dust beneath her belly.

"Whoever tried to kill Lars went through an awful lot of trouble," I explained. "They had to steal the apple seeds. They had to make the cyanide. They had to poison the lutefisk without being seen. Injecting the right amount of poison should have been the easy part. But that's where they made their mistake."

"Maybe there weren't enough seeds to make enough poison," Violet said.

With a heave I flipped Violet onto her back. "Maybe. But what would be the point of only partly poisoning someone?"

"Maybe the person hated Lars, but didn't want to be a murderer."

"I don't think so," I said. "I think that they must have—"

"Dash!" Violet screamed suddenly. "Look out!"

A shadow fell over me. My reflex was to spin around, but that was almost impossible to do in the space suit. Especially from a kneeling position. I couldn't even turn my head to look behind me.

I felt something tug on the back of my suit.

A second later, an alarm sounded inside my helmet. "Warning," the same calm computerized voice from the base announced. "Your oxygen hose has been detached. If it isn't reconnected in three minutes, you will asphyxiate."

I knew the hose couldn't have simply come loose. My family and I had checked it four times, making sure it was tightly attached. Whoever was behind me had pulled it out on purpose.

Someone was trying to kill me.

Excerpt from *The Official NASA Procedures for Contact with Intelligent Extraterrestrial Life* © National Aeronautics and Space Administration, Department of Extraterrestrial Affairs, 2029 (Classification Level AAA)

OFFICIAL GREETINGS

In the (hopeful) event that the secondary contact proves to be friendly, rather than hostile, the primary objective of the encounter ought to be to welcome the IEL to earth and begin to foster peaceful relations between our species. Therefore, the first message will most likely be to extend warm greetings to the IEL (though what form this message is delivered in will be left up to DEXA's linguistics team). Ideally, the president and other world leaders (including the leader whose country contact has occurred in—assuming they are not despotic) will be among the first members of humanity to communicate with the IEL, but given travel times, it may not be feasible to wait for them. Therefore, the senior US government representative on location will most likely be tasked with extending the initial message of greetings, and they (as well as all other representatives of the USA present) should do all they can to make the IEL feel welcome and comfortable on our planet.

18

IMMINENT SUFFOCATION

Lunar day 252

Quite possibly the last minutes of my life

"Stop it!" Violet screamed at whoever had attacked me. Her voice was high-pitched and terrified. She understood what was going on, but she couldn't do anything to help me. She was still stuck on her back. "Leave my brother alone!"

On the radio channel, along with her screams, I could hear something else: the sounds of my attacker breathing heavily. They had been listening in on the same channel we had been using. Either the exertion of attacking me was forcing them to breathe louder than before—or I stupidly hadn't realized they were eavesdropping until it was too late.

"Violet!" I yelled. "They pulled my oxygen hose! You need to . . ."

I actually said "put it back," but Violet didn't hear that part. And neither did anyone else. My radio went dead as my attacker killed that, too. And then they shoved me down on top of Violet.

My helmet slammed into the ground. Luckily, there were no moon rocks to break the face plate, but I ended up facedown in a pile of moon dust, which clung to the glass and practically blinded me.

"Warning," the voice in my suit announced. "You have approximately two minutes and thirty seconds to repair your oxygen hose or return to the base." A graphic showing my rapidly depleting oxygen supply appeared on the heads-up display inside the helmet.

So, basically, worst-case scenario. Two minutes and thirty seconds was very little time to get back to the base, enter the air lock, and repressurize it, especially when someone else was doing their best to make sure I died on the lunar surface. I tried to scramble to my feet anyhow, but they shoved me right back down again.

I struggled against them, wondering how I had managed to end up in yet another life-or-death situation, wishing that I had never left the moon base, wanting desperately to be safely back inside . . .

And then, suddenly, I *was*. There was a flash and the strange sensation of being pulled through something, and then I was standing inside the air lock, without my space suit, safe as could be.

Only, when I looked through the air-lock window, I could see that everyone else was still out on the surface—including someone lying on their stomach, who I realized was actually *me*.

I had transmitted myself via thought again, only this time I had done it without Zan's help, and I hadn't projected *to* someone like Riley. I had simply projected myself—or my mind—to exactly where I wanted to be: the safety of the air lock. In the heat and desperation of the moment, I had managed to pull off the trick of traveling via thought once again.

Unfortunately, my body was still dying back on the lunar surface. So I didn't have time to savor the moment. Or even focus on how I'd done it.

I thought myself back into my own body, which was far easier to do. Once I stopped trying so hard to think myself away, it was as though my mind homed right back in on where it was supposed to be. One second I was in the air lock. The next I was back in my space suit, two minutes from death.

I fought to survive. I heaved myself up to my knees. My attacker tried to shove me back down again, but adrenaline was now surging through me. I braced against their attack, then

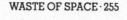

swiveled toward MBA. The air-lock door was probably forty-five seconds away, and it would take another minute to repressurize inside. Then I'd have fifteen seconds to unlock my helmet. . . .

Only my attacker was still between me and the air lock.

Since I was on my knees, they loomed over me. And since their reflective visor was down, I couldn't see their face. I had no idea who they were, or what they were thinking. It was like facing a robot, rather than a human being.

In the warped mirror of their visor, I saw myself, kneeling helplessly before them.

But there was other movement as well. Behind me, Violet was struggling to her feet, probably having an adrenaline surge of her own. I couldn't quite make out what Violet was doing, but she seemed to be reaching for my oxygen hose.

My attacker turned slightly, noticing Violet. And then they lunged for her as well.

"No!" I screamed. Without my radio connection, I was the only one who heard it. My voice echoed in my helmet.

I reached for my attacker, but they easily brushed past me, heading for Violet.

"Warning," the computer said. "Ninety seconds left."

Violet tried to run from our attacker, making the mistake of turning her back on the enemy. Now her fragile network of life-sustaining hoses and other equipment was exposed. The attacker grabbed her oxygen hose and tugged on it.

It didn't come free, but I figured another good yank would do the trick. And if Violet lost her oxygen supply, she probably wouldn't have the ability or mental calm to make it to safety.

My own oxygen was going fast, but I wasn't about to let someone take down my sister, too. I staggered to my feet, determined to defend Violet to my last breath.

Only, before I could attack, someone else did it for me.

Another Moonie suddenly raced into view and body-slammed Violet's attacker. Once again, due to the reflective visor, I had no idea who our savior was. Both Moonies went flying due to the impact. They sailed ten feet and then tumbled across the lunar surface, plowing through the moon dust.

Violet's oxygen hose was still attached. She was safe.

"Warning," my suit computer said. "Sixty seconds left."

I turned back toward the air lock, wondering how long I could hold my breath. And worried that if I saved myself, I would be leaving my savior at the mercy of the killer.

Something tugged at the back of my suit. For a brief, terrifying moment, I feared a second killer had attacked, but then I realized that I could no longer see Violet, and it must be her behind me. There was a metallic click, followed by a sudden whoosh of air.

"Crisis averted," the computerized voice announced. "Your oxygen hose has been properly reconnected. Please exercise caution: Your oxygen level is now only at forty-two percent."

The heads-up display changed. My oxygen level was revealed to be decent, and I was shown a nice little smiley-face emoji, as well, to indicate that I was no longer about to die.

Violet might have only been six, but she had obviously been paying attention to the safety checks. She had just saved my life.

"Thanks, little sister," I said, forgetting that she couldn't hear me, because my radio was still unplugged.

I didn't have time for her to fix that, though. Whoever had saved me was still fighting whoever had tried to kill me.

The problem was, I wasn't sure who was who. I had lost track of which was my attacker and which was the one who had come to my rescue. In their space suits, they appeared exactly the same. The two of them were wrestling on the lunar surface, so covered with moon dust that they looked like they'd been dipped in batter. They were rolling over each other and pounding on each other.

By now the other Moonies had realized what was going on. They were coming our way, moving as fast as they could, which wasn't fast enough.

I bounded toward the fighting Moonies.

And then Zan suddenly flickered into view. She appeared

in her usual human form—although, since she didn't need a space suit, she was simply standing on the lunar surface, which looked almost as odd as her jellyfish form would have been.

There was a look of shock and astonishment on her face. She seemed horrified that we humans were trying to kill one another yet again. "Dashiell!" she cried. "Are you all right?"

"Yes."

"And Violet, too?"

"Yes."

"Is there anything I can do?"

"Keep an eye on Violet. Make sure she's doing okay."

"All right." Zan vanished from my sight, perhaps worried that she'd be a distraction otherwise.

Ahead of me, the other two Moonies were still fighting each other. One seemed to have gotten the upper hand, however, sitting on the chest of the other, who was laid out flat on the ground. The one on top grabbed a large moon rock and raised it above their head, ready to smash it down on the other's glass face plate.

I figured that was probably my attacker. Anyone willing to smash the face plate of another Moonie was a pretty bad person.

I dove at them, driving my shoulder into the attacker, knocking them to the lunar surface. I lost my balance and went down with them, plowing back into the moon dust.

Unfortunately, they didn't let go of the rock. Instead they thumped me on the helmet with it.

"Warning," my suit computer said. "A blow to the structural integrity of your helmet has been detected—"

The attacker thumped me again.

"Warning," my suit computer repeated. "A blow to the structural integrity—"

"I know!" I shouted. "Shut up! I get it!"

There was another thump on the helmet, but this one wasn't as hard, as though the attacker had been interrupted in the middle of it.

I struggled to my hands and knees to find a lot more Moonies around us. In fact, it appeared that almost everyone from MBA had joined the party now. Three were restraining the Moonies who had been fighting, while others were still racing over to help intervene.

My attacker, who still had the rock in their hands, was now being pinned to the lunar surface by two Moonies. Again, I had no idea who anyone was due to the visors, but given that one of the Moonies who had come to the rescue was several inches taller than anyone else, I figured it was Dr. Balnikov.

He looked at me in a way that, even with our faces hidden from view, seemed to indicate that he was talking to me.

I did my best to convey that I couldn't hear anything

and pointed to the back of my suit, signaling that my radio was shot.

Another Moonie slipped around behind me. A few seconds later, there was a crackle as my radio came back on.

I could immediately hear Violet talking to Zan on channel 17. "That was *scary*," my sister was saying. "Like really really scary."

"It's over now," I assured her. "We're safe." Then I flipped to channel 1, which was the basic channel for communication, and was instantly overwhelmed by a flood of voices. Everyone was talking at once.

"Be quiet!" Dr. Balnikov roared. He sounded like *he* might start knocking people around if they didn't listen.

Everyone immediately fell silent.

"That's better," Dr. Balnikov said, then pointed at me. "Who are you?"

"Dashiell."

There were a few hushed gasps over the radio. People seemed surprised that I was the one who had been attacked.

"Are you all right?" Dr. Balnikov asked me.

"Yes."

"Good." Dr. Balnikov shifted his attention to the person who had saved me. "And who are you?"

"Cesar Marquez."

This time *I* gasped a little. Cesar had never struck me as

the type who would go out of his way to hand someone else a napkin, let alone risk his life for them.

One of the other Moonies burst from the crowd and threw their arms around Cesar protectively. "Are you all right?" she asked. It was Dr. Brahmaputra-Marquez.

"Sure, Mom. I'm fine."

Dr. Balnikov now turned his attention to my attacker. "Who are you?" he demanded.

There was no answer. The Moonie simply lay on the ground beneath Dr. Balnikov. They didn't speak. They didn't move. Dr. Balnikov might as well have been talking to a department-store mannequin.

"Who are you?" Dr. Balnikov demanded once again.

The Moonie didn't respond.

Dr. Balnikov grunted angrily, then yanked the Moonie to their feet. He did it with such ease, it appeared that the Moonie weighed nothing at all. Dr. Balnikov planted the Moonie on the ground so hard that their boots sank several inches into the moon dust. Then he reached to the back of their helmet and flipped a switch.

My attacker's mirrored visor sprang up, revealing their identity.

Lily Sjoberg.

Excerpt from *The Official NASA Procedures for Contact with Intelligent Extraterrestrial Life* © National Aeronautics and Space Administration, Department of Extraterrestrial Affairs, 2029 (Classification Level AAA)

ALIEN ABDUCTIONS

Although the idea of being abducted from earth by IEL is most likely the fantasy of Hollywood movies, it cannot be ruled out completely. There is a chance (however slight) that the first contact with IEL will be via humans who have been physically removed from earth. Therefore, anyone you encounter who claims to have been the victim of an alien abduction must be taken seriously until proven otherwise.* They ought to be quarantined, closely examined, and carefully interviewed to assess the veracity of their story.

If *you* happen to be the one who is abducted, be gracious and accommodating to your hosts, try to remember everything you can, and contact DEXA immediately upon your return to earth.

---

* Within reason. If someone claiming to have been abducted is obviously a raving lunatic (and there are many such people), then their story can probably be discounted without expending the time or energy of further analysis.

FACE-OFF

Lunar day 252

T minus 11 hours to evacuation

It took another two and a half hours to repair the base oxygen system and another thirty minutes to confirm that it was safe to allow everyone back inside MBA once again. During that time, we had little to do but wait on the lunar surface.

Since more than half my oxygen was gone, I didn't want to exert myself too much and burn through the rest of it. I also didn't want to turn my back on anyone. Dr. Balnikov was keeping a very close eye on Lily Sjoberg, but that didn't mean someone else might not take a crack at me.

Lars was one of the few Moonies who hadn't witnessed

at least some of Lily's attack on me. Most everyone had missed the beginning of it, where she unplugged my oxygen hose, but they had seen what the fight had devolved into. However, Lars had been on the other side of the base; in his haste to evacuate MBA, he had abandoned his own children and raced off to the emergency backup air lock. Now, Lars tracked me down and spent much of our remaining time on the lunar surface shouting at me. I think he might have been accusing *me* of starting the fight and of possibly even trying to kill Lily, but I don't know for sure because I switched off my radio three seconds into his tirade so I didn't have to listen to him. Lars didn't notice. Instead he continued gesticulating angrily for another hour, until he had screamed so much that his own oxygen supply dropped to dangerous levels and he had to stay silent simply to keep from asphyxiating.

To conserve my own energy, I sat by the air-lock door. It occurred to me that I was squandering some of the last, precious time I had on the lunar surface, and that I should have been off exploring the moon or at least enjoying the feel of wandering around on a foreign celestial body while I could still do it. But I was too exhausted, physically and mentally. It had been a very long day, and, frankly, there wasn't too much to see around MBA anyhow. It was the one part of the entire lunar surface that had been polluted by humans, and thus it looked more like an industrial wasteland than a pristine moonscape.

Meanwhile, Kira and Violet were relishing every moment of their time outside. If Violet was upset at all by our ordeal, she didn't show it. But then, Violet hadn't been out of MBA since we'd arrived, so it was possible that the excitement of this trumped any other emotions. First the girls made history by being the first humans to do cartwheels on the moon, and then they attempted several other gymnastic moves as well, with varying results. After that, they tromped off to a nearby patch of virgin moon dust and made the first human footprints there. I thought about radioing them and telling them to stay close to base, but I could still keep an eye on them from where I was, and I figured Violet deserved some fun after our near-death experience.

Once we were given the all clear to come back inside, I was allowed to enter first due to my depleted oxygen supply. The other kids—Violet, Kamoze, Inez, Kira, Roddy, and Cesar—were also given priority status.

After a normal trip onto the surface, we would have spent at least fifteen minutes in the air lock, trying to vacuum the moon dust off our suits before returning them to storage. However, there were too many other people waiting to come in behind us. Plus, keeping MBA free of moon dust wasn't such a big priority anymore, seeing as half of us were scheduled to evacuate the next day. So we passed through the air lock as quickly as possible, then removed our suits in the staging area instead, getting moon dust all over the nice, sterile moon-base floor.

Mom was waiting for us anxiously in the staging area. She had heard almost immediately over the radio that Lily Sjoberg had tried to kill Violet and me, but she hadn't been able to come to comfort us because of the urgency of the repair work on the oxygen system. Now she looked exhausted and racked by guilt. She wrapped her arms around both of us tightly and sobbed, "I'm so sorry. I'm so sorry."

"Why are *you* sorry?" Violet asked innocently. "You didn't do anything. Lily Sjoberg did."

"I'm sorry you had to go through that at all," Mom explained.

"We weren't in that much danger," Violet said reassuringly. "Well, Dash kind of was, but I saved him."

"You did," I said, tousling her hair.

Violet then told Mom everything that had happened. In truth I knew Violet had been a lot more scared than she was letting on. When she got frightened, she had a habit of overstating her bravery. On our rocket to the moon, she had been so scared during liftoff that her hands had gone cold, but she later insisted that she hadn't been scared one bit and that the ride had been a hundred times better than any roller coaster on earth.

While she chattered to Mom, I noticed Cesar Marquez

close by, trying to figure out how to unlatch his helmet from his suit. I wandered over to him. "Thanks for helping Violet out there."

Cesar shrugged. "I saw someone picking on a kid and thought it wasn't cool. I had no idea it was Lily. I figured it was someone psycho, like Patton or Dr. Goldstein."

"Dr. Goldstein?" I repeated, surprised by this accusation.

"Yeah. She's so weird, always working with her plants."

"Well, she *is* a botanist. . . ."

"She *talks* to them."

"Lots of people do that. And it especially makes sense here. It gives them carbon dioxide."

"Carbon what?" Cesar asked dully.

"It's what plants take in to make oxygen. . . ."

"Whatever," Cesar said, already seeming bored by the conversation. "I still can't believe it was Lily." He shuddered. "I can't believe I fought a *girl*." He tried to yank his helmet off without unlatching it first, which was impossible.

"I can help you with that," I said, reaching toward him.

"I can do it fine by myself," Cesar said curtly, even though he couldn't. It seemed that the whole idea of fighting Lily had put him on edge. Or maybe he was upset to find out that Lily had tried to kill someone. After all, she and Cesar had spent a lot of time together at MBA.

Cesar stormed away from me, straining against his own

helmet, oblivious to the latch that was still connecting it to his space suit. When he couldn't get it off, he angrily pounded it with his fists.

"Wow," Violet said, coming over to me. "How did someone as smart as his mother ever have someone as dumb as him?"

"Be nice," I said, more for Mom's benefit than Violet's. "He saved our lives out there."

"He's still a moron," Violet said.

I noticed that Mom didn't correct her.

The next batch of Moonies poured into the air lock from the lunar surface. Within fifteen minutes, everyone was back inside MBA, safe and sound—and I found myself in Nina's office, having an emergency meeting with my parents, the Sjobergs, Dr. Balnikov, and Chang. (Dr. Merritt agreed to look after Violet and took her to the mess to get space ice cream.)

It was a meeting I had been dreading the entire time on the lunar surface, but one I knew we had to have. The fact that Lily had attacked me needed to be dealt with immediately. The meeting was called in Nina's residence with the intent of keeping it secret, but of course anyone who wanted to (like Kira) could hear everything that was said by standing on the catwalk outside and listening through the door.

There weren't enough InflatiCubes for everyone, so we all stood awkwardly. The moment the Sjobergs came through the door, Lars started yelling at the rest of us. His voice was still hoarse from all the yelling he'd done at me out on the surface, but that didn't stop him. "Lily didn't attack anyone!" he declared. "She was acting in self-defense!"

"By all accounts, that does not appear to be true," Nina said coldly.

"It *is*!" Lily exclaimed. "I was minding my own business when the Gibsons attacked me!"

"That's right!" Patton agreed, lamely trying to back up his sister. "I saw the whole thing! Dash and Violet just jumped her!"

These were such bald-faced lies that even Lars couldn't bring himself to agree with them. Instead he shot his children a withering look, apparently annoyed at them for pushing things too far.

Nina gave the Sjoberg twins a withering look of her own. Both instantly fell silent.

"I have already examined the security footage from the cameras mounted outside," Nina said. "It is clear that Lily attacked first, and without provocation. Furthermore, I have reviewed the radio transmissions from right before the assault. It appears that Lily was eavesdropping on the conversation between Dashiell and Violet. Dashiell was about to reveal that Lily was behind the murder attempt on her father, so Lily attacked him to keep him quiet."

This provoked a variety of reactions around the room. Most of the adults seemed stunned by the accusation, although Lars and Sonja were particularly mortified. Meanwhile, Lily turned even paler than usual, while Patton gaped in astonishment. "*You* tried to kill Daddy?" he accused.

"I didn't!" Lily gasped.

Patton didn't seem to believe her. But then, he didn't seem to be upset with her either. Instead he burst into a fit of hysterical laughter, as if his sister trying to kill his father was the funniest thing he'd ever heard.

"I *wasn't* about to accuse Lily," I announced, trying to be heard. "She's not the one who poisoned Lars."

Patton stopped laughing. "She's not?"

"No," I said. "She was only trying to protect the person who *did* poison him."

Now everyone's attention shifted toward me.

"So who did it?" Mom asked.

"Lars Sjoberg poisoned himself," I said.

This produced a whole new round of shocked, stunned, and astonished reactions.

For a moment Lars Sjoberg looked like he'd swallowed a whole bag of human excrement. Then he recovered and started shouting again.

"That's a lie!" he yelled, jabbing a finger at me. "This boy is a menace! He simply cannot be trusted!"

"*I* trust him," Nina said. This caught me off guard, as it was the closest thing to a compliment I had ever received from Nina. In fact, it might have been the closest thing to a compliment *anyone* had ever received from Nina. "And I am going to listen to what he has to say. If you don't wish to stay here for it, you are free to leave."

"But—" Lars began.

"On the other hand," Nina told him, "if you *do* choose to stay for it, then I expect you to keep your mouth shut and not make a scene for once in your life. If you can't do that, then I will have Dr. Kowalski and Dr. Balnikov forcibly escort you from the room."

Lars fell silent, although he was obviously still enraged. I half expected to see steam pouring from his ears.

Chang smiled. He seemed excited by the prospect of getting to forcibly escort Lars out.

Nina looked back to me. "Please, Dashiell. Tell me how you arrived at this conclusion."

Everyone's attention returned to me. I took a step back, uncomfortable with being on the spot and wondering if I was right. But then I looked to my parents, who smiled at me reassuringly, giving me confidence. "I figured it like this," I said. "If someone was actually looking to kill Lars, they didn't do it right. They didn't put enough poison in the lutefisk, even though there was poison left over in the syringe. That was a dumb mistake. But this whole base is full of very smart people. They wouldn't have made a mistake like that. In fact, I'm sure pretty much everyone here could have come up with a better way to kill Lars than poisoning his lutefisk. A way that wouldn't have left any evidence behind, maybe. Instead, the killer botched the job, which doesn't make sense—unless they were *trying* to botch the job. The craziest thing about this crime is that nearly everyone here at MBA was a suspect. Almost everyone had a good reason for wanting Lars dead. But I could only think of one person who would want Lars *sort of* dead."

"Why are we even listening to this?" Lars exploded. "It is utter nonsense! Why would I want to be sort of dead?"

"Because you wanted all of us to *think* someone was trying to kill you," I said. "But you didn't actually want to die."

"Of all the idiotic things I have ever heard," Lars said, "this has to be the dumbest!"

"Gentlemen," Nina said to Chang and Dr. Balnikov. "Please escort Lars out."

"It'd be my pleasure," Chang said happily. He and Dr. Balnikov seized Lars by the arms.

Even though Lars was a big man, he was no match for

both of them. "All right!" he cried as they dragged him toward the door. "You win! I will be silent!"

Chang and Dr. Balnikov looked back to Nina, waiting for orders.

"Let's give him one more chance," she said, then glared at Lars. "But one more word and we finish this without you."

Lars nodded meekly.

Chang and Dr. Balnikov didn't toss him out the door, but they both kept vise grips on his arms.

Dad looked to me. "Why would Lars want us to think someone had tried to kill him?"

"So he could go home," I said. "He definitely hasn't been happy up here, but NASA hasn't been able to find a spot for him or his family on any of the rockets back to earth. . . ."

Mom piped up, realizing where I was going with this. "But if there's a threat to his life, NASA protocols mandate sending a rocket, no matter the cost."

Everyone looked to Lars, aware that this made a twisted sort of sense. Lars didn't give anything away, though. He just glared angrily at Nina.

Dr. Balnikov looked at Lars curiously. "You were willing to poison yourself to get a rocket home?"

Lars stubbornly refused to answer.

"It could work two ways," I explained. "Either it would create a medical emergency for Lars without killing him, or he could claim that his life would be in jeopardy if he stayed here. I actually overheard Sonja claiming that to Nina this morning."

"That wasn't a plot!" Sonja argued. Her broken nose was still swollen, but she had regained her ability to talk properly. "I was legitimately worried for my husband!"

"I doubt that," Dr. Balnikov grumbled. "You were just looking for an excuse to get home."

"Either way, she had a valid argument," I said. "Lars was counting on that when he poisoned himself."

"So this was only about getting off the moon?" Chang asked. "Not about framing me for murder?"

"I think framing you was kind of a bonus," I said. "Lars thought he could go back *and* send you to jail."

This didn't seem to surprise everyone nearly as much as some of my other revelations had. Everyone knew Lars had a serious grudge against Chang.

"Lars stole the apple seeds from the greenhouse a while ago," I went on. "He could have made cyanide at any time. He's definitely smart enough to have figured out how to do that. But he waited for just the right moment to poison himself. He didn't do it on a random night. He did it on a night when he knew Chang had already been sneaking into the mess hall."

"How did he know that?" Mom asked.

"The Sjobergs' room is directly over Chang's room," I explained. "I realized today that you can see through the greenhouse into the mess hall from Chang's door, which means there should be a similar view from the Sjobergs'. The walls are so thin here, I'm sure the Sjobergs could hear Chang leaving his room at night. Any one of them could have simply opened the door a bit and watched him enter the mess hall. Once they saw him go into the storage unit that held the lutefisk, they knew the time was right to set him up."

"Why was Chang getting lutefisk?" Dad asked.

"He wasn't," I replied. "He was getting rassolnik."

"Rassolnik?" Dad repeated, confused.

"It's a pickle-and-kidney soup," I said. "It's some kind of Russian delicacy."

"Oh," Mom said, then looked to Dad with understanding. It seemed that both of them already knew about Chang and Dr. Balnikov.

"Pickles and kidneys?" Patton Sjoberg cringed in disgust. "Blech. That sounds horrible."

"It's a lot better than your horrid lutefisk," Dr. Balnikov said defensively.

"*I* never said lutefisk was good," Patton shot back. "I think it tastes like cat pee."

Nina stepped in before the discussion could get out of hand. "There's no point in arguing which culture has the worst food

here." She looked to me. "You think Lars poisoned himself last night because he saw the opportunity to frame Chang?"

"Right," I agreed. "He—or someone else in his family—saw Chang fiddling around in the food storage and realized the time was right. So Lars waited a few hours, then went down to the storage area, got some lutefisk out, and returned to his room to poison himself with it. Which explains why he was eating lutefisk in the middle of the night, instead of during normal waking hours."

"Lots of people snack in the middle of the night," Sonja Sjoberg said protectively.

"Maybe," Chang said. "But very few of them snack on lutefisk. That's just weird."

"You should talk!" Sonja howled. "You were getting pickle-and-kidney soup in the middle of the night!"

"Anyhow," I said. "It was all done to set Chang up." I turned to Nina. "This morning you told me that there wasn't any point in going through the video footage to see if anyone had poisoned the lutefisk. But then, later on, you said you had changed your mind. What made you do that?"

Nina looked surprised to be put on the spot like this. "I'm allowed to change my mind."

Mom asked, "In the middle of preparing for an emergency evacuation, you suddenly decided to take the time to go through last night's security footage?"

Nina wavered for a moment, then said, "I got an anonymous tip. Someone slipped a note under my door suggesting that I check the footage from midnight to one a.m."

"And you didn't think that was suspicious?" Chang asked.

"On earth, the police get anonymous tips all the time," Nina countered.

"I'm guessing this one came from Lars Sjoberg," I said. "Or maybe Lily delivered it for him. And then, to seal the deal, one of them planted the syringe with cyanide in Chang's room."

"But Chang's door was locked," Mom argued, then looked to Chang. "Wasn't it?"

"The security protocols at this place are crap," Chang said. "Anyone with half a brain can override the door locks. The override is built into the system in case Nina ever needs to do it. And Lars knows his way around a computer system. He's fiddled with the one here before. He might be a pig, but he's not an idiot."

Lars bridled at this, but he still remained silent. It was obviously getting hard for him, though. With Chang's latest needling, he began to tremble with rage.

Dad returned his attention to me. "Why do you think Lily was involved? Why not just Lars?"

"Because Lily must have known what Lars was up to all along," I said. "And she knew Nina was having me investigate. So she eavesdropped on Violet and me out on the lunar surface, and when I started to say who the real killer was, she tried to kill me herself to keep it quiet."

"Then what's to say Lily wasn't the only killer all along?" Dr. Balnikov asked.

"What?" Lily gasped.

"Everything that has been mentioned, she could have done on her own," Dr. Balnikov said. "Watching Chang get the rassolnik, tipping off Nina, planting the syringe. And we *know* she tried to kill two people: Dashiell and Violet. So maybe this all started because she tried to kill her father first, and she simply got the amount of poison wrong. Everything else she has done has been to protect herself."

I hadn't thought of that.

The adults all paused to consider that as well. Rattled, Lily looked to her father. It seemed to me that she was expecting him to come to her defense.

He didn't. Instead he lowered his eyes to the floor.

Lily instantly flooded with rage. "You don't have anything to say to that?" she demanded.

Finally Lars spoke. "It seems possible," he said.

Lily went ballistic. "How dare you?" she screamed. "After all I've done for you, you're going to throw me to the wolves?" To everyone's surprise, she launched herself across the room at Lars, seized him by the neck, and started choking him.

Chang and Dr. Balnikov had to let go of Lars and direct their attention to prying his own daughter off him. Only Lily turned out to be stronger than they expected. Despite their best efforts, her hands remained firmly clamped around Lars's neck. She shook him angrily, screaming at him in Swedish.

Lars's eyes bugged out as his own daughter choked him. His pale flesh quickly purpled.

Most of the other adults leaped into action to separate Lars and his daughter. Only Sonja appeared unsure what to do. She looked back and forth between both family members, torn as to who to help.

Patton leaned against the wall, laughing hysterically, enjoying the show.

Everyone finally managed to pull Lily off Lars. Lars stumbled backward, gasping for air. "It was her all along!" he told all of us. "My own daughter . . ."

Lily pleaded her case to the rest of us simultaneously. "It was him! He wanted to frame Chang! When I caught him doing it, he forced me into helping him! He said he'd cut me out of his will if I didn't!"

"Those are lies!" Lars argued. "We have always known Lily had a homicidal streak. But we can no longer protect her. You have seen for yourself how dangerous she is—"

"You low-down, dirty snake!" Lily screeched, then

launched herself at him again. This time Chang and Dr. Balnikov intercepted her, but she still struggled against them, determined to throttle her father. "I didn't try to kill you before, but I obviously should have! What type of monster poisons himself and then lets his own daughter take the fall for it?"

"What type of daughter tries to kill her own father and then claim that he did it himself?" Lars retorted.

"Stop it!" Sonja wailed. "Stop it *right now*!" Her words were so shrill and desperate, everyone obeyed, no matter what they were doing. Even Lars and Lily froze in the midst of their fight.

Sonja apparently couldn't take this anymore. She was quivering in anger. Slowly she raised an accusing finger and pointed it at her husband. "You have done a lot of terrible things in your life, and I have stood by you, but not this time. Not now. I don't care if you take all my money away. I am not going to let you do this to our daughter."

"Sonja, please . . . ," Lars pleaded.

"No!" Sonja shouted. "Enough is enough!" She looked to all the rest of us. "Lars isn't well. He has spent the last few weeks here plotting and brooding, determined to do anything he could to get us off this stupid moon."

"Sonja . . . ," Lars said, angrier now.

"I told him this would never work," Sonja continued.

"But there was no talking him out of it. Being trapped up here has been driving him crazy. So I let him go ahead with it. But I never expected it would come to this. To accusing his own daughter of murder just to save his own pathetic skin. Lily never tried to kill anyone."

"Except me and Violet," I said.

Sonja ignored this, as though it wasn't that important. She glared at Lars. "Lily is innocent. This is all her father's doing."

"Sonja!" Lars bellowed. Unable to hold his tongue any longer, he started shouting at her in Swedish. Sonja shouted right back at him, and then Lily joined in for good measure. Swedish is a very guttural language. Three people yelling at one another in it sounded kind of like a room full of geese trying to hock up phlegm.

Patton sat on an InflatiCube and watched. He seemed to be having the best day of his life.

It occurred to me that there was an irony to all of this. Lars had gone through so much trouble to get off the base, unaware that steps were already under way for everyone to evacuate. If he had only waited another day, he would have found out his whole plot was unnecessary.

Dad came over to me and put an arm around my shoulders. "Come on," he said. "I think our work here is done."

"I do too," Mom said, and we started for the door.

"Wait!" Nina yelled after us. "Where are you going?"

Dad said, "You forced my son to help solve this crime, and he solved it. It's your job to deal with the aftermath."

Nina shifted her gaze from us to the shouting Sjobergs. She didn't look happy to have them all in her office.

"Don't worry," Chang told Nina. "Viktor and I will be happy to help you take care of these idiots." He cracked his knuckles and smiled, like he was hoping Nina might ask him to knock some heads together.

My parents and I stepped out onto the catwalk and shut the door behind us.

Most of the other Moonies were gathered in the staging area below us. Since we could all clearly hear the Sjobergs arguing through the thin walls, it seemed that everyone else had a very good idea what had happened in Nina's office.

Meanwhile, Kira and Violet were right outside the door. Violet had chocolate ice cream smeared around her face. Daphne stood nearby, looking a bit embarrassed. Obviously, they had all been eavesdropping.

"Is it true?" Violet asked. "Lars poisoned *himself*?"

"Looks that way," Dad replied.

"Why would he do that?" Violet asked.

"He was trying to manipulate NASA into getting him off the moon faster," Dad explained. "And to frame Chang for doing it."

"It's a shame he didn't get the dose wrong and off himself for good," Dr. Janke said, and a lot of the other Moonies echoed agreement.

"We'll be free of the Sjobergs soon enough," Mom told the crowd. The she turned her attention to me. "You still have a few hours of your birthday left, Dash. Is there anything special you'd like to do?"

"Yeah," I said. After my exceptionally long day, there was only one thing I could think of. "More than anything else in the whole world, I want to go to sleep."

CONTACT BEYOND EARTH

As humanity begins to expand our frontiers, colonizing our moon and Mars and traveling to planets even farther out in our solar system, the possibility exists that our first contact with IEL may not occur on our own planet. (Of course, there is also the potential for encountering *non*intelligent life on other celestial objects—e.g., bacteria and viruses beneath the crust of Mars—but while that would no doubt be an incredible event, it does not require the cautionary procedures laid out in this manual.) Should you encounter IEL while not on earth, DEXA should be contacted immediately. Obviously, many of the steps laid out here will not be feasible beyond earth, but DEXA can still be extremely helpful in facilitating contact between our species—and perhaps directing the IEL to earth, where further, more practical communication between our species can take place.

THE GIFT

Lunar day 253

T minus 3 hours to evacuation

I slept better than I ever had in my previous 252 nights on the moon.

Maybe it was because I was exhausted from the extremely long day and all the time on the lunar surface and the fact that Lily Sjoberg had tried to kill me. Or maybe, after eight months, I was finally getting the hang of lunar sleep, just in time to leave. Whatever the case, I was out cold until my parents shook me awake at seven a.m.

"Sorry to do this," Mom whispered, "But we have a lot to do today."

And we did. There was still a lot of prep for evacuation,

which was more complicated than expected because of the emergency evac we'd done the day before. Our space suits, which were still piled by the air lock, all had to be reorganized, cleaned, and examined for damage. There were many more experiments left to break down in the science pod, and there was still equipment to pack. Plus we were shorthanded, due to the Sjoberg situation. In addition to the evacuation, Nina now had her hands full dealing with Lars and Lily, her two newest criminals.

While I had been asleep, NASA had floated the idea of having the Sjobergs sent down on the rockets that day instead of my family, so they could be jailed immediately back on earth, but it was ultimately decided that leaving children in a potentially dangerous moon base (one that had already suffered a life-threatening oxygen leak) while sending criminals to safety would make NASA look bad. Besides, it wasn't as though the Sjobergs would end up in jail immediately anyhow; they had more than enough money to post bail back on earth. For the time being, the best punishment seemed to be to keep them at MBA for as long as possible.

Meanwhile, NASA public relations was freaking out that they now had to handle an emergency evacuation *and* Lily's attempt to murder me. Unlike the Dr. Holtz murder, there was no way to sweep this one under the carpet. Then, Dr. Holtz's death had been proclaimed an unfortunate accident, and Garth Grisan, a little-known government employee, had been quietly tried and convicted by a secret tribunal. In contrast, the Sjobergs were world-famous, and any attempt to bring them to justice was going to be big news.

Therefore, what would have otherwise been a chaotic and tense preparation for evacuation was now an *extremely* chaotic and tense preparation for evacuation.

To my surprise, I found myself feeling a little sad about leaving.

The whole time I'd been at MBA, I had never found much to like about it. But now I realized there were things I would miss: the view through the skylight in the greenhouse, the marathon games of holographic Risk I'd played with Kira, helping Violet do low-gravity gymnastics when Nina wasn't watching, and having conversations in the mess hall with some of the smartest humans alive. (True, these were often about how repulsive the food was, but I'd learned some fascinating cutting-edge science as well.) I found myself taking any spare moments to wander into the science pod or the gymnasium, just to spend a few last minutes there.

Zan found me in the greenhouse.

Although I'd helped uproot most of the plants, Dr. Goldstein had repotted a few to bring back with us, so she could examine them more closely on earth and study how low gravity had affected them. It wasn't much, but it was still a nice little oasis in the midst of the bustling base.

"Hello, Dashiell," Zan said. Although she was smiling and her bright blue eyes were radiant, I got the feeling that she was very sad.

"Is something wrong?" I asked.

"Do you have time to talk?"

I looked through the glass of the greenhouse into the rest of the base, watching my fellow Moonies bustle about. I had probably wasted too much time hanging out in there already, but I desperately wanted to speak to Zan. "Sure," I said. "A little." Then, because I wanted privacy, I had no choice but to exit the greenhouse and cross the hall into the bathroom.

Thankfully, there wasn't anyone else in there. I slipped into the middle stall and sat down on the space toilet.

I wasn't going to miss those things one bit.

"I'm happy to see that you are all right after yesterday," Zan said.

"Thanks." It seemed that, since the fate of humanity might be on the line, I should do my best to defend us. "Zan, you need to realize that, even though people have tried to kill me up here twice, that's not really normal. It's a factor of being up here on the moon, I guess. Space madness or something. All of us living up here in this little confined space with nowhere else to go."

"I suspected as much."

"Back on earth, most kids my age have never had even *one* attempt on their life. In fact, lots of people never have anyone try to kill them."

"I know that. But I am actually pleased to have witnessed what I did yesterday."

I suddenly understood why Zan had seemed so sad. "You're not going to help humanity, are you?"

Zan blinked, surprised. "I'm afraid you have things backward. What I saw yesterday convinced me to give you what you need."

I sat up, so thrown by this that I couldn't quite make sense of it. "But you saw Lily trying to kill me."

"Yes. However, I am aware that the Sjobergs are not normal humans. And in your moment of need, I saw something else more important than Lily's behavior. Cesar Marquez came to your aid. And Violet's. To protect you from Lily."

"And that surprised you?"

"I have always gotten the impression from you that Cesar didn't like you very much."

"Right."

"And yet, when he saw you were in trouble, he came to your rescue without any hesitation. Even though that meant he could have ended up in danger too. And others were also rushing to help; Cesar simply got there first. That doesn't strike you as extraordinary?"

"Well . . . no," I admitted. "I mean, I would have done it for Cesar—or anyone else."

"Even the Sjobergs?"

"If I saw one of them was in danger, yes, I would help them." I wasn't saying it merely to make myself sound good. I really meant it.

It seemed that Zan could tell. She smiled warmly. "In the galaxy, that behavior is far more unusual than you realize. Of course species will protect members of their own families, and when a community is at risk from a threat, we will come together to defend it, but it is rare to see a species that is willing to protect random members so readily."

"So . . . ," I said, still trying to comprehend what was going on, "you weren't horrified when you appeared to me on the moon yesterday?"

"Not at all. In fact, I was amazed. I know that I have spoken to you many times about the flaws of humanity. It is possible that I have spoken to you far too rarely about the positive aspects."

"Well, you've mentioned music and art. And love."

"Yes, love. I am still fascinated by how strong the emotional bonds can be between humans. And yet, yesterday showed me that there barely has to be any bond between humans for one to save another."

"Actually, there doesn't have to be any bond at all," I said. "My parents have both rescued drowning tourists off the beach in Hawaii. They didn't know those people. They had never met until right then."

"It's fascinating," Zan said. "Your species can be so terrible and brutal to one another, and yet be so loving and kind. I wonder if those two impulses are connected in some way. There is no darkness without light."

"So you're going to save us?"

"I can't promise that. But I will do my best. If you can avoid wiping yourselves out, you might just be able to that teach the rest of us something."

I immediately felt as though an enormous weight had been lifted off me. The stress of having to answer for all of humanity gave way to an incredible feeling of joy. This, combined with the knowledge that I would soon be leaving MBA, was almost overwhelming. I had to fight the urge to leap to my feet and start dancing, if only because I didn't want anyone to find me doing that in the bathroom.

And yet I still felt sadness emanating from Zan.

"This is all good, right?" I asked.

"Of course it is."

"Then why aren't you happy about it?"

"Because, after this, I will never be able to see you again."

And just like that, I didn't feel so happy anymore. "Why not?"

"Some time ago, I told you that there were many of my kind who didn't want me to be in contact with you."

"And that you were taking a big risk to talk to me."

"Yes. Well, giving this information to you is even riskier. And if you and I remain in contact, they will *know* I gave it to you."

"And they'd punish you for it?"

"Yes."

"How?"

"That's not important—"

"Yes, it is!"

"It's not. There's nothing you could do about it, one way or the other. But you *can* help protect me in the first place. Once I give this to you, you can't share it with anyone for at least two of your years. You'll have to keep it a secret. I know that won't be easy, but it's absolutely necessary. I need that time to cover my tracks and conceal any evidence of contact between us."

"I don't understand. . . ."

"Perhaps you will someday. But I don't have the time to explain it now."

Outside the stall, the door to the bathroom opened. I

heard my father's voice. "Dashiell? Are you in here?"

"Yes!" I called out.

"We're getting close to time," Dad said.

"I know," I replied. "I'm just trying to take care of business before we have to get on the rocket. That zero-g toilet's even worse than this one."

"Good point," Dad said. "It's gonna be two days to the next decent restroom." Then he entered the stall next to me.

I tried to return my attention to Zan and ignore the fact that my father was using the toilet close by, even though I could hear him attaching the various hoses to his body parts.

It occurred to me that I should probably really be using the toilet myself, rather than just sitting on it, because the zero-g toilets really *were* more awful than the low-g ones.

But things with Zan were even more pressing. I couldn't believe this was going to be the last time I ever saw her. I had always imagined she would be able to visit me on earth. After all, in galactic terms it wasn't any farther away from her planet than the moon. I had looked forward to showing her my favorite places, having thousands of other conversations with her, and perhaps even learning how to control traveling with my thoughts the way she did. Or maybe, one day, getting to reveal her existence to the world.

But that wasn't going to happen. Now I had mere minutes left with her, if that, and we were stuck in the MBA bathroom, of all places. With my father doing his business in the next stall.

I felt myself beginning to cry. "I don't want you to go," I told Zan, only using my thoughts.

"I don't want to go either."

"Isn't there some way we can at least meet a few more times? You can't visit me on earth before giving me this information?"

"I wish I could, but I have taken enough risks as it is. Even being with you now is dangerous for me."

"It's not fair."

"I know. I'm sorry you have to feel this way. To be honest, these emotions you have—your joy, your love, this sadness— they are very different from what we experience. We care for each other, but in a way that is much less powerful. I had never felt anything like it until I connected with you."

"Even though you connected with Dr. Holtz first?"

"Yes. His relationship with me was more . . . scientific. Whereas you have, well . . . you have love for me . . . and I have love for you in return."

"You do?"

"I do. And it is an absolutely wonderful thing. You humans should cherish this feeling. I am so thrilled that I have been able to experience it with you. It is as though you have given me the most amazing gift in the universe. Even if it means that I have to feel this terrible sadness, too."

Zan's image flickered, though in a different way than I'd seen before. It appeared as though she was losing control of it. The form wavered, and I caught extremely brief flashes of her true self.

"Zan? What's wrong? Are you in danger now?"

"No . . . I . . . I think I'm crying."

"Crying?" I repeated. I had never heard Zan mention doing this before. And from what I had seen, her actual form didn't seem to have eyes, let alone tear ducts.

"I'm not doing it the way that you do it, but I'm experiencing a physical manifestation of sadness. This has never happened to me before."

"I'm sorry," I said.

"Don't be. Please. It is worth the other feelings I have experienced through you."

In the stall next to me, Dad finished his business and hiked up his pants. "Dash, you almost done in there?" he asked.

"I just need another minute or so," I said.

"All right," Dad said. "But don't take too much longer. We need you out there." I heard him leave the bathroom and close the door.

"I think the time has come for me to finish our business as well," Zan said.

"No!" I cried.

"Yes. I need to go, and all that will come of delaying this is more sadness." Zan took a moment to compose herself. Her avatar reformed, appearing as bright and vivid as usual. "Now then, I need you to relax and open your mind to me."

"All right," I said, and then I did my best to do as Zan had asked.

Suddenly my head was full of information. I had no idea how Zan had done it, but it felt as though I had instantly memorized an encyclopedia. For a few moments I was over-whelmed. It was like when you get a brain freeze from eating ice cream too quickly, only in this case I had learned too much too fast. It left me reeling. I almost fell off the space toilet.

"Are you okay?" Zan asked.

I steadied myself and focused. There was a jumble of numbers in my head, but when I concentrated, I began to see connections between all of them. I didn't understand it, but I recognized that there was an order to the chaos and that, somehow, I had it all memorized.

"I've got it," I said.

Zan seemed relieved. In a sense she had shifted the burden of this information to me. But her sadness also deepened, and now I understood why.

"Don't go," I said.

"I have to," she replied.

Nina Stack suddenly came over the MBA intercom system. "Attention all lunarnauts," she began—as if, perhaps, there might be someone else to speak to at MBA. "It is T minus fifteen minutes to touchdown for the rockets. All travelers on the first wave, please report to the staging area immediately." She had even less emotion in her voice than the base computer.

Zan looked to me, her form wavering even worse than before, which I figured meant she was crying harder now.

I was crying myself.

"If you can't talk to me," I asked, "can you at least still keep an eye on me? Visit earth now and then?"

"No. To protect myself, I will have to cut all ties with earth."

I heard the pounding of footsteps outside the bathroom. Then Roddy, Cesar, and Kamoze burst through the door. I could tell it was them from their voices and laughter. Obviously, they'd been sent to take a last toilet break before heading back to earth. Cesar and Kamoze beat Roddy out and ducked into the stalls on either side of me. "Ha-ha!" Cesar taunted. "You lose!"

Roddy banged on the door to my stall. "Dash, is that you in there?"

"Yes."

"Stop hogging the toilet! I've got to go."

"I'm almost done."

"C'mon! The rocket's almost here, and it's two hundred fifty thousand miles back to earth."

I looked to Zan. It was bad enough that she had to leave, but I hated to think that *this* would be one of her last memories of humanity.

"Hold on," I said, then stepped out of the stall.

Roddy barely waited for me to clear the way before shoving past and slamming the door on me.

I realized that, for all the time I'd just spent in the toilet stall, I hadn't actually gone myself.

Zan had stepped out into the bathroom with me. It wasn't exactly private, though, with the three boys in the stalls. This wasn't the way I wanted to end things at all.

"Good-bye, Dashiell," Zan said.

"Wait—"

"I can't. The time has come." Zan gazed at me sadly with her piercing blue eyes. "Have a nice life," she said.

Then she vanished for good.

Excerpt from *The Official NASA Procedures for Contact with Intelligent Extraterrestrial Life* © National Aeronautics and Space Administration, Department of Extraterrestrial Affairs, 2029 (Classification Level AAA)

FAILURE TO COMMUNICATE

A cautionary note: Any IEL we encounter may be from a civilization so radically different from ours that our systems of communication are indecipherable to each other. Perhaps we simply won't be able to understand their language, or maybe they will communicate in a way so alien to us that we will be unable to even process it.* In this case, it may take a great deal of time to establish a rapport, although in time our top scientists will certainly be able to figure it out. In cases like this, do not get frustrated—and certainly do not take your frustrations out on the IEL. Instead, do your best to convey kindness, friendliness, and excitement that contact has been made.

---

* For example, they might use a range of the aural or visual spectrum that we can't detect, or communicate using senses that we don't even possess.

NOT-SO-FOND FAREWELL

The very last lunar day

Evacuation time

We didn't even see the rockets land. We were too busy suiting up in the staging area, and there were no windows aimed toward the launchpad, save for the small one in the air-lock door. Since there was no atmosphere on the moon, we couldn't hear the landing either. The only way we knew it had happened was when Nina announced it.

"Touchdown is complete," she said. "Prepare for evacuation."

Despite her flat, emotionless monotone, the words were still among the most wonderful I had ever heard.

Our suiting up went much less chaotically than it had

the day before. Partly this was because we had just done it and partly it was because there was no emergency this time. Since only half of us were leaving, the others were available to help us get our suits on.

The Sjobergs were nowhere to be seen. Lars and Lily had a decent excuse—both were locked up—but Sonja and Patton had simply wanted nothing to do with us.

Of course, it wasn't like any of us really wanted to see *them*, either.

Dad and Chang had spent the past few hours stacking all the gear that was being returned to earth outside the base, making repeated trips back and forth through the air lock. Now they were back inside. Dad was helping Mom suit up while Chang assisted me.

Meanwhile, Daphne worked with Violet. Daphne was obviously trying to hold back tears. "I'm going to miss you so much," she told my sister. "You've been like a little ray of sunshine around here."

"We'll still get to see each other back on earth," Violet told her.

This wasn't really true. Once we returned, there would be a two-week quarantine period at the Kennedy Space Center in Florida, followed by a few weeks of rehab while we rebuilt the strength in our bodies to handle earth gravity. But after that we would all be returning to our real homes, which were scattered all over the world. My family would be going back to Hawaii, while Daphne would be going to NASA Mission Control in Houston. Chances were, we'd barely see her again, if ever.

Violet hadn't put this together yet. Even though we'd only been on the moon for eight months, that was still a significant portion of her young life; she was only six and a half years old. After spending so much time in a cramped space with everyone close by, she seemed to have forgotten just how big the earth was. And no one wanted to burst her bubble by telling her the truth yet.

"Maybe we can have a slumber party!" Violet said excitedly.

"I'd like that," Daphne told her. "It's a date." She tousled Violet's hair one last time, then placed the helmet on over her head and locked it into place.

"Daphne's right," Chang told me. "Things are going to be pretty dull here without all you guys around."

"Oh, there'll still be plenty of fun things to do," I teased. "You'll have all the Sjobergs to play with. And there's always the danger of asphyxiation to keep you on your toes."

"You know what I'm not gonna miss?" Chang asked. "That attitude." He smiled to let me know he was joking, then leaned in close and whispered, "You've got a good head on your shoulders, Dash. Keep in touch with me when we're back on earth. NASA could use a brain like yours."

I was so stunned by this, I wasn't sure what to say. Having a supergenius like Chang tell me that *I* was smart was one of the most amazing things that had ever happened to me. All I could manage was, "Okay."

"Good." Chang held up my helmet. "Take one last good breath of Moon Base Alpha air, and then I'm closing you up."

"Wait!" Kira bounded over. She had her entire suit on except for her helmet. "We're not going to see each other on the ride back."

"I know," I said. "But we'll see each other in quarantine."

"Still, it's going to be a few days, so . . ." Kira gave me a hug. Or the closest you could get to a hug while wearing a space suit, which wasn't much of a hug at all. We were more like two sumo wrestlers bumping bellies. "Thanks for being my friend up here. It's been wild."

"It has," I agreed.

To my surprise, Kira gave me a quick peck on the cheek. "Have a safe ride," she said, then turned to Violet. "You too," she said, then gave her another sumo hug and, since Violet's helmet was already on, a kiss on the face plate.

"Bye, Kira! See you on earth!" Violet yelled to be heard through her helmet.

"Yeah. See you down there." Kira bounded back over to Dr. Alvarez, who helped her put her helmet on.

"Y'know," Chang said to me thoughtfully, "if I liked girls, and I was your age, that's the kind of girl I'd like."

I didn't know what to say to that, either. So I simply told Chang, "I'm ready to go."

He put my helmet on and locked it into place.

Nearby, my parents were wrapping up their safety checks for each other. They came over and made sure that Violet and I were properly suited up as well, then said their good-byes to Chang and Daphne. There was lots more hugging.

Nina emerged from her office, but she didn't make a move to say good-bye, or give anyone a hug, or do anything else remotely human. She didn't even wave to us. Instead she ordered, "Let's move it, people. You don't want to miss your liftoff window."

So we headed for the air lock. The Howards and the Goldstein-Iwanyi family entered it first. While we waited for them, I took my last look around Moon Base Alpha.

"What a dump, right?" Roddy Marquez asked. He was wheezing heavily under the weight of his suit.

"It wasn't so bad," I said.

"Please. This place sucked. The veeyar system was five years out of date. I couldn't even play the latest version of Warp War. Or Space Pirates of Xenon. Or anything. Which is exactly what I'm going to do when we get back to earth. The moment I get home, I'm jacking in for a week straight."

"You're not going to go outside?"

Roddy looked at me as if *I* was from another planet. "Why? There's nothing out there that's anywhere near as cool as what I can experience online."

I shouldn't have been surprised, but I was. The *last* thing I wanted to do when I got back to earth was stay cooped up inside. When I got home, I was going to head right to the beach. And then climb a mountain. And maybe sleep out under the stars for the first few nights.

I noticed that the door to the Sjobergs' tourist suite was now open a crack. Patton Sjoberg was peeking through it, glowering jealously at us. He gave me one last mean stare for the road, just to let me know that he was always going to be a jerk, no matter what, and then slammed the door.

The first group exited the air lock and shut the outer door.

"Next wave," Nina said. My family moved inside the air lock with the Brahmaputra-Marquez family, and Nina closed the door behind us.

There was one last whoosh of air as the chamber depressurized. The light flashed green. We opened the outer door and left Moon Base Alpha forever.

Once we stepped onto the lunar surface, we could see the rockets. Two enormous, shimmering craft that loomed over the blast wall.

All the gear that was returning to earth was stacked right outside the air lock. The Howards and the Goldstein-Iwanyis had already grabbed what they could and were hauling it to the launchpad. Although I noticed one of them—it had to be Kira—set their load down for a moment and attempt some lunar gymnastics.

The pilots, Buster Reisman and Katya King, had emerged from the rockets to help with the loading. They said some quick, warm hellos to us and then grabbed what they could.

I grabbed some gear myself, as did everyone else except Violet. She was too little to help, and besides, my parents wanted to give her one last chance to bound around on the surface.

"You can take a quick run too," Mom told me.

"Really?" I asked. "What about Nina?"

"Nina can stuff it," Dad said. "She's not our commander anymore."

So I set my box of gear down. "Check this out. This is going to be one *enormous* leap for mankind," I said, then bounded a few steps and leaped as far as I could.

I probably didn't go that far at all, but in the low gravity, it *felt* like I did.

"Ladies and gentlemen!" Dad announced over the radio, in his best sportscaster voice. "Dashiell Gibson has set a new lunar record in the broad jump!"

"Not for long," Mom said. Then she dropped her crate of gear and took a flying leap as well.

Dad joined us a second later. And then everyone else noticed what we were doing, dropped their gear, and went to take one last romp on the moon as well. Even Katya and Buster.

For the next few minutes, we all completely defied protocol and goofed around. Moonies were doing somersaults and pirouettes and having contests to see who could jump the highest. Cesar pegged Roddy in the helmet with a clump of moon dust, and the next thing we knew, a moon-dust fight had broken out. It was kind of like a snowball fight, but since no one had ever done it before in human history, it was extra fun.

Everyone was happy and laughing and getting along great. It was exactly the kind of thing we had imagined when we had dreamed of coming to the moon—and the sort of thing that, up until that very moment, we hadn't done at all.

Of course Nina didn't like it one bit. "Stop that at once!" she ordered us over the radio. "This behavior is completely against official regulations."

We ignored her. Instead we continued to romp and play and bean each other with handfuls of moon dust while Nina droned on and on about how we were in violation of some protocol or another.

Eventually, we all realized it had to end. We grew tired from the exertion, and our suits were getting creaky from all the moon dust in the joints. We returned to the cargo that we'd dropped, hoisted it back up, hauled it to the rockets, and secured it in the cargo bay.

Then we climbed aboard, sealed the air locks, shed our suits, and strapped into our seats.

It took another twenty minutes for all the safety checks to be done. And then Mission Control said the words that I had been dying to hear for the past eight months:

"Raptor Twelve, you are cleared for launch."

Since we were inside the rocket, as opposed to the moon base, we could hear the thrusters fire this time. We certainly felt it. The whole craft shuddered, and then we were pressed back into our seats as the rocket lifted off.

Unlike the designers of MBA, the designers of the rockets had realized that the lunarnauts would want windows. I had one right next to my seat. I pressed my face up against the glass and watched Moon Base Alpha drop away beneath me.

It didn't take long. From above, the base looked even smaller than I'd realized, a tiny outpost in a massive sea of moon dust. The solar arrays were much bigger than the base itself, but even they were smaller than your standard mall parking lot. The rocket quickly broke free of the weak lunar gravity, and soon I could barely even make out the place I had lived in on the vast, barren expanse of moon.

Due to the angle of the rocket, I couldn't see the earth. Instead, as the moon dropped from sight, my view was of the endless void of space, speckled with a million stars.

I kept thinking that Zan might show herself to me one last time. After all, she wasn't bound to the laws of physics when she appeared. I half expected to see her float by outside the window, or to zoom past riding a meteor—but she didn't.

It saddened me that she was gone, but I didn't dwell on it. After all, she had given me what she had promised. I had represented humanity well, and hopefully I now had the tools to save us from destroying ourselves.

On any given day, that would have been more than enough to be happy about. But I had something else wonderful on the horizon.

Within two days, I would be back on earth, where I could breathe air that wasn't canned and eat food that actually tasted good and take a real shower and swim in the ocean and see birds and insects and other animals and do a million other wonderful things that I had taken for granted.

I was going home.

Excerpt from *The Official NASA Procedures for Contact with Intelligent Extraterrestrial Life* © National Aeronautics and Space Administration, Department of Extraterrestrial Affairs, 2029 (Classification Level AAA)

SUCCESS

Ideally, with your hard work and that of all DEXA employees, successful rapport will be established between our species and the IEL, leading to an exchange of ideas and technology, and ultimately a great new chapter in human history. However, the process certainly will not go perfectly. In fact, there will doubtless be many hitches, hiccups, and mistakes along the way.

So try to keep in mind throughout this endeavor that even though it may be troublesome at times, you are participating in one of the greatest moments of our existence—and possibly the existence of the IEL as well. Your efforts here will go down in history, so act accordingly. Be the best representative of humanity that you can possibly be.

Epilogue Part One

TRANSMISSION

November 13, 2043
From: Dr. Chang Kowalski, PhD
Department of Lunar Science
National Aeronautics and Space Administration
Jet Propulsion Laboratory
Pasadena, CA
To: Dashiell Gibson
Subject: Re: Can you take a look at this?

Dash!
Just took a look at the equations you sent me. Holy cow! I knew you were
smart, kiddo, but this is off the charts. We're talking game-changing stuff
here. Huge implications for humanity.
To be honest, some of this is even a bit beyond me, so I guess it's a
good thing you sent it to Dr. Brahmaputra-Marquez too. Together, we've
been able to analyze it all, and she's in agreement with me that this is
Einstein-quality work.
We have to talk about this ASAP. I'm dying to know how you even came
up with it. I just tried to call you, but didn't reach you. I'm betting you're
surfing. Or maybe chasing girls.
Anyhow, genius, call me IMMEDIATELY when you get this.
Chang

Epilogue Part Two

FAR-FLUNG DESTINATION

Earth year 2075

Bosco day 1

The planet is bigger than I expected.

I am used to looking at earth from space, and while the earth is certainly not small, it is significantly smaller than this. This planet's circumference is about 50 percent larger than earth's, which means there's a lot more planet.

And nearly the entire surface appears to be water.

There is some land, most likely formed in similar ways to the land on earth: by volcanic eruptions and the smashing together of continental plates. This planet, like earth, has a dynamic surface. However, the land masses are dwarfed by the oceans, and they are few and far between. Even the biggest mass, one the size of North America, looks puny compared to the enormous blue sea around it.

It's no wonder that intelligent life here stayed in the oceans.

I can't believe, after all this time, that I am finally here.

This has been my whole life's work, figuring out how to think myself here. It was evident, right after I returned to earth from MBA, that the human space program was never going to get me this far. Not in my lifetime anyway. Even colonizing our own moon was far more difficult than we'd hoped. It was years until NASA could even get MBA re-established, and five times that before Moon Base Beta was up and running—and things still aren't working perfectly there. Interstellar travel might be a possibility someday, but that day is centuries away, if not more.

So I have been working at this instead. I've been practicing for decades now, taking what I learned from Zan and combining that with things I have figured out by myself. I realized, after that time on the moon when Lily Sjoberg was trying to kill me, that it was tied into the extreme desire to be someplace else, although it obviously wasn't as simple as wishing yourself there. It was more about channeling that desire—and some extremely complicated subatomic physics. I worked on it all through middle school and high school, making very little progress at first, doing whatever I could to recreate that brief moment when I had made contact with Riley Bock on Hapuna Beach, or when I had projected myself to the safety of the air lock.

Well, actually, I didn't make *any* progress at first. But I kept trying, because I'd done it twice, and so I knew it was possible.

I didn't have any trouble getting into college, given my work on what became known as the Kowalski-Gibson equation. (Chang had made some refinements, and though he always tried to give me the bigger share of credit, he was the famous genius, and I was just a kid, so people tended to assume he was the brains of the operation.) I went into astrophysics and studied under Dr. Brahmaputra-Marquez. Together we made a lot of amazing discoveries about space and time and distance, though I never let her know that I had an ulterior motive throughout, that the only reason I was doing this was to see if I could master thinking myself across the galaxy the same way that Zan had.

The only one I told about that was Violet.

She has become a world-famous scientist herself, although in a very different way than I have. Violet has always had a flair for the dramatic, and people have always loved watching her, so it was never a surprise to me that she ultimately became one of the great spokespeople for science, lecturing to huge crowds at conferences, hosting the fifth incarnation of *Cosmos*, and making the occasional cameo in *Star Trek* movies.

Violet is the only one who has ever known about Zan besides me. She never had the chance to think herself anyplace, the way I did, but she always accepted that it was possible, and she worked at it with me. It took decades, but eventually, one day long after we had returned to earth from the moon, when we were both home visiting Mom and Dad in Hawaii, I thought myself across the house to her mind.

In a sense, figuring that out was the hardest part. Once I knew how to do it, I simply had to hone the skills. After a while, I could think myself across much larger spaces to Violet, and then from one side of the earth to the other, and then I could project myself to other minds as well, to dogs and rabbits and wildebeests. (Zan was right, wildebeests don't have much going on. Although communing with dolphins was amazing.)

Occasionally I could think myself to another person, but I had to be careful about that, because I didn't really want other people to know I could do it. I figured it would be way too unsettling, or that the CIA might try to recruit me to work for them. I never even told Riley what I'd done. She simply assumed that she had dreamed my visit to her that one day on the beach, and I always let her believe that was true. It was much easier than explaining what had really happened. I still dropped into her mind from time to time, though, just to freak her out and make her think she was having visions of me.

So I had mostly communicated to Violet, and after a while she had learned how to do it and think herself back to me. She wasn't as good as I was, but we definitely got to the point where we didn't need the telephone. (Although we still used the phone most of the time, because thinking yourself into another person's mind is always a little weird, and there was always the chance that I might accidentally appear to Violet while she was on the toilet. Or vice versa.)

And now, all those years of hard work, those hundreds of thousands of hours of practice, have finally paid off.

Bosco's star is hotter than the sun, so the planet's atmosphere is sweltering. The seas are wonderfully warm. While I can sense the water, I can't really analyze it, but it seems to be exactly the same as water on earth. At least, it should be. There aren't that many forms of water in the universe.

The sea life is wildly different, however. At first glance it all looks vaguely like life on earth; after all, in our own seas, there is a tremendous variety of life in all shapes and sizes, ranging from sharks to starfish to sea cucumbers. But when the life forms come closer, I realize that each and every one of them is like nothing I have ever seen before, and occasionally like nothing I—or anyone else—have ever imagined. Some of them are gloriously beautiful, while others are the stuff that nightmares are made of. But it is all amazing and incredible and overwhelming. Kira, who is now a marine biologist, would go out of her mind.

Kira is an expert on humpback whales—as well as one of the earth's most aggressive environmental activists, leading rallies and protests all over the world. And though it has never been proven, I'm pretty sure she was behind the suspicious sinking of several corporate whaling ships. Kira has never been a big fan of following the rules, especially when they stand in the way of what's right.

For now, I don't bother to focus too much on the life around me. Hopefully, there will be plenty of time for that in the future. In the meantime, I am on a mission.

I plunge onward through the seas, thinking myself forward, homing in on the signal I know by heart, the signal that has called to me from all the way across the galaxy.

As I get closer to it, I begin to see signs of intelligent life.

There are structures under the sea, but structures far different from anything that we have on earth. Instead of bending nature to their will, the way we humans have done, by cutting down forests and paving the land, these creatures have built things in harmony with the natural world. Their buildings aren't blocks of concrete and steel, but seem to be made of crystals and films of bubbles.

Back on earth, we humans haven't fully given up our destructive ways. We're still generating huge piles of garbage, and the rain forest has shrunk to a fraction of what it used to be, and the last gorillas and rhinos and elephants are gone. But thanks to the Kowalski-Gibson equation, we've made progress. We aren't heating up the earth the way we used to. Our population has stopped growing to unsustainable levels. We might just make it after all.

Perhaps the most surprising thing about being one of the people behind the equation is how long it took for humans to put it into use. The scientists all backed it right off the bat. They recognized how revolutionary it was. But a startling number of people had problems with the new. Old-fashioned corporations didn't want to change, so they hired lobbyists to strong-arm Congress and spent millions on disinformation campaigns. Chang and I were made out to be bad guys. People got confused and rejected the science. Some even railed against it as unnatural. And the politicians actually listened to them. So it took a lot longer to implement the changes than I had ever expected it would.

Thankfully, Zan's greatest fears didn't come to fruition. No one has tried to use the information to destroy other people. At least as far as I know.

I see the first inhabitants of the alien community. Like Zan, they are all beautiful, only now I can observe how they glide through the water. Their movements are graceful and hypnotic.

I am immediately overcome by a strange sensation. It is impossible to explain, but it feels like—for want of better words—an intensely good vibe, like hundreds of souls all feeling the same way at once. It is like being at a concert or a sporting event, where everyone is happy for the exact same reasons, only far more intense.

It is coming from the aliens, I realize. They communicate differently than humans do, using thoughts rather than words, and I am picking up on it. I am feeling them, and what I am getting is a sense of kindness and harmony.

It is almost as though I am in a world without an unkind thought, or a flash of anger.

It is overwhelming, like being plunged into a beehive, surrounded by the hum and thrum of the bees. Save for their size, the aliens all look exactly alike to me. I have to take some time and really focus to find who I am looking for.

But when I sense it, there is no doubt in my mind that I am right.

I lock onto the signal and connect with it. There is a brief sensation of being pulled through something, and then I am in her mind.

She is startled at first, the same way I always was when she appeared to me. And then there is a flood of other emotions, some of which I recognize, some of which I don't. There is disbelief, amazement, even a tiny bit of fear, but once she realizes what has happened, who I am and what I have done, there is relief and warmth and boundless joy.

Even though she can't smile the way that I do, I know she is smiling. And I project the image of myself smiling into her mind as well.

"Hi, Zan," I say.

HELLO FRIENDS~

As part of my continuing study of earthlings, I am transmitting the following conversation with Dashiell Gibson (age 12 in human years) to you from my memory. I believe it illustrates, once again, what a bizarre and fascinating species humans are. Every time I think I am beginning to understand them, I learn something else about them that is strange and unusual.

This conversation took place at human outpost Moon Base Alpha on Lunar Day 246, after the events in which Nina Stack had gone missing but before the events in which Lars Sjoberg had been poisoned. I had yet to reveal my true form to Dashiell or give him much information at all about our species or our planet.

Your devoted companion,

ZAN

(Translated from the original Bosconian)

Zan: Would you mind if I asked you some questions about food?

Dashiell: Food? Really? Why?

Zan: Humans seem to think about it a great deal. You're always complaining about the food here on the moon.

Dashiell: That's because it tastes like boiled cardboard.

Zan: Is that bad?

Dashiell: Er . . . yes.

Zan: You have eaten boiled cardboard?

Dashiell: No. I was just being, uh, metaphorical. I think. What I meant was, it tastes terrible.

Zan: This is what interests me. Why is the taste of food so important to you? The primary importance of food is to provide sustenance and thus fuel to keep your body functioning, correct?

Dashiell: Yes, technically . . .

Zan: Then why should taste even matter? It is of no importance to your survival.

Dashiell: It can help us avoid things that are poisonous. Those tend to taste bad.

Zan: Perhaps. But your sense of taste often seems to be working against you. For example, I am sure that your space food is not poisonous. From what I understand, it has been designed to keep you fit and healthy. And yet you still detest it. What purpose is your sense of taste serving there?

Dashiell: None, I guess. But when food does taste good . . . it's one of the greatest pleasures in life. Your species doesn't care at all about what your food tastes like?

Zan: No. But then, our alimentary systems are very different from yours. We do not have taste buds, like you. Or even tongues.

Dashiell: Really? Because you're missing out. Food can taste *incredible.*

Zan: Let's talk about this. What are some of your favorite things to eat?

Dashiell: Well, a lot of kids my age would probably say hot dogs or hamburgers, but my favorite thing to eat is Chinese.

Zan: Chinese people?!

Dashiell: No! The food! Chinese food. It's a whole cuisine. . . .

Zan: I apologize for my misunderstanding. There *are* cases of humans eating other humans, correct? I believe it's called cannonballism?

Dashiell: Cannibalism. And I'm not even sure that it exists anymore. If it ever did. It's gross.

Zan: Really?

Dashiell: Yes, really! You don't eat others of your species, do you?

Zan: No. But then, remember that we are far more highly advanced than your species. You have barely even begun to understand subatomic particle physics. And you often pick your noses and eat the boogers. Even the adults.

Dashiell: Good point.

Zan: So . . . this Chinese food. What is it, exactly?

Dashiell: It's all kinds of great stuff. There's moo shu pork and beef with black bean sauce and egg rolls and dim sum! Oh man, dim sum! You go to a place, and there's like two dozen different kinds of dumplings you can pick. . . .

Zan: There are two dozen types of dumplings alone?

Dashiell: Maybe more.

Zan: How many different meals are there in this Chinese food?

Dashiell: Thousands, I guess. And people are inventing more all the time!

Zan: People are inventing new foods?

Dashiell: Well, different ways to cook it. Like, my folks tell me that when they were kids, there was no such thing as a pastrami egg roll. But those are amazing. I would kill for a pastrami egg roll right now.

Zan: You are being metaphorical again, yes?

Dashiell: Yes.

Zan: So there are thousands of types of food in this Chinese food—and that is only one cuisine on earth, correct?

Dashiell: Correct.

Zan: And you have access to all these cuisines at once?

Dashiell: You do in a lot of places on earth. Even in Hawaii, which is kind of remote, we could get all sorts of different kinds of foods. Though I suppose that might not be the case everywhere. Like maybe in rural China, you can still only get Chinese food. Although, I guess they wouldn't call it "Chinese food" there. They'd probably just call it "food."

Zan: With all these options, how do you ever decide what to eat?

Dashiell: It's not easy. But you usually go with what you're in the mood for.

Zan: You can be in the mood for different foods?

Dashiell: Sure. Sometimes you want Chinese, but maybe others you want Indian. Or French. Or just a handful of Doritos.

Zan: What are Doritos?

Dashiell: They're a snack food. They're chips flavored to taste like nacho cheese. Or cool ranch. Or salsa.

Zan: And what are these chips made of?

Dashiell: I have no idea.

Zan: And you eat them anyhow?

Dashiell: Yes. Everyone does.

Zan: I suppose they must be extremely nutritious for you to do that.

Dashiell: Uh . . . no. In fact, they're not nutritious at all. They're actually kind of bad for you.

Zan: Then why would you eat them?

Dashiell: Because they're delicious!

Zan: You eat things that are knowingly bad for you at the expense of your own personal health? That makes no sense.

Dashiell: I guess you'd have to taste one to understand. If you had taste buds. Or a tongue. Or actually existed here instead of being a thought projection.

Zan: Sadly, that is not the case. Let's return to these moods of yours as they pertain to wanting different foods. What determines these moods?

Dashiell: I have no idea. You just want what you want.

Zan: And you have access to all these foods at any time?

Dashiell: Pretty much. If you're in a decent-size city.

Zan: Because I have heard that there are millions of people starving on earth as well. Possibly billions.

Dashiell: Oh. Uh . . . yes. That's true.

Zan: So . . . some people on earth have access to more food than they could possibly eat at one time, while others have so little that they are dying?

Dashiell: Yes.

Zan: How is this allowed to happen?

Dashiell: I don't know.

Zan: Could you limit your own intake of food in order to pass some on to other humans who need it more?

Dashiell: It's more complicated than that. I don't know why the food ends up where it does. But it's not like, if I pass up an appetizer at dinner, then someone else across the world can have it instead of me.

Zan: What is an "appetizer"?

Dashiell: It's like a little meal you eat before your big meal. Like salad, or soup.

Zan: I thought that was called "dessert."

Dashiell: No. Dessert is what we eat *after* our meal. It's usually something really tasty, like ice cream or cake.

Zan: Ah yes. I have heard your sister talk about this ice cream at length. She wrote a whole song about it. And another one about something called "scummy bears"?

Dashiell: Gummy bears. Yes. I've heard that one. A lot.

Zan: What are these gummy bears?

Dashiell: They're just candy. Shaped like bears.

Zan: Why?

Dashiell: I don't know. You'd have to ask the people who make them. Gummies come in all sorts of shapes, really. There's gummy sharks and gummy worms . . .

Zan: Are there gummy walruses?

Dashiell: No.

Zan: Gummy orangutans?

Dashiell: Not that I know of.

Zan: Gummy kangaroos?

Dashiell: Maybe in Australia. I'm not sure how anyone decided what shapes to make gummies into.

Zan: Is there any actual bear in the gummy bears?

Dashiell: No. It's just sugar and . . . uh . . .

Zan: This is another food you consume that you have no idea what is in it?

Dashiell: Yes.

Zan: And it is also bad for you?

Dashiell: Yes. But very tasty.

Zan: So you will have an appetizer, and a full meal, and a dessert, all at one sitting, while there are people starving other places on earth?

Dashiell: I guess so.

Zan: I would suppose that, at the very least, you would never let any food go to waste, knowing that others of your species are going hungry.

Dashiell: Um . . . You know what food I *really* like? Pizza. That's Italian food. From Italy.

Zan: You're trying to change the subject.

Dashiell: I'm still talking about food. . . .

Zan: But you don't want to discuss the horribly unequal distribution of food that results in some people having none while others are gorging themselves on pointless gummy objects shaped like random animals?

Dashiell: Correct. It's kind of embarrassing for our species.

Zan: Like the fact that you all try to kill each other on a regular basis?

Dashiell: Well, not quite that embarrassing. And we don't *all* try to kill one another.

Zan: All right. I suppose we could return to the topic of gummy bears.

Dashiell: Really? Out of everything we humans have created, you want to discuss gummy bears some more?

Zan: We could discuss nuclear weapons if you'd like.

Dashiell: Gummy bears would be fine.

Zan: You are aware why I thought there might be actual bear in them, correct? You humans eat other animals on your planet.

Dashiell: Yes. But not bears so much.

Zan: There *are* animals that you humans hunt for food, though?

Dashiell: Yes. On occasion.

Zan: Like elephants.

Dashiell: Elephants? No.

Zan: Then why are they extinct in the wild and only seen at zoos? As far as I understand, they were hunted to death.

Dashiell: Yes, but not for food.

Zan: Then why did humans kill them?

Dashiell: Uh . . . for their tusks.

Zan: Those giant modified teeth that protrude from their faces? Why would anyone want those?

Dashiell: Some people liked things carved out of ivory, which is the substance the tusks were made of.

Zan: Is this ivory the finest carving material known to man?

Dashiell: Not really.

Zan: Then why was it worth the extinction of a species?

Dashiell: I really can't defend humans on this one. To be honest, we really don't hunt animals for sustenance much anymore. We mostly rely on domesticated animals.

Zan: Ah yes! On farms. I have seen those. You raise animals there for human consumption. Cows and pigs and chickens and dogs.

Dashiell: Dogs? Whoa! We do *not* eat dogs.

Zan: But you have domesticated them, yes? Millions of them.

Dashiell: Yes.

Zan: But you don't eat them?

Dashiell: No! I would never eat a dog.

Zan: But you would eat a pig?

Dashiell: Yes.

Zan: Why would you eat a pig and not a dog?

Dashiell: Um . . . well . . . first of all, a pig is delicious.

Zan: Violet has sung about this as well. Some part of a pig called "the bacon"?

Dashiell: Yes.

Zan: There is no delicious bacon on a dog?

Dashiell: No. We don't breed dogs to eat. We breed them to be our pets.

Zan: Ah. Pets. I have observed these as well, but I must admit I find them confusing. I really thought they were for you to consume. If not, what is the point of them?

Dashiell: Well, they're fun. And loyal. And we love them.

Zan: You *love* your dogs?

Dashiell: Oh yes. It's like they're members of our families.

Zan: You feel just as much emotion for a dog as you might for your parents? Or your sister?

Dashiell: Maybe not quite that much. But close. Before we came up to the moon, we had a dog on earth. Titan. He was the best.

Zan: What happened to him?

Dashiell: He died a year before we left earth.

Zan: Are you crying?

Dashiell: A little. I miss him.

Zan: You feel that strongly about a dog?

Dashiell: Yes. Lots of people do.

Zan: And would you feel the same way about cats?

Dashiell: Cats? Not quite. But some people do.

Zan: Why wouldn't you feel that way about a cat?

Dashiell: That's just how people are. There are dog people, and there are cat people.

Zan: And the two tribes are at war?

Dashiell: No! We just have differences of opinion as to which is better.

Zan: Why don't you like cats?

Dashiell: I don't *dislike* them. I'd just rather have a dog. Dogs are fun, and you can play fetch with them and stuff. You can't play fetch with a cat.

Zan: What is this "fetch"?

Dashiell: That's where you throw a ball for the dog, and the dog runs and gets it, and then you throw it for him again, and he runs and gets it again, and so on.

Zan: Why would a dog want to do that?

Dashiell: I guess they think it's fun.

Zan: Why? It sounds like a pointless waste of energy.

Dashiell: It's just what dogs do. Some of them, at least.

Zan: What else do dogs do?

Dashiell: You can teach them all sorts of tricks. Like sit and shake and roll over.

Zan: To what purpose?

Dashiell: There isn't one, really. You can also take dogs for walks.

Zan: What are those?

Dashiell: You go out with your dog and walk around the neighborhood.

Zan: That's it? There's no other point to it?

Dashiell: Not really. I guess you get some exercise. And the dog gets a chance to go to the bathroom.

Zan: Ah! That makes sense. I suspect that dogs do not know how to use toilets.

Dashiell: They don't. So they have to go outside.

Zan: So they expel their waste product, and then you can let the elements dissolve it, as would occur in the wild?

Dashiell: Um . . . not quite.

Zan: What do you mean?

Dashiell: You're not supposed to leave dog poop out in most neighborhoods, or people might step in it. So you have to pick it up in a little bag and bring it home.

Zan: You collect the undigested refuse that comes out of your dogs' bottoms and bring it back to your homes?

Dashiell: We don't keep it there. We throw it in the garbage.

Zan: Are dogs the dominant species on your planet?

Dashiell: No. Humans are.

Zan: But you raise them in your homes and walk them when they need exercise and carry their waste around for them. It certainly *sounds* like they are dominant over you.

Dashiell: Well, they're not.

Zan: Are you sure? Maybe they are much smarter than you realize and have figured out how to take advantage of your propensity for affection in order to survive.

Dashiell: Ummm . . . I can see how it might seem that way, but trust me; dogs aren't that smart. They drink out of the toilet bowl, for Pete's sake.

Zan: Sounds to me like they have figured out how to get you to create bountiful sources of water for them as well.

Dashiell: No! We're the ones in charge.

Zan: Really? Do they provide anything for you except affection?

Dashiell: Er . . . no.

Zan: Do you provide them with anything?

Dashiell: Yes. Pretty much everything.

Zan: Sounds like they're dominant to me. They at least forage for their own food, yes?

Dashiell: Not really.

Zan: You mean you feed them too?

Dashiell: Yes. We give them food and water and shelter and take care of them, and they give us nothing in return. Except affection. Although cats don't even give you that.

Zan: Is it possible that cats are the dominant species, then?

Dashiell: Maybe.

Zan: Out of interest, what do you feed your dogs?

Dashiell: Dog food.

Zan: Which is . . . ?

Dashiell: I'm not sure. I think the stuff we fed Titan had beef and nutrients and maybe even some venison. And we always gave him our leftovers after eating dinner.

Zan: So . . . on your planet, pet dogs eat better than all the people who are starving?

Dashiell: Um . . . yes. I guess that seems bad.

Zan: It certainly isn't a good thing that so many people on your planet are going without food. But I'm intrigued by your ability to feel emotion for a species that isn't your own. You humans are very unusual creatures. You wipe out one species of animal, like elephants, for questionable reasons. You raise another, like pigs, for food. And you take exceptionally good care of other species, like dogs and cats, because you have formed emotional bonds with them. It is very hard to understand why you would interact with the fellow denizens of your planet in such radically different ways.

Dashiell: I suppose. Though I should point out that those categories shift for different people. Most people are horrified that elephants are extinct. Lots of people like animals so much that they won't eat them. And there are people who don't just have dogs or cats as pets, but snakes and ferrets and guinea pigs and goldfish and all sorts of other animals.

Zan: Really? There are so many strange nuances of behavior in your species. Sometimes it seems as if I could study you humans for centuries and never fully understand you at all.

Dashiell: That's probably true. Heck, there are things that we don't even understand about ourselves.

Zan: Like the fact that you think it's hilarious when someone slips on a banana peel?

Dashiell: Exactly.